Praise for

JOHN S. MCFARLAND

"McFarland is adept at creating unsettling scenarios within very human, everyday contexts. The horrors that plague his characters feel like something that could happen to anyone, anytime, which is a great way to creep under a reader's skin and stay there awhile."

— Philip Fracassi,
Author of *Behold the Void*

"McFarland's style definitely whispers of older writers, like Lovecraft, but his handling of language is much more crisp and focused. The perfect combination of literary and contemporary. One of the great, undiscovered talents of horror fiction."

— C. P. Dunphy,
Gehenna and Hinnom

"... a brilliant writer..."

— Jodie Rhodes,
Jodie Rhodes Literary Agency

"McFarland's writing is lush and sensual, filled with textures, sounds, smells, and primal terrors that have lurked beyond the firelight since prehistory. It is filled with wit, psychological insight, and intelligence, counterbalancing the deepest dreads that curse our collective nightmares."

— Kenneth Anderson,
Editor of *Charon II*

Praise for

THE DARK WALK FORWARD
and tales from the collection

historical horrors, exploring the plight of WWI veterans in the title story and cancer-stricken factory workers in "The Radium Girls." Wandering farther afield, "Saturn Devouring His Son" tells of artist Francisco Goya tripping over his child's forgotten toys, and "Hakudo Maru" sees a Japanese fisherman atoning for his son's neglected funeral rites. McFarland tempers his frights with the mercy of familial love and sympathy for outsiders and victims. Horror readers will be riveted.

~ Publishers Weekly

THE DARK WALK FORWARD

A Harrowing Collection by

John S. McFarland

From

Dark Owl Publishing, LLC

Arizona

ISBN 978-1-951716-14-1

Also From
Dark Owl Publishing

Anthologies
A Celebration of Storytelling
The anthological festival of tales.

Something Wicked This Way Rides
Where genre fiction meets the Wild West.
(coming October 1, 2021)

Collections
The Last Star Warden:
Tales of Adventure and Mystery from Frontier Space, Volume I
Sci-fi pulp fiction at its finest by Jason J. McCuiston.
(coming March 1, 2021)

Bottled Spirits & Other Dark Tales
A collection of strange fiction from the mind of Adrian Ludens.
(coming May 1, 2021)

No Lesser Angels, No Greater Devils
Beautiful and haunting stories collected from Laura J. Campbell.
(coming May 1, 2021)

Novels
The Keeper of Tales
An epic fantasy adventure by Jonathon Mast.
(coming March 1, 2021)

Buy the books for Kindle and in paperback
www.darkowlpublishing/the-bookstore

Table of Contents

Forward

It is always a pleasure to find a writer whose work is relatively new to you, and who offers a content which intrigues far beyond the usual passing interest. With this collection, John McFarland demonstrates a mastery of mood and detail, exploring the lives of outcasts, victims, and troubled souls—very troubled souls. And he does so with craft, drawing us into the mistakes of strangers, for this is also a collection ripe with terrible decisions—some born of hate, others of love.

Many of the tales within are set in the period between the two World Wars, in the vicinity of a small American town, Ste. Odile, and though each can stand alone, they are often interlinked in subtle ways, evoking the changing nature of life and society. Do not visit Ste. Odile, however, for neat picket fences and neighbourly greetings, for you are more likely to encounter madness and malformation, hopeless struggles, and the occasional bitter victory. And do not seek the services of anyone called Dr Treves. Trust me.

Finally, although McFarland has a fine hand for the uncanny and the supernatural, which are generously represented within, where he excels is in documenting the small natural tragedies which beset ordinary people, amplified by yearning and resentment. If you read only "Oblivion", "The Radium Girls", and "The Dark Walk Forward" itself, you will be well served.

Some of these stories may disturb you.

And they should.

John Linwood Grant
Yorkshire, July 2020

The Little Dead Thing

Abel Edwin Jarre
128 Constantinople St.
St. Odile

Mr. George M. Nance
441 William St.
Pittsburgh

Nov. 16, 1922, Thursday

George:

If I can't discover how to heal the wound God has put in my heart
to know Him, to understand and satisfy my longing for Him and
finally feel I am a part of His creation. I don't know how I will face the
years to come. I'm sorry to make these ravings (or musings) the main
part of my letters lately, and perhaps that is why you have not
answered me in so long, but I find I can hardly think about anything
else.

You've heard this before, ever since Fismette. Before the war I never
questioned that I knew the heart and will of God. I knew God kept me
apart and disconnected from the world for some reason, which would
someday be apparent to me. So arrogant when you think about it, that
any of us can understand the will of God! That day in Fismette when
the Germans finally crossed the river and that boy, that German
soldier of maybe twenty years of age who was carrying the flame
thrower canister—remember when the bullet struck the tank and the
lad went up in flames, remember how our boys cheered? It was a
spectacle, an entertainment. We cheered and laughed as he, the
enemy, screamed in the most horrific and pitiful agony. I aimed my
rifle at his head to put an end to his suffering, but I hesitated. He was
an enemy soldier, yes, but would not the act of shooting him in that
way be something other than the accepted barbarity of war? I knew, as
the Church says, I would have a murder on my hands, a mercy killing.
This boy who may have been raised a Catholic, as I was, who only
thought he was doing his duty to his country, must die slowly and
painfully so that I may not have a mortal sin on my soul. Lieutenant
Allen shot him, mercifully, so his immolation only lasted a few
seconds.

I killed two men that day, two I know of. Acceptably as a protocol of battle. I shot them on the bridge, and they fell into the river. It didn't affect me any more than putting my boots on that morning. They were strangers, objects, targets, the enemy. But that night, I could only think of the burned boy who died in such a different way. I wondered how is the suffering and loss of an enemy, the *other*, different from ours? Of course, it isn't. An obvious enough proposition, but I didn't really *understand* it before then. But the war was full of moments like that, wasn't it? As we said on the ship home that night when our time in the 111th was nearly over: war is moments where familiar things became understood in a different way, or understood more deeply. It's that connection that must be made to this world, to all of life which I have been seeking and turning over in my head for four years. I'm sorry to refer to it so often. One day, I hope to put it out of my mind.

With your wife's serious illness, maybe you have had these pointless "metaphysical" thoughts, too? I am glad Mae is feeling better (per your last letter in March), and her consumption was relieved by your trip to Arizona. Perhaps you will move there? I would hope to see you again and to meet her on your way west, if you do. I wish we had been able to do that on your first trip, but there it is.

I write to Eustace Kirby, too, as you may remember. He was as near as the landing at DeCastres Island in my very town in June, according to the visitor list in the newspaper, and he didn't visit me. "Eustace Kirby of Bremen Ridge Pennsylvania who served with distinction in the 111th Pennsylvania in the recent war, travelling to San Francisco, California with his wife Kate. The Kirbys came by boat down the Ohio then up the Mississippi to catch the train in Ste. Odile and travel north to their connection in St. Louis to continue their journey." I have written him seven or eight times since getting reestablished here in Ste. Odile. He was a few blocks away and chose not to visit me. I am at a loss to understand this.

I mentioned in my last letter, also, that my hopes of a future with my Lucy were fading. Her father has never approved of me. She says he wants no veteran of the war for her husband. He suspects that no man who lived through it would be unaffected enough to make a suitable mate for his daughter. He would never trust such a man to be capable of a normal family life after all we experienced. I have asked her for a final answer, asked that she consider only her own feelings, not her family's. I am still waiting to hear from her.

My work continues at the assay laboratory at Osage Lead Company. Mr. Karl, my supervisor, has hired a new technician; Roualt is his name. He is supposed to be my assistant, and I am to train him to process samples. The young man is concerned with details and organization and is good enough at arithmetic, so he is learning quickly, as I expected he would. It seemed to me there were barely enough samples to keep me occupied, as our production has fallen off so drastically since the war, but Karl has insisted that we will be much busier in the future, that there are prosperous times ahead, and we must be prepared. He has said there will soon be a push to add lead to gasoline, as it makes automobile engines run smoother, and our production will soon increase. However, I was unconvinced by this assertion and I asked Karl if he is dissatisfied with my work, or has come to dislike me for some reason, but he says I am imagining it. He says I spend too much time imagining plots against myself. I don't know what it is, George, but the town has not accepted me since I returned from the Army. Treves has noticed it, too, noticed that he is ostracized now. In his case, his injuries have changed his appearance so terribly; perhaps that is what is behind his situation. His surgery has fallen off to nothing. But as far as I can tell, I am unchanged, outwardly at least. But Ste. Odile has changed toward me. I am an outsider here.

Though I still harbor some concern for him, even Treves seems alien to me. What are the chances that two fellows from a tiny village on the Mississippi should find themselves, at the outbreak of a great war, in the same unit in a Pennsylvania battalion? I would have taken no bet on it! You would think with that great coincidence and the unifying experience of what came after, we would be brothers or fast friends thereafter, but we hardly have two words to say to each other. There it is.

I will close now so I do not miss the mailman.

Your Friend,
Abel

November 17, Friday

George:

I dozed off and missed sending yesterday's letter. Much has happened today. My suspicions were correct. Karl dismissed me this morning. He said my work had suffered recently, which I know is not true. He said Roualt can replace me very well now and at a lower rate of pay. And Karl is hiring a friend of Roualt's to be *his* assistant at an even lower rate. There it is! Dismissed! A veteran rewarded for his service. I had few personal things to retrieve, collected my seven dollars in wages, and walked the several blocks home to Constantinople Street.

It turned much colder overnight and the wind whipped in from the river as I made my way home. I have saved forty-two dollars which might sustain me for a few weeks, but as I walked against that cold wind I knew I must find other employment quickly, and that this new development will damage my prospects with Lucy even further unless I succeed. As I approached my front gate, I saw the ancient Mrs. Zell, my landlady, on the front walk. With some obvious revulsion, she was

3

examining something on the ground near the porch stairs. She looked up and saw me and waved urgently for me to hurry to her.

"I'll swain I've never *seen* such an ugly thing!" she said. She seemed awestruck and unwilling to take her eyes off the thing on the ground.

"What is it?" I could just see part of it behind a boxwood bush.

"I never *seen* such a thing. It's some ugly little thing, some little *dead* thing." Mrs. Zell's manner of speaking is to emphasize at least one word in every phrase or sentence. "What *is* that? I wonder how long it's *been* there? I *never* noticed it until just now."

"It looks like it's been dead a while," I said. "Maybe the cat dragged it here?" That prospect seemed unlikely. The creature was not as large as a cat but looked formidable. It was unlike anything I had ever seen. It was hairless except for a few patches of a gray, coarse fur near its hindquarters and on its feet... its *six* feet. It had forepaws armed with long, curved talons and two sets of hind legs, similarly armed. There was a short set of hind legs in front of a longer, more powerful set. The short legs seemed to be vestigial, or perhaps some sort of malformation, because like the forelimbs of the great Tyrannosaurs found in the West lately, they seemed to have no practical use.

The head of the creature was beyond classification. It had a short, muzzle-less face, two bulging eyes, filmy and gray in death, and a round mouth much like a lamprey's, with many needle-like teeth. Below the weak jaw were two appendages tipped with bony barbs that reminded me of the stinger of a scorpion. Its skin was gray with a bluish tinge, sagging and wrinkled and showing the first stages of decay.

"It's a chimera," I said. "I've never seen such a collection of deformities. What *is* it? We had many monstrous specimens in jars at the university, but nothing like this. Doesn't have much of a smell, does it?"

"I can't *touch* it," Mrs. Zell moaned. "Please get *rid* of it for me, Mr. Jarre."

"I wonder if we should notify someone? Some county official or the sheriff, or even one of my old professors at the Carthesian University?"

"I don't want to *see* it again. Just dispose of it *immediately*, please, and... why are you home from work in the *middle* of the morning?"

You may remember my interest in natural history and zoology. It was I who always cared for the war horses when I had the chance and looked after cats and dogs displaced by battle. In school I loved zoology more than chemistry, my major field of study, but couldn't foresee a way to make a living at it. I could not see myself dumping this horrific and unique creature in a grave or disposing of it in the city dump. I assured Mrs. Zell I would dispose of the dead thing.

I went up to my room and found an old lidded laboratory jar with a two-gallon volume I had retrieved from the lab after Karl threw it out. I had a supply of denatured alcohol, too, which I had brought home for cleaning and as lamp fuel. I poured about a gallon of this into the jar. In the shed back near the alley, I found a burlap sack and a shovel. From just outside the kitchen window I could hear Mrs. Zell speaking to her niece on the telephone, telling her the story of the discovery.

I slid the shovel under the body of the creature and lifted gently. It was so fragile with putrefaction that the gray skin tore as I lifted, revealing a swarming and disgusting mass of maggots inside. My gorge rose and I thought I might eject my breakfast on the spot! It seemed odd to me that with the weather turning colder the maggots would still be active in the body, but I soon saw a wisp of steam rise from the torn skin as though the body were still warm inside. As I held the top of the sack open and passed the laden shovel under it, one of the barbs on the creature's jaw scraped below my left thumb. I gently lay the burden inside the sack and immediately started to notice that the punctured place on my hand was going numb. By the time I lifted the sack off the ground, my left hand had gone completely dead and had become nearly useless. I reckoned the barbs deliver some sort of anesthetic or paralytic agent, as some insects and spiders do, which may aid in the killing of its prey.

I carried my burden up the front stairs so Mrs. Zell would not see me. Once in my room, I locked my door and lowered the sack into the jar which I had placed on my worktable. With a shears, I split the sack on both sides of the carcass and with a little twitching of the sack, the body slipped out. It drifted gracefully into the fluid, tatters of decayed flesh fluttering about it like tiny wings. One of the small rear legs fell off and wafted slowly to the bottom of the jar. The body settled against the side of the glass: its head and left shoulder near the top of the surface of the alcohol, and its hindquarters resting on the bottom. Soon, the body and the fluid into which it had been placed, were still. Its filmy eyes seemed to be looking at me. By this time, I had begun to notice the feeling returning to my left thumb.

I turned my desk chair around and sat in it, looking at the jar. The eyes of the creature still seemed fixed on me; they are an opaque gray-blue. I was struck again at what a chimera the thing is, at what impossible biological inheritances had come together so unbelievably and implausibly to create it. Now, at least, it is preserved in its jar and it will decompose no more but remain forever in its present suspended state until I can decipher its mysteries further. I think you will be the only person I tell about this thing George, at least for now. I will cover the jar with a sheet when I am away. I cover the whole table most of the time, and the Morstan girl who cleans up for Mrs. Zell never disturbs the sheet when she's in here. I think there is little chance she will discover my secret.

Yours,
Abel

November 22, 1922

George:

I wonder when you will receive my last letter and what your response will be? I hope you will respond, as I would like to have your reaction and opinion of the little dead thing. I will try to sketch it today and include that with this message.

The first action of a man displaced from his livelihood is to try to find his next employment in that same field. There is a limeworks in Ste. Odile; Seraphim Lime, it's called. Their offices and small laboratory are on Mal Ardents Street. I walked there after mailing Friday's letter. Mr. Arnot, who is in charge of the office and laboratory, agreed to see me, if grudgingly. His office is a glass-walled cubicle and it was freezing in there. He asked me to sit in an oaken chair opposite his desk. His face was purple, and his corduroy vest could scarcely contain his stomach.

"Abel Jarre," he said. "I have heard of you."

"I am surprised."

"Yes, I am in the Knights of Columbus, and one of my brothers there is Mr. Karl, your former supervisor."

"Ah." I felt my prospects here fade suddenly away. "I am surprised my name should come up between Lodge brothers."

"He mentioned you Friday night, the day he dismissed you. He thought you might come here seeking work."

I felt the anger rise inside me, but I did my best to suppress it. "So, he was warning you then," I said.

"He said you were not gregarious, not a joiner or a mixer. In fact, he said you have an argumentative and disagreeable nature. He mentioned you as a free thinker, an eccentric..."

"He and I have had our disagreements. I am nervous, high strung as my Lieutenant Allen used to say. But... I am not an atheist, if that's what you mean by 'free thinker,' sir. Far from it."

"I don't see you in church. You're not a Protestant, are you? In which case you are as *good* as an atheist."

"No, I was raised a Catholic. I speak to God in my own way. A more personal way. In the war, I started to see God differently than I had before, and I saw... that He wishes me to understand Him in a new light, different from the manner in which I was raised."

"That does sound a little eccentric to me," Arnot stifled a yawn. "We all need the Church whether we know it or not. Those who think otherwise are mistaken. Pure and simple. Isn't up to each of us to interpret Scripture. Then everyone would do whatever they wanted. You are a single man... yes?"

"Yes. I have asked a young lady to marry me, but she hasn't answered me yet. If I get a new position, perhaps..."

"Karl told me you were in the 111th Pennsylvania. How did that come about?"

"There was nothing for me here... at the time. I had no family, or... I went to Pittsburgh for a new start, to see if I could work in the laboratory of a coal company, but the only job I could get was as a hand loader underground. Backbreaking work. Then we got into the war."

Arnot looked at me as though he either didn't believe my story or was not the least interested in it; I couldn't tell which.

"I know you have experience and I could make a place for you immediately," he finally said, "but I have to think about it. It's a small space here to be closed up together all day. I don't like to rock the boat. A different personality can rock the boat. I didn't want to take Karl's word alone about you. I wanted to hear your responses to his assertions for myself. I am a fair man, and as I said, there is work you could do now. But... I don't know. Let me think it over. Your boarding house has a telephone? I will call in a few days if I decide to proceed. Thank you for coming in, Mr. Jarre."

It had turned much colder in the brief time I had been at Seraphim. The walk home took me past Boyer's Butcher Shop, and I thought of stopping in to ask if there was any work available there, but I argued with Boyer a year ago about some spoiled mutton he sold me, and he has never seemed to like me much since. And besides, I was anxious to get back to my room to study the creature more and sketch it for you.

Before I could get back home, it began to snow: large, fluffy flakes that quickly blanketed grass, trees, and the brick, stone and iron fences and gates of Ste. Odile. I stood on the front porch of the boarding house watching the snow fall. I was transfixed by the look of it, by the beautiful silence, and only when it struck me how cold my face and feet were, did I realize I must have been standing there for a very long time. I find that my attention wanders more and more lately, and I often forget what I am about. Back in my room, I uncovered the jar and for all the world I could swear that the creature had moved a little. Its head seemed deeper below the surface of the alcohol, and its left forelimb wasn't in the same position as before.

Its eyes had seemed to move, too. I stared at it in mild disbelief for fully five minutes, but I detected no twitch or tremor. The animal's filmy orbs seemed to be looking deeply into my own eyes. As I stood looking down at it on the tabletop, it was peering directly back at me. When I pulled my chair next to the table, sat and looked at it again, it was still looking at me. I sat as still as I could for thirty minutes and didn't take my eyes off of it. I saw not the slightest suggestion of movement. I removed my sketching diary from my desk, found a pencil and started to draw the thing. As I sketched, concentrating on getting just the right curvature of the odd skull, in my peripheral vision, I thought I perceived the creature twitch slightly. When I looked directly at it, I could see there was some little disturbance to the liquid in the jar, but saw no sign of change in the creature.

The snow continued to fall heavily. There are but a handful of automobiles in Ste. Odile, and I could hear that one of them had become stuck in a snowbank on the street below. I looked out my window and saw the yellow Packard of Robert Dufresne half-buried in a drift, tires spinning uselessly. This was the same Dufresne I mentioned in a letter of last spring who objected to my membership in the Ste. Odile Ethical Union and was solely responsible for my rejected application. He got out of his car and examined his predicament. The solution, of course, was a push. He was in need of someone to push him out. After a second, he glanced upward and saw me looking at him from my window. After a few seconds more, when I was sure he recognized me, I turned and resumed my seat. Did I do the wrong thing, George? It was spitefulness, wasn't it? It was a prideful and vengeful sin, and I wish now I had done otherwise.

I heard a rustle of paper behind me. I turned to see that Mrs. Zell or one of her girls had slipped a note under my door. It was from Lucy. It read:

Dear Abel:

> *My family has helped me realize that the affection I have felt for you for the past year is more in the nature of friendship than romantic love. I am honored by your proposal of marriage, but given the limitations of my feelings for you, I know it would be a mistake to accept it, one which we would both soon regret. In addition, we have heard of your being terminated from your job, news which further sullies any notion of a comfortable future with you which any woman might entertain. My greatest wish is that you find a lady who can return your feelings in kind. Thank you for your attentions to me and best of luck.*

> *Your Friend,*
> *Lucy*

So, there was my answer. I am a poor prospect, and it seems she never loved me anyway! I always suspected as much, and her note came as no great surprise. Still, it was painful, to see it written out like that. I will go for a walk in a little while and try to clear my head or distract my thoughts, whichever seems more appropriate at the time. I sat back down at my desk.

I added a few finishing touches to my sketch of the creature. Satisfied I had reproduced it accurately, I will include it with this letter and get it in the mail to you.

Sincerely,
Abel

December 4, 1922

George:

It has been so long since I have heard from you. I check the mail anxiously every day, and with some excitement, yet nothing comes. Of course, Mrs. Zell knows of my unemployment now. She has said if I have no new job by the end of this month, she would prefer that I find other lodgings because she has no place for transients—as I will shortly be! No house will take in an unemployed man when I am put out of here, so it is becoming almost certain that I must leave town.

Yet, I start every day with more hope than the day proves to warrant. There is expectation of some boon or positive helpful thing, that *could* happen, but what that could specifically be, I cannot define. All I know is that no such thing *does* happen. Every day is the same. I awake at four or five in the morning. I toast some bread and fry an egg for my breakfast, and I sit for an hour or more and look at the dead thing in the jar. I still have no notion of what it is or where it fits into Nature. I sketched it again and sent that to John Stubbs, one of my zoology professors at Carthesian, but no response, yet. He may think I am trying out some practical joke on him. I will need to buy a camera and photograph it.

The most striking thing about the creature, I say again, is what an impossible mixture of heritages it is. It defies what little I understand about genetical science. I wonder how intelligent it was. I wonder if it had thought processes of a predator, which are necessarily more complex than those of prey animals. And I wondered where more of the species might be or if it was the last of its kind. I still own a copy of *The Classification of Higher Vertebrates* by Hawkins, from my undergraduate days, and an antique copy of *Compendium Naturalis Mundi* by Van Der Meet, which I found in a bookseller's stall a few years ago in St. Louis. I found nothing in either of these which in any way corresponds to my creature. I walked to the small Ste. Odile public library on Bucephalus Street, but their sad collection of volumes on natural history also contained no reference or image of anything I could relate to my animal. I hope that Stubbs will take an interest and help me with this. Perhaps my letter will induce him to come look at it, as I can't quite imagine carrying the jar with me on the train. On my way home from the library, I asked for work at the bakery and Broussard's Pharmacy, but was given no encouragement from either. Back at home, I clipped tatters of flesh from the creature in three different places and have prepared slides for such a time when I may have access to a microscope and examine them in detail, or send them to Stubbs for examination.

I watch the thing and watch it. Sometimes for a moment I am distracted by something, perhaps something I have never noticed before in my surroundings. Something unextraordinary elsewhere in my room, like the smoothness of my desktop or the weight of my pocket watch or penknife, or even re-reading Lucy's note, and my attention wanders. It is only at those times that I think I notice that the thing moves, almost imperceptibly. If there is some spark of life in it and it wishes to deceive me, it is failing at that, because I know what I am seeing is real.

And at night in my bed when the room is dark, I sometimes think I hear the movement of liquid, a slight sloshing sound, but I can't be sure about that. At those moments it seems there is no other sound in the world, no human activity in the street, no animal noise or boats on the river, nothing but the sound in the jar, that *liquid* sound. A terror strikes me that if the thing would turn out to be alive, the lid of the jar could not contain it, and in the dark while I sleep, it could be abroad in the room with me. By the time I get the light on to investigate, there is nothing to be seen. Then I must take some of my bromide to settle into sleep again.

Dec. 5

I have started to duplicate everything I have written you in a journal. I wanted to have my own copy of this experience, otherwise it may be lost. It seems less likely every week that you will ever answer these letters.

I should start packing my things, but most days I don't have the energy or concentration to do it. Mrs. Zell hardly speaks to me at all now, except to remind me of what day of the month it is. I told her I have inquired at most of the other boarding houses in town but they either have no room for me or do not want me. I continue to have no luck in finding any kind of job. Since my dismissal from Osage Lead, my reputation has spread across town. An undeserved reputation, an unfair one, I hope. I should consider moving to St. Louis or maybe back to Pittsburgh. The society of this little town is closed and unwelcoming. Humans are social creatures, and when an individual is ostracized by his group and cast out, it leaves an emptiness in his soul which defies description. There is no more certain way to kill a man than that, I think. I have a little more than thirty dollars to my name.

Yes, I should begin packing, but sometimes I don't think I move for hours at a stretch. From time to time, I wonder if I should go out or stay in. I ask myself where I would go if I went out? If I went out, I would pass men in the streets who have wives and families, friends and coworkers. Yes, they have all of those gifts from above, they have a place in the order of things, the clear and well-understood blessing of God. I will not have my Lucy, nor anyone else, most likely. So it seems to me now. But none of those men have what I have. None of them have this secret. I stare for hours at the thing in the jar because now I know, I am sure it must be watching me. I want to *see* it move directly, not *suspect* it has moved. I want to know unambiguously that there is some little glimmer of life in it. I possess this thing. I have a connection to it, and no one else on earth may say that. If my prospects are few and unpromising, maybe there is some way I can exploit that connection, or use it to secure some livelihood, some sort of future for myself? This creature was put in front of me for a reason, surely. Finding it, classifying it, and describing it to the world is obviously what I am meant to do. Most of the time I am certain of this. Other times I am not so sure. Maybe exploitation of this animal would be wrong. I am a private man. Maybe God put it in my way *because* I am so private. Maybe God's plan for me in His creation has always been with regard to this creature. It is so hard to know what God wants. Why would this responsibility be given to me? The only reason I can imagine is that this is the answer I have been seeking these four years. I just have to *understand* it.

I will go to sleep now. The silence is what is so oppressive. Any little sound can become frightening, can seem to be a threat or be distorted by my imagination. Did I hear the lid of the jar move? Did I hear the movement of liquid? If I hear activity on the street or the sounds of other people in the house, the troubling sound is masked or hidden. There is none of that now, so I try to sleep so I will hear nothing that will unsettle me. Tomorrow, I will pawn anything I still have which may be of value and pack my things. I will buy a train ticket to St. Louis. It appears I must go to St. Louis.

Later

This morning, I carried a bundle of things with me to LaHaye's Pawn Shop on Rouen Street close by. I took some trouble to bring some lidded jars and an old burner and even my copy of Van Der Meet, which I thought might be of some value. LaHaye scowled and studied the things and in the end refused to buy anything I had brought. Now what am I to do? I will soon have no place to live and no means of establishing myself elsewhere.

Afternoon

George, the creature moved! Just as I was awakening from a nap, I saw it, clearly and without doubt. It twitched and some white particles floated up from the tear in its skin. A stab of terror shot through my stomach as I watched it floating in its liquid until the ripples in the jar subsided. Slowly, I got out of my bed and approached it. Now its filmy eye did not seem to be watching me, but only staring vacantly at the wall behind me. As I neared the jar, I could see that the white particles which had floated up from the tear in the creatures skin were bitten-off fragments of the maggots I had seen inside it the day I recovered it from under the bush. Slowly and carefully, I lifted the heavy lid from the jar and looked down at the thing inside. I looked into the torn flesh of the back. The tissue inside it was a nondescript blue-gray confusion of subcutaneous fat and muscle and collapsing gray blood vessels. But something else beyond these caught my attention. It was a familiar shape, but one I could not quite define or make sense of. Suddenly, the shape quivered and slid downward across a glistening and awakening orb. It was an eyelid blinking across a yellow, sensate eye!

I withdrew in horror and disgust across the room from the thing. I stood at my window looking back at it trying to understand what I had seen. I was breathing frantically. I tried to steady myself. After a few moments, I approached the table again, slowly and tentatively. I looked down into the jar. The tear in the dead creature's skin was a little wider and cleaner now, and I could see that this was so because the smaller one inside had eaten away the edges of the wound. Shivering with revulsion, I looked at it, and in a moment, its minute wriggling and writhing to feed revealed that it was an immature version of the dead thing which had served as its host. I clapped the lid back on the jar and withdrew again to my window. I sat at my desk, never taking my eyes off the jar.

This was the creature's nature. It reproduced itself by growing an embryo inside which slowly consumed the host body of the mother: a type of matriphagy as some spiders practice. Or perhaps this carcass was the father and the fertilized zygote is placed within him while he is alive, to grow as is seen in some marine animals, I believe. The males in nature are usually more disposable than females. This conjecture makes the most sense to me. And the growing fetus must be anaerobic if circumstances warrant, even after it is viable, otherwise it could never survive in the alcohol.

A knock at my door. "Mr. Jarre?" It was Mrs. Zell. "I have a *letter* here for you. Just arrived." She pushed it under the door. "And Mr. *Jarre*, I have a young lady coming up from Cape Girardeau on Monday. Miss *Connolly* is her name. She is to be the new *housekeeper* at the rectory. I want her to have *this* room. I would be *obliged* if you could be out by the weekend."

"But I was counting on having the full month, Mrs. Zell."

"We rent by the *week*, Mr. Jarre. I can put you out at my *discretion*. By the weekend, if you *please*."

"I need more time, Mrs. Zell. I have nowhere to go."

"To be *honest*, Mr. Jarre, I regretted bringing you in here almost *immediately*. You have always been an *ill* fit. I don't know *why* you would want to stay in a *house*, or a *town* for that matter, where you weren't wanted. I shouldn't repeat this, but now I hear from Mrs. *LaHaye* that you have tried to sell goods to her *husband* which were obviously stolen from your last employer. She believes Mr. Karl has pressed a complaint against you, and the Sheriff has a *warrant* for your arrest which he will execute when he returns from that *shooting* business on DeCastres Island in a day or two. Perhaps I shouldn't have *mentioned* it, but I have always spoken *plainly,* and you are hardly in a position to run away from the *justice* awaiting you... and I suppose you have a right to know. I will have no *undesirables* in my house."

I am to be arrested? The old woman's words were like a judgment from Heaven. It was like that moment on the transport ship when we realized that the war made us understand everything in a new way. The entire town wants me gone, and I have no means to go elsewhere. So, what will I do?

There was a slight sloshing sound in the jar. I could see the gray, slippery body of the dead thing twitch a little as the offspring inside it fed. I arose and went to my door, picking up the letter Mrs. Zell had pushed under it. It was from Professor Stubbs at Carthesian. It said:

Mr. Jarre:

> *You claim to have been in a vertebrate zoology class of mine some ten years ago, but I have no memory of you. Your letter is obviously a hoax as the creature you describe is a biological impossibility, as someone with a true knowledge of natural history would certainly know. Please find better ways to occupy your time than by dreaming up nonsense to waste the time of persons more productive than yourself.*

> *Signed,*
> *J.S.*

So, there it is George. I am soon to be homeless or arrested, and I have no prospects but to take this thing in its jar and try to show some scientific or academic person that it is real and I have made a great discovery. But who will listen? I am exhausted. I must rest.

Dec. 7

George: This will be my last letter. I will leave it on my table for Mrs. Zell to find. And what *else* will she find? I am not well. I am not strong, but I am content. I feel such peace now. I am holding a towel to my face as I write. My face is numb but bloody. Covered in blood. I slept a deep, undrugged sleep last night. I scarcely moved all night and only awoke ten minutes ago. As I started to awaken, I noticed that the lower half of my face was numb, completely without feeling. There was a small weight on my chest and neck. As my eyes slowly focused, I was horrified to see the young creature from the jar sitting on my chest, just at the collarbone. Its dark eyes watched me indifferently. Its small body was a perfect copy of its dead parent, except it had more fur. Its mouth and face were covered in blood. My blood! It had deadened my face with its stingers! I gasped and choked on the blood I inhaled with the breath. I jumped out of my bed and saw that the mattress was splattered in red. The little thing fell to the floor with a soft, flopping thud, and seemed unhurt and unperturbed.

I pressed myself to the wall and moved away from it to my front door. I opened the door and looking out into the hallway, I could see no one was about. Mrs. Zell was probably downstairs, and it was too early for the Morstan girl to come and clean. I slipped down the hallway to the lavatory and turned on the light. To my horror I saw that my lips had been eaten away in a ragged pattern revealing bloody teeth within. A little cry escaped my tattered mouth, spattering blood on the mirror.

At first, I could not think of what to do. I could not think of calling Mrs. Zell, or returning to my room. After a few minutes, I made my way back down the hallway to my door. My fear and sense of revulsion had suddenly subsided. Now I could not define how I was feeling, except to say there was no panic. I was suddenly calm and clear-headed. I opened my door and edged into my room. The little creature was still where it had fallen, and seemed completely oblivious to me.

I watched it for many minutes. It was cleaning the blood from the edges of its mouth. It seemed so purposeful and focused on its natural function, on the undoubted, perfect fulfillment of its nature: its God-ordained purpose, as the Bible says. I don't know if I smiled at it or not as I peacefully watched it. If I did, it would not have been recognizable as a smile. I locked my door and braced my one dining chair against the knob. I sat at my desk and wrote this account for you. This action, this perfect, natural action had begun, and I must not interfere with it. I am filled with the love of God at this moment, and so grateful for His blessing... George my friend... or one whom I once thought of that way, a deep, deep sleep is what is needed, that I may better comply with my part in this. My bromide powder is on the table...

One Happy Family

Dr. Ellison's eyes burned. He squinted into the darkness, into the low-lying mist on the desolate gravel road ahead of his car, and it seemed the harder he concentrated on avoiding the gullies and potholes that regularly appeared out of nowhere, the sleepier he became. His vision was becoming more difficult to focus after each blink of his eyelids, and he realized that for several moments he had been mesmerized by the white mists drifting through the beams of his headlights. He rolled his window down a few inches and turned off the heater. This never made him less sleepy; it just made his physical discomfort more important than his sleepiness for the time being.

Three-twenty a.m. Babies, of course, always come in the middle of the night. Probably seventy-five percent of all children he'd delivered in the past six years had been born between midnight and five a.m. If Mrs. Knoss was as far along as her husband had described on the phone, then maybe hard labor would start soon. After all, she'd had four children. This one would probably come a little quicker than the last, and the last had, as Mrs. Knoss had told him, been an easy, fast birth. If this were over by six, he could get home and get a couple of hours' sleep before he had to be at the office—no, hospital. Tomorrow was the day he had to reinforce Mrs. Lupke's cervix. Later in the day, he would remove and insert IUDs, check for tiny heartbeats through the taut skin of swollen bellies, and possibly deliver another baby. Mrs. Grasse was due within the week, and she was always unpredictable. Hysterical and unpredictable. You'd think that after eight kids she wouldn't fall apart every time, but she'd been raised that way: to think of her labor as her "sickness," and to scream during delivery whether she really needed to or not. Ellison was sure that Mrs. Grasse's mother had been the same way, and her grandmother, and he knew that she would teach her own girls to think of themselves as inferior to their brothers, to regard sex as a distasteful duty to their husbands, and to bring forth children, as the Bible says, in pain: affected, if necessary, but certainly underscored in hysterics. He dreaded the thought of having to deal with her—he'd been too tired and depressed lately to be patient with her righteous ignorance.

Mrs. Knoss was not like that. Though she was well into her forties, she was as excited about this baby as many young women are about their first. There was no doubt in Ellison's mind that the child he would deliver tonight, as well as all the Knoss children, was the product of genuine, unself-conscious love.

She'd first visited Ellison when her pregnancy was in its fifth month. She and her husband, Luther, had moved to the Arkansas Ozarks from some place in Kentucky, where they had briefly lived, having come there from West Virginia. Merrilee had wanted only the most superficial care from Ellison. She'd shown no interest in having an ultrasound image, or in learning about PKU testing or any of the other modern medical assurances that other expectant mothers usually required. The couple had been peculiarly elusive in answering many of Ellison's questions about their monthly visits. He knew they were poor: their clothes were dated and shabby. He'd also gathered that they were virtually illiterate. And all they would say about Luther's professional was that he was a "wildcrafter," selling herbs and roots gathered in the woods at flea markets and county fairs, along roadsides, or wherever he could set up a table.

Ellison shifted in his seat uncomfortably. Driving these winding gravel roads always exhausted him. He was accustomed to wide, well-lit asphalt streets and sidewalks. In the past few months, he had begun to regret his decision to leave his profitable but relentless Chicago practice to become a country doctor. Things had not been as idyllic as he had imagined. The air was clean and the countryside beautiful, but the workload was no easier. In fact, the work seemed more oppressive because there were no cultural distractions, no nightlife, none of the urban things he was missing now, things that he was certain only a couple of months ago that he would not miss. And there were poverty and ignorance, two things he hadn't encountered much in Lake Forest. He had felt genuine compassion for these people at first, but no he found himself growing annoyed and resentful. of having to treat patients who believed that opossums mate through their noses, and that urinating in the road will result in a stye in one's eye. Still, some of his patients, like the Knosses, made it more bearable. He rather envied their affection for each other, and their apparent indifference to their poverty. He smiled to himself, remembering Merrilee's enthusiastic optimism after her last examination. "I know I'm going to do everything right. With you there a-keepin' an eye on me, I know I'll do it right."

Ellison had been getting more involved with home births lately than he really wanted to be. Yes, he believed that women should have an alternative to the regimentation and assembly-line rapidity sometimes found in hospital deliveries, but he never dreamed the idea would catch on to this extent, and that he would be called upon to give up so much sleep. The Knosses didn't belong to the generation of new parents who had rediscovered home birth. They were from some sequestered, unchanging place in the Blue Ridge or Smokey Mountains, a place unaware of or unconcerned with national trends. Ellison doubted whether either of them had ever seen the inside of a hospital.

Ellison's head felt numb, and he was finding it almost impossible to concentrate on his driving. He thought for a moment that he heard a new tapping or clicking noise coming from his engine. He shuddered at the thought of being stranded out here, ten or eleven miles from the highway and another eight from Staleyville. His mind drifted back to Mrs. Grasse—back to her first visit after he had set up his practice the year before last. She had been a long-standing patient of Ellison's chief competitor in town, Dr. Castellano, who was notoriously brusque with histrionic women. "He's an odd bird," Mrs. Grasse had confided. "All that money and he married an Oriental!"

Ellison started. For a moment he wasn't sure where he was. He had made a trip out to the Knosses' cottage only once before, in daylight. He rubbed his eyes and stared into the dark woods. Off to the right, down in a small hollow, he spotted a dim yellow light. A porchlight. He remembered now. A few feet farther there should be a drive.

As soon as Ellison turned his car into the nearly washed-out gravel drive, a light came on in the front room of the cottage. The front door opened, and Ellison could see Luther peering out anxiously toward him.

"Jest pull 'er up here anywhere, Doctor," Luther called, scurrying out to pull open the car door almost before Ellison had stopped the car. Ellison groped for his bag with his right hand as Luther tugged at his left arm, trying, it seemed, to lift him off the car seat. Ellison had forgotten how tall Luther was. Tall and amazingly thin, with a whiskerless face whose age was impossible to guess. Ellison intended to say something about nearly getting lost, but Luther, guiding him anxiously toward the house, was talking nonstop.

"Her water broke at ten minutes to two. The pains is down to six minutes. The kids is so excited. I thaink I got everthaing ready for ye..."

***

The inside of the cottage was as dreary as Ellison had remembered. It had apparently been abandoned for ten or twelve years before the Knosses had moved in, and they had done little to restore it, except for having the electricity turned back on. There were boxes of dusty jars on the floor, as well as various automobile engine parts. Most of the original wallpaper had long ago been pulled from the walls or had fallen from the weight of the slowly crumbling structure behind it. In its place, dirty sheets of corrugated cardboard had been nailed up to contain the dust of disintegrating plaster. A clothesline had been tacked across the corner of the west and north walls in the front room, and several articles of Merrilee and Luther's clothing hung from it. Conspicuously absent were any children's clothes, and Ellison wondered for a moment if the children might be self-sufficient enough to wash their own laundry. Alongside the front door stood the aquarium that had puzzled Ellison on his first visit. It seemed absurd to him that people as impoverished as these would keep pet fish. The ten-gallon tank was so green with algae that nothing distinct was visible within. The dark, nondescript shapes which were suspended motionlessly in the water could have been weeds and mosses, though some of the mass looked like thick, wide clumps of dirty cotton. Vaguely disgusted, Ellison assumed that the contents of the aquarium filter had been dumped into the water. The children must have done it. Did Luther and Merrilee let their kids run wild, and were they not expected to clean up the results of their vandalism? Surely, they had noticed the mess. Ellison was certain that there was nothing left alive in the tank except the algae and perhaps a few hopelessly overworked snails.

Something else about the house seemed familiar and in place. From out in the nearby woods—or perhaps it was the small strip of yard bordering the drive—came the mewing of a cat. The sound never became the scream or meow of an older cat, but was the mewing of a kitten, though the resonance and volume of the sound suggested an adult animal. Ellison remembered reading somewhere, *Natural History*, probably, that tiger cubs at a certain stage in their development must be taught to kill with one bite by their mothers. A cub that does not learn this never matures emotionally. *Perhaps the same is true of domesticated cats*, he thought.

Luther led Ellison into the bedroom where Merrilee sat naked in their sagging double bed, propped up by pillows and partially covered with a sheet. She looked old in the harsh light of a bare lightbulb, which dangled tentatively from the ceiling. The room was filled with the smell of stale sweat. She smiled broadly as they approached her.

"Sorry ta call ye out in the 'idle of the night like this, Dr. Ellison," she said in a voice cracking with weariness.

"Don't worry about that. How are you doing?"

"I'm fine. I don't thaink I'll keep ye a-waitin' fer long."

Luther sat beside her on the bed and began to dab at her face with a cloth he had dampened in a bowl of water on the floor. Ellison placed his bag on a trunk that stood against the east wall, and, snapping it open, he removed his stethoscope.

"Let's see how he's doing," he said in a tone which was intended to sound soothing, but instead seemed to him over-rehearsed and mechanical. He fixed the stethoscope earpieces in place and listened to Merrilee's stomach.

"It's good and strong, as usual. Now... if he's in position..."

He slid his hands over the smooth orb of her belly. As in previous examinations, he could not tell in what position the child lay inside her. He sighed heavily to himself.

"Is somethin' wrong?" Luther asked nervously.

"This is a tricky little guy in here." Ellison smiled wearily, dreading the possibility of a breech birth. "In four months, I haven't been able to plot his position. I ought to check your dilation..."

"Not jest yet," Merrilee said and winced as another contraction began. "I don't want to be touched jest yet."

Ellison nodded his assent. He knew better than to press the point with her.

"Three minutes apart now," Luther noted as he looked at his pocket watch.

"It shouldn't be too much longer," Ellison said, suppressing a yawn. "Are your other kids going to witness the birth?"

"Oh, yes," Merrilee gasped.

"Are they in bed? I'd think with all the excitement..."

"No, they're awake," Luther interrupted. "They're as excited as we are."

"Where are they?"

"They're around."

Ellison was annoyed—and a little insulted—by Luther's elusiveness. Surely, they felt close enough to him by now to show him the courtesy of answering his questions. Why were they so secretive? He felt like telling them that he had only been making conversation, that he really didn't give a *damn* about where the kids were. He had assumed when he asked the question, that they were peeking out at him from behind their door, having been told to keep out of the way until their mother could cope with their presence during the delivery. He felt himself getting a headache.

The contractions continued to come at three-minute intervals for the next hour and a half. Ellison sat on the trunk against the wall and his eyes felt as if hot blasts of air were hitting them. The harsh light in the room was making his headache worse. He craved a cup of coffee, but if Luther had offered one, he would have refused it. He'd have rather fallen asleep during the delivery than consume anything prepared in the Knoss home.

If he were still in the city, he would have spent the event at the Schubert with a late dinner at Benihana's. He thought of Piper's Alley and Old Town, of the jazz bands at Rick's, and the sight of the moon on Lake Michigan from atop the Hancock Building. He rubbed the back of his neck. His nerves were fraying slowly, and he knew it. Over the past weeks, he had begun to notice it more and more. The less sleep he got and the greater his workload, the more difficult it was for him to face his daily responsibilities. Two weeks ago, he had started taking lithium to stabilize his moods. If only he could take one now...

The cat could be heard mewing at the rear of the house, just beyond a window behind the bed. As he stood to retrieve his bag, Ellison glanced toward the front room. He hadn't noticed it before, but nearly the entire inside of the house was visible from his vantage point. There was the front room with its doorless, empty closet, the kitchen-dining area, and the bedroom in which he stood, with the bathroom adjoining it. He saw no other doors. There were no children's rooms. Suddenly and inexplicably, Ellison felt a stab of fear in his stomach. For a reason he couldn't pinpoint, he found himself compelled to act as if he hadn't noticed anything. The four Knoss children for whom he had imagined names and personalities were abruptly and brutally wiped out of his mind. Almost against his will, his eyes darted around the house again. If the children *were* hiding, there was no place for them to conceal themselves. They *must* be outside. But it was no warmer than forty-five degrees outside, and Ellison had been there nearly two hours. It wasn't possible. They must in the house *somewhere*.

Merrilee and Luther hadn't noticed the momentary shift in Ellison's attention. He knew his exhaustion was distorting everything. *They are simple, good people*, he thought, repeating it in his mind, though they were beginning to seem filthy and malevolent. The problem of the children dogged him; maybe they had never existed, or maybe they had died. They might even have been killed. These ignorant, inbred mountain families, isolated from society and immune to the law, could be capable of anything. Ellison breathed in and out deeply in an attempt to regain control of his thoughts. After a moment, his mind cleared, and he smiled to himself. "I've got to start getting more sleep," he thought. "I'm getting as hysterical as Edna Grasse."

He pulled the sheet that covered Merrilee back to her knees and for a second, he was sick at the thought of giving her a pelvic examination. He removed a roll of thin plastic gloves from his bag, tore one off and slipped it over his right hand.

"I've got to check your dilation now."

This time, Merrilee nodded obligingly as Luther continued to dab at her flushed cheeks. Ellison probed gently for the cervix. One, two, three centimeters. She would have to be nine or ten centimeters to give birth to a normal-sized child. Why wasn't she dilated? He felt further. He should have been able to feel the child's head, unless it were a breech birth. He felt nothing recognizable.

The cat's mewing had continued nonstop for many minutes. Ellison found the sound was distracting him.

"You're not dilated," he said in an abrupt, almost accusatory tone.

"I'll be all right," she cooed softly. "I know I'm going to do everything right."

Ellison found himself annoyed with her placidity. *He* was the doctor. *He* was the best judge of whether or not she was going to be all right. The throbbing in his head intensified.

"You're going to have the baby in the next ten minutes or so, and there isn't enough room for it to come out."

"We really thaink she's a-goin' ta be all right this time," Luther interjected. "We're proud of our other kids, but this one's a-goin' ta be the best."

Ellison suddenly wondered if these people were mocking him. Their expressions, their vocal inflections, no longer seemed genuine. Perhaps Merrilee wasn't in labor at all. He realized he hadn't felt her stomach during a contraction yet this evening. She couldn't fake the feel of a contraction. If she were faking, he'd know. Perhaps they intended to isolate him out here for some sinister reason. *This is preposterous*, he thought. *If ever a woman looked like she was in labor, Merrilee does. I've got to get a hold on myself. I can't believe I'm thinking these things.* Ellison breathed deeply again until he felt himself calming. *This is great. She's having a baby and I'm the one who has to do the breathing exercises!* He felt the need to say something offhanded and chatty.

"Those kids of yours must be hiding from me."

He felt immediately that this was not the chatty thing he wanted to say. Whatever was going on here between these people and their children, he didn't want to know.

"They ain't hidin'," Luther said.

"Oh... well, all I meant was..."

"Only three lives with us; that's Lester, Lonny, and Virgil. Walter's at college."

Ellison grew angry now. They'd been toying with him, lying to him for no reason. The thought of a Knoss child in an academic setting was ridiculous, and somehow offensive.

"*You've* got a son going to college?"

"He ain't a-goin' there, he's there!"

"How'd you pay for it? By selling roots and weeds on the roadside?"

"We don't pay for it," Luther said, looking puzzled. "They pay us."

Ellison was so angry he couldn't think clearly for a moment.

"They pay you? They pay students to attend this college?"

"He ain't a student. He's there to be... studied."

The mewing from the back of the house had reached a maddening crescendo. Ellison could think of nothing else. He stood and faced the window.

"Can't you shut that..." Ellison's voice failed him.

The mewing thing that peered in at him from the darkness was a filmy-eyed glistening mass with three or four appendages dangling limply off the windowsill. Several black orifices punctured its nearly gelatinous body; these were partially veiled in shimmering mucous membranes. Ellison was transfixed. He felt the muscles in his back and shoulders freeze and tighten to the point of pain.

"There's Lonny now." Luther smiled, nodding toward the window. "And Lester's in there."

He tapped the trunk that stood against the wall with his foot, and an animated scratching and gurgling sound arose from within.

"And in there, in the 'quarium, that's Virgil."

Merrilee grasped Luther's hand tightly as another contraction began.

"This time," she said weakly, but in a voice tentative with joyous anticipation, "this time I'm going to get it *right!*"

The Thing Under the Seat

Dr. Ellison thought Merrilee, the laboring woman, was making a tasteless, stress-induced joke until he saw the child she delivered. "I don't know what it is but I'm gonna get it *right* this time!" she said through her teeth, moments before the birth. But she wasn't joking. The infant was a conglomeration of deformities Ellison hadn't seen outside of his medical school textbooks. It had flap-like appendages where arms and legs should be, a single yellow eye and what appeared to be gill-slits behind its ears. It gasped for breath a few times and died. As Ellison adjusted to the shock of what he was seeing, he realized that Merrilee had died too. At that moment, his hand was on her stomach, and he could feel it growing colder by the second.

For a few moments, Ellison's thoughts, his awareness, left his body. The previous hour couldn't have been real. He'd just been thinking earlier that day that he was reaching his limit. He had one overworked week after another, and his body never seemed to have the chance to recover. He had nightmares most nights, balanced by insomnia, depression, and loss of appetite. Exhaustion was overtaking him, and obsession with his own physical decline, and in the last three weeks he had begun hearing things he knew couldn't be real and seeing things in his peripheral vision that turned out to be nothing.

Why did he ever start doing home deliveries again? They were taxing enough back in Chicago, where you just had to find a street address, but why did he move down to this country backwater where you had to find a shack or a trailer on a dirt road out in the woods somewhere? He had done his time in VISTA and The Peace Corps. That was all before he went into private practice in Lake Forest and switched to hospital deliveries only. It was a comfortable life and he never fully accepted that he had done his humanitarian duty as a physician; he should feel no guilt in leaving it at that. But he knew he couldn't leave it at that. He found himself checking listings weekly for retiring country doctors needing younger partners in the Ozark foothills. He found Dr. Estes's practice listed and purchased it within a week. At age eighty-six, Estes died before Ellison could relocate, so he had a backlog of work before he ever took possession of his new office.

So now he was doing the right thing again, the work he was meant to do. He had given up his comforts, but he had found himself wondering every day if it was worth it. Yes, there was a great need, but these people who needed his help so much often distrusted him as a stranger and outsider. They often didn't do the things he advised them to do to ensure their own health and the health of their babies. These home births were taxing and dangerous under these conditions. You often didn't have what you needed if anything went wrong. Like tonight.

He brought his mind back to this shabby room where he was standing over a monstrous stillborn infant and a dead woman.

Ellison regained control of his thoughts, and he knew tonight had been no hallucination. It had been real, and there was nothing he could have done to prevent it. And now he began to understand that his own life might be in danger.

And Ellison wasn't imagining the pain and rage on Luther's face. Merrilee's husband: that rage, that emotion, were unmistakably real. Luther's shock had given way to sorrow, and finally rage, and that rage now was all directed at Ellison.

"You kilt her!" Luther said. He looked slowly up at Ellison. "*You!*"

"No, Mr. Knoss. Luther. The child had... extreme deformities. Something was very wrong here. I told the both of you the development seemed abnormal, but you wouldn't agree to the testing I..."

"You come out here to our home an' you kilt her! They weren't nothin' wrong with that baby. She delivered all the ones before and come through 'em fine until you come along. Both dead. You done this."

Ellison felt his exhausted mind drifting away from the moment again. Hours ago, as soon as he pulled his car into their overgrown yard, something seemed wrong about the Knoss home. It was a ramshackle clapboard farmhouse so far from the county road out in the woods that he almost couldn't find it. Ellison remembered thinking he was being watched as he approached the front door of the dilapidated, filthy house. Once inside, he thought he glimpsed some wet, misshapen creature watching him through the window. He knew that must have been his mind tricking him again. It was only a fleeting glimpse. Probably a mangy dog or wild animal.

But how to account for the thing in the murky aquarium? It could have been a Hellbender salamander or eel twitching around in the dark liquid. He watched it a long time, though he couldn't see it clearly. Whatever it was, Ellison knew it was really there, and though people often refer to pets as their children, he remembered having the distinct impression that Luther and Merrilee were telling him that this dark mass actually *was their child.*

Ellison struggled to bring his attention back to Luther's face. He had never seen anything like that expression before. It was clear to him that this man was angry enough to kill him. Ellison's medical bag was on a chair behind Luther. Ellison decided not to try to retrieve it. He could replace the bag and everything in it. He just needed to get out of the house.

Luther suddenly moved to a pine wardrobe against a wall near the bed. He threw its doors open and began rifling through it. Ellison ran out of the bedroom and out the front door. His keys were in his sport coat pocket. He fumbled with them as he jumped into his car. Luther appeared on the front porch of the house with a shotgun. He leveled it at Ellison and fired as the car swerved around and sped back out to the county road. A little of the lead shot hit the windshield and sprayed small fractures in the glass in front of Ellison's face.

In a few seconds Ellison glanced at his rearview mirror and saw Luther's old Dodge pickup with one headlight out pull onto the road behind him. He pressed the gas pedal hard.

If he could find his way back to Staleyville and the police station ten or twelve miles away, he'd be safe, but he had taken a couple of wrong turns trying to find the Knoss house earlier and was already suspecting he was lost. Since he'd started doing so many home births, he had been carrying a breakdown kit with flares, a flashlight, tools, and maps in case he ever needed them. There was a county map in the canvas kit, but it was in the floor on the passenger side. He needed to lose sight of Luther behind him before he could look at the map.

It was still a couple of hours until dawn. Driving so fast on a twisting, country road terrified Ellison, but every time he thought he had lost Luther, the single headlight would reappear in his rearview mirror. And it was closer now than it had been a few minutes ago.

"How can that old heap keep up with me?" Ellison mumbled. "Must be a '53 or '54."

At the bottom of a steep hill Ellison suddenly came upon a low-water concrete bridge that crossed a sluggish creek. The car hit the bridge hard and bottomed-out against it. A good way to destroy the car's struts or driveshaft, Ellison thought, but as he climbed the hill on the far side of the creek, there didn't seem to be any damage. A beam from a single headlight pierced through the dust Ellison had raised on the road behind him. Luther had an advantage chasing him on these rough, half-paved country roads. If he could get to the blacktop state road that leads to Staleyville, he could put some distance between himself and the old truck.

At the top of the hill above the creek, the road turned east and ran along deep woods on the right side and open fields on the left. Ellison thought he could pick up some speed on this straight stretch. As he accelerated, he heard a scratching sound coming, it seemed, from under the front passenger seat. At first, he thought he must be dragging a tree branch under the chassis, but the sound was too close, and definitely inside the car. Definitely under the passenger seat.

The scraping sound soon turned into a sound of muffled movement, and a metallic twang, as if something were pushing itself past the springs under the car seat. Ellison knew his imagination wasn't playing tricks: there was something in the car with him.

His first thought was that it might be a squirrel or an opossum. He had left the passenger side window down while he was inside the Knoss house. He needed to pull over and get the creature out before it panicked and attacked him, but Luther was no more than three hundred yards behind him now. He thought about trying to reach the kit in the floor. There was a flashlight in there, but Luther was now noticeably gaining on him and he had to speed up.

A washed-out gully hidden by shadows suddenly appeared in the road and Ellison hit it hard. He turned the wheel sharply to the left to keep from going off the road, but he could tell the steering was off now. The impact had thrown off the car's front alignment. As he accelerated again, something seemed wrong with his right foot on the gas pedal. Something was interfering with his pressure to accelerate.

Ellison was suddenly aware of a tightening pressure around his right ankle. He reached down into the darkness below him and felt a wet, muscular band of flesh tipped by something like boneless fingers, wrapping themselves around his ankle. Ellison jerked his hand back as the car tore through some weeds and bushes on the side of the road. As he righted the car, he could see Luther's truck was now no more than three hundred feet behind him. There was a flash of light in Ellison's rearview mirror and the ticking sound of lead shot hitting his trunk and rear window.

Now Ellison was sure. His imagination and exhausted mind hadn't been deceiving him earlier that night. What he had seen had not been a mangy dog or huge salamander at the Knoss house. The creatures he had seen were just what Luther and Merrilee had said they were: children, monstrous offspring. And one of them had hidden itself in the dark, under his car seat.

Ellison struggled to shake his ankle free of the fingered tentacle that held it and still maintain steady pressure on the gas pedal. The glow of the dashboard lights reflected a soft, green illumination on his hands holding the steering wheel. He knew he would have to reach down into the darkness again.

The pressure around his ankle increased and now seemed to be forcing him to accelerate. He stepped on the brake with his left foot, but felt that foot being dragged off the brake pedal. He struggled to keep the car on the road. He reached down and found the boneless fingers in the dark. He tried to pull them away from his ankle. He heard a damp, sucking sound, and then felt a tearing pain across the edge of his hand. In the dashboard light he could see jagged bite marks and lacy ridges of tattered flesh along the side of his hand.

Just ahead the county road ended at State Highway 67. Ellison would go north there. On a better road, he could put some distance between himself and Luther. Six or seven miles ahead, across the River Auxvasses bridge, was Staleyville. The police station was on Business 67 in the middle of town.

Ellison struggled to control the pressure on the gas pedal. The speedometer read just over 80 miles per hour. He couldn't tell if the creature consciously wanted him to accelerate or if it was even capable of deciding on any kind of course of action. Ellison swerved to the left onto Highway 67. The car fishtailed dangerously as he tried to maintain control. Luther pulled onto the highway some distance behind him. Ellison doubted the old pickup had the horsepower to keep up with him on an open highway.

Ellison felt a pressure move across the back of his left shoulder. He could feel more boneless fingers on the back of his neck. He swiped at the fingers with his right hand. Ellison remembered that he had a screwdriver in his emergency kit. He could use it as a weapon if he could reach it.

As Ellison topped a hill, he could see the highway ahead of him for another mile or so. He could see the Staleyville bridge. There were several sets of flashing lights visible on the bridge. They must be police cars, or state patrol. An accident maybe.

The highway was straight and wide. Ellison made a lunge for his kit in the passenger side floor. He grabbed it and dropped it on the seat next to him. The fingers were moving along his neck again. He unzipped the kit and reached inside. In the darkness he recognized the screwdriver. He pulled it out and stabbed savagely at the fingers on his neck. He felt the screwdriver pierce the muscular flesh, but he had also stabbed himself across his trapezius. He dropped the screwdriver between the car seat and door.

The bridge, the emergency lights were less than a quarter mile away now. Reaching back into the kit, Ellison felt the signal flare. He removed it. His foot was being pressed harder on the gas pedal. He could see a figure up ahead, state patrol officer or policeman, waving a flashlight at him to stop. Steadying the steering wheel with his left hand, Ellison wedged the end of the flare between his hand and the wheel and twisted the cap off with his right. He struck the flare tip with the cap and it burst into sputtering flame. He jammed the flare under the seat. There was a gagging, sucking sound and Ellison could smell flesh burning.

A flame sprung up from under the right side of Ellison's seat. He had mortally injured the creature, it seemed, but the seat was on fire. As he approached the bridge, Ellison could see where the shoulder along the road widened, approaching a bluff that overlooked the River Auxvases. The fire had spread to the back floor of the car and the passenger seat. Ellison could feel nothing gripping his ankle now. The fire flamed up between Ellison's door and his seat. He cut the steering wheel hard to the right and the car crashed through the weeds and over a red clay precipice careening the fifteen feet down into the black water.

The shock of the car hitting the water smashed Ellison's face and chest against the steering wheel, but he barely felt the impact. He struggled for breath as the car settled into the water, listing nose first and barely moving in the slight current. It would be completely submerged in a few seconds. Ellison rolled his window down. He reached for his seat belt but realized he had never buckled it. The pressure of the water coming in the window was tremendous and Ellison knew he could not overcome it. He waited until the car was completely submerged and he pushed his way out of the window.

The water was warm and soothing. A comfort to his shattered body. Through the dark water he could see the police lights on the bridge above rippling and distorted by the current. He pushed himself toward the surface. He heard voices from above and saw figures looking down toward him from the bridge. He was almost to the surface of the water. He would break free in another second. He could almost hear the words the figures were saying. And there was another sound, muffled and wounded in the black water below him. His foot brushed a soft obstacle. He kicked at it to no effect. Its muscular, boneless hand wrapped itself irresistibly around his ankle.

Kafiri Road

Most summers Rudy Benko went west and southwest on Highway 66. Some years he did the southern and southeastern circuit, which was actually more lucrative, but he preferred going west, and in the last few years of doing so, had started calling the highway Kafiri Road. That was shorthand thinking to him, because the trailer he was hauling was emblazoned with garish images and the luridly painted legend: THE BEAST OF KAFIRISTAN.

He loved his new car, but what a mistake he'd made in buying it. His old pickup shot craps two years ago just as Dot, his wife, was dying of uterine cancer. Dot thought a flashy car would comfort him. She persuaded him that he was justified in buying it, and that the increased revenues his exhibit had brought in the previous year predicted he would be more than able to pay for it. It was February when Dot died, and a month later Rudy bought the Hudson.

The car was a cream-colored dream of elegance and refinement. It was a new 1952, solid as a tank and shaped like a torpedo in reverse. The interior seats and ceiling were a muted green cloth, and the steering wheel and gearshift knob were shiny, substantial combinations of that green and the cream color of the exterior. Rudy was thrilled that he could sit in his back seat, legs extended, and his feet would not touch the back of the front seats. He had never owned a car like it in his life.

The dealer added a trailer hitch for a little extra charge, and with the H-145 high compression engine, towing a large trailer across country would be no problem at all. Paying for the car was proving more difficult, though.

The two touring seasons since Dot died had been lean. His car note was a burden, and the expense of traveling and feeding both himself and the Beast was considerable. Mississippi, Alabama and up through Georgia were where the real money was. Get a permit and set up in any small town, then just try to keep the rubes away. But even the more sophisticated citizenry, the lawyers, bankers, doctors, could not resist the lure of The Beast of Kafiristan. Every time Rudy visited Loomis, Alabama, a local high school biology teacher, a Mr. Sheiner, would bring his class and lecture them on the human/ape hybridization experiments of Ivanov in Stalin's U.S.S.R. Sheiner wanted more information on the Beast than Rudy could provide, and when he asked if Rudy was sure the creature came from Kafiristan, all he would say was, "That's what the fellow told me," then shrug and smile.

But Dot was born and raised in Tucumcari, New Mexico, and she grew homesick, as her strength left her, for the wide-open spaces and desert landscapes. Rudy grew to love them too, and since his wife had been gone, the only route he could really imagine for the tour at the start of each season was in the West.

This season, Kingman and Flagstaff had paid off in Arizona, but Albuquerque, Glenrio, Amarillo, and Groom were disappointments. Heading east into the dark and the Texas state line, Rudy figured he had only a little better than a hundred dollars more in his pocket than he'd started out with three months before.

It was fully dark as he approached the turnoff for State Road 73 and a town called Traynor to the north. He remembered noticing the sign for Traynor the year before, because it was Dot's mother's maiden name, and thinking he might take a look at it this trip. He was exhausted and hungry and had less than a half tank of gas, so he took the exit.

The road was in a bad state of repair, and after driving on it for ten minutes and seeing the small white sign: TRAYNOR, POP. 27, he started to look for a place to turn around and head back to the interstate. There was a turnout on the right side of the road about twenty feet wide, but the opposite side of the road had only a ditch, and Rudy didn't thing he could turn the car and trailer around in that small a radius. A few hundred feet further along, he saw a gravel drive or road on the left. That looked more promising.

As Rudy pulled up and took a wide turn onto the road, he could see it was a drive for a farm or ranch. He saw what looked like a piece of twisted angle-iron on the shoulder too late to avoid hitting it. He heard it flip up as he rolled over it and hit the sidewall of his right-front tire.

"Oh... no!" Rudy gulped. "I hope it didn't... that's the last thing I need!"

He stopped the car and found his flashlight in the glove compartment. He got out to look at the damage. Sure enough, there was a visible gash in the whitewall, and he could hear air seeping out of it. Rudy felt his stomach sink.

"Another setback I can't afford!" he groaned. "I'm gonna be broke by the time I get home. They won't patch a hole on the sidewall. I'll have to buy another tire. More expense!"

Rudy could hear a deep, gargling whimper coming from inside the trailer. He could see a dark shape watching him through the trailer's upper vents. The Beast could always sense when Rudy was sad or distressed, and she whimpered and whined until Rudy was comforted. A sudden blast from a car horn startled Rudy. His foot slid off the edge of the gravel shoulder.

"Git thet goddam thang off'n my road!" It was a thin, angry voice coming from an ancient Dodge pickup that had appeared, unheard, behind the trailer. Rudy came around the front of the Hudson and waved at the driver.

"Hey, buddy! I was turnin' around and cut my tire on that iron yonder. Just need to get the spare on there. Sorry!"

Rudy could just make out a skinny old man sitting in the truck in the darkness.

"Iff'n you ain't got that rig outta my way in two minutes, I'll shoot out the other three an' you into the bargain!" The old man fumbled through the truck's glove compartment for a moment. He climbed out of his truck. He was holding what looked like a .45 revolver in his hand. "You're a carnival man, an' I won't have you on my propitty!"

"Aw... come on, mister. Why would you pull out a gun on me? I'm kinda between a rock and a hard place here. You can see the fix I'm in! I'll ruin my wheel if I drive on it like that. Won't take me ten minutes."

"You know Jimmy Dumar, operates the carousel for Odeon Shows thet comes through here every other year?"

"No. How would I... I ain't really a carney. I ain't with a carnival.,"

"You all know each other. He said so. He cheated me outten four hunnerd dollars. At cards. Then he laughed at me. Kinda games you all play on people thet trust. I had to lose my new fan mill, Belcher and Taylor. Had to sell it! Git out!"

The old man aimed the .45 at Rudy's left front tire. As he leveled the gun, he grunted a little. He moved in front of his truck's headlight and examined the pistol. He grunted again, an irritated sound, and quickly scurried to the truck's passenger door. He opened it and threw the gun inside. He grabbed something from under the passenger seat. He ran back to the front of the truck holding a large ball-peen hammer. "Don't need to waste my ammo on the likes of you anyways," he said.

Rudy turned and he could see the truck's headlights glinting off the wet eyes of the Beast behind the trailer vent.

"Whatever you say, mister," Rudy sighed. "There ain't no need for any of this, but whatever you say. It's your road."

As he backed the car onto the road, the gashed tire went completely flat, and he could hear the sound of the wheel cutting into the rubber as it rolled over it.

"Move it!" the old man yelled. Rudy could hear the Beast make an angry growl, melting into a mewling sound inside the trailer. He backed out into the dark road until he heard branches brushing the top of the trailer. There was no saving the tire or the wheel, so Rudy decided to go back to the turnout and pull over there. As he pulled past the old man's driveway with the front end of the Hudson wobbling wildly, he saw the farmer climb back into his truck and turn onto his road, driving up the hill and out of sight.

Rudy pulled into the turnout on the left side of the road, stopped the car and got out. He examined the damage with his flashlight. The flat tire was shredded and the wheel on which it was mounted, bent and warped. A total loss. Rudy sighed and he fought the urge to be overwhelmed by this.

"More expense!" he whispered. He suddenly gasped loudly to

suppress a sob. He'd thought about discontinuing touring after Dot died. She could manage the money and get them through one season to the next. Rudy knew he had no real talent for those things. He was good at talking to people and selling the rubes, but no good at business, and had too weak a nature to be a success on his own. He was devastated by any setback, and now he was all but certain that he couldn't continue to do all this touring and exhibiting alone.

He decided to camp on the turnout for the night. He didn't want to put on the spare in the dark, and he was exhausted. He gathered twigs and branches from the edge of the stunted forest that bordered the turnout and quickly had a campfire going on the gravel, behind the car and trailer. It had been dark for nearly an hour now, and it was time to feed the Beast.

Henson had named her Klava, which he said was Russian for something or other. In those days, before Pearl Harbor, Rudy was exhibiting what he was calling a Giant Sumatran Rat, which was an old beaver with a tail deformity. When the beaver died, Rudy drove back up to Hugin, Minnesota, where he'd bought the first one, to look for a replacement. Rudy wasn't able to find another beaver to fill the bill, but a trapper told him about Henson, who had an exhibit he might want to sell.

Henson owned the ramshackle remnant of what had once been a farm north of Hugin near the Canadian border. The property was littered with car parts, derelict appliances, blueberry bushes, and weeds. Henson was a man of about fifty. He was in the last stages of cirrhosis and looked two decades older.

Henson said he had tried a little of everything in his life. In 1934, he was prospecting in Yakutat, Alaska. As he told Rudy, that was where he met Yuri, an old Russian army deserter, and where he first laid eyes on Klava, the Beast.

Yuri's English was almost indecipherable, but Henson understood that the old man had owned Klava since she was weaned, and that she was now, when Henson first saw her, about two years old. Yuri wouldn't say where he had found her, but Henson understood that it hadn't been in Alaska. The old Russian originally intended to exhibit her but was unsure how to legally do this in a U. S. territory, or even if he still felt it was the right thing to do. The odd child had deformities that required a certain amount of care, and the old man had reached an age where he thought the responsibility of keeping her was too much for him. He had only spoken Russian to her, but she'd learned a few English words recently. Henson gave Yuri two hundred and twelve dollars, all he'd made prospecting, and brought Klava back with him to Minnesota. Henson exhibited Klava along the Canadian border until his own health started to fail. By the time the war started, he was ready to pass her on to someone else. Rudy's timing couldn't have been better.

Klava was about nine years old when Rudy first saw her. He guessed she would have been six feet tall if she had been able to stand up straight. Her weight must have approached 250 pounds. Henson said she always refused to wear clothes, no matter the season. Her right leg was withered, and her left hand was a long hook, consisting of only a single finger and thumb. She appeared to have the skin condition vitiligo, as her brown skin was splotched everywhere with pink patches. Her nose was broad and flat, and she had no chin or forehead above heavy brow ridges. Her ears were exceptionally small, and her body was nearly hair-covered. A thick mane, ranging from black to auburn, grew down the back of her neck and between her shoulders, although the top of her head was nearly bald. Except for her withered leg, she was powerfully built. She could not speak, but uttered only whistles, grunts, growls, and a mewling sound. She showed something like an expectant smile when she first saw Rudy from inside her cell. Her teeth were white, flat and strong.

Rudy called Dot on the telephone that night and she agreed that he should purchase this new oddity to exhibit. It was Dot who thought of the name, "The Beast of Kafiristan."

"Just remember," Henson warned, "she's got a few more years' growing to do."

The campfire was burning high now. Rudy opened the trunk of the Hudson. Inside was a cooler. He removed some raw fish fillets. From the back seat of the car he collected several turnips, a cabbage, carrots and four large potatoes. He laid these on a towel he had spread out near the campfire.

He unlocked the rear gate of the trailer and opened it. Klava ambled out excitedly. She whimpered happily as she threw her arm around him and gave him a brief, crushing hug. It seemed to always take her a second to remember he had trained her to be gentler in her affections. She stroked the top of his bald head once or twice.

"Food's over here, Klava," Rudy said, and he led her toward the campfire. She limped noticeably and, after a day in the trailer, Rudy held her hook hand to steady her. He knew if she ever did fall over, she would nearly crush him.

As the years went on, Rudy had grown to trust Klava enough that he let her roam free out of her trailer or cage. Back home in Ste. Odile, he rarely caged her, and on the road, if he was camping, he always let her out to sleep on the ground near him. She sat on the ground roughly and started to eat her food. Rudy had no appetite. He sat next to her. He stared into the campfire.

"Sometime I think it's only meanness in people," he said quietly. "It's what comes most natural to them and it's the one thing you can always count on. Niceness is harder to find. I didn't think much about it when Dot was alive. She softened everything. Made it all tolerable."

Rudy removed a folded letter from his vest pocket and opened it. It was a note he'd found inside his screen door when he left on tour in the spring. He'd meant to dispose of the note as soon as he read it months ago, but hadn't managed to do it yet.

Dear Rudy:

It pains me every day to think of you across the street, alone and missing your Dot. You know, I think she was my best friend in town. It's odd how you don't know things like that about a person until they are gone from this Earth and they are called into the embrace of our Lord. I admit that for years I thought that since she was Catholic, she was condemned to hellfire for false doctrine, but in later years she said a few things that made me think she had got right with the Gospels and embraced the true message of Scripture. I pray it is true. And I pray the same for you. Miracles happen to those who accept the embrace of Jesus.

But let me get to what I'm getting at. I think of myself as an open-minded person. The fact is, my Delbert has been gone for ten years. You seen me across the street, living a quiet life, having few visitors, never giving the gossips nothing to wag their tongues about. I have embraced my lot in life and thanked the Lord for the challenges I have been given. Dot has been gone two years. I guess your period of mourning is over. Isn't it? I think the Lord is putting us together. Why should me, a widow, and you, a widower, live separate and lonely lives 150 feet apart? I think if we tried, we could make a life together.

As you may know, I do not approve of the work you do. Carnival people are well-known to be immoral, and I think that ugly cripple you exhibit is spawn of the Devil, if not the Devil incarnate. But you were misguided and can put that behind you. You can embrace a righteous life and be saved. You may not know that my dad runs a dry-cleaners in St. Louis. He is nearly eighty years old and has blood cancer. He will sell his business unless I move up there and take it over. I need a man's help. Will you come with me? Will you leave behind a life displeasing to the Lord and make a new one with me?

Cat Merton
221 Gentian Street
Ste. Odile.

Rudy frowned. He crumpled the note and threw it into the fire. "Ignorant cow," he mumbled.

***

Klava ate her fish quickly. She had been watching Rudy's face as he read the letter, and her fathomless brown eyes began to glisten.

"I don't think I can take the meanness all on my own," Rudy said. "I couldn't never make a go of nothin' on my own, neither. Dot kep' us afloat. Saved money and kep' a good outlook. It's nobody out there will ever replace her. Not a glamor girl, not a holy-roller neighbor.

Nobody." He tossed more branches into the fire. "I'm not strong. Never have been, and I know it. Life is empty as a drum, old girl," Rudy looked warmly at Klava. "I do my best to protect you from it. As much as a weak man can do, since I'm all you got of humanity. Thanks be to God you don't know what I'm talkin' about. That old man up the road yonder who run us off... that's the whole world in one little man, right there."

Klava reached tentatively toward Rudy. She stroked his arm a few times, then touched his bald head. He touched her hand. She seemed to need the reassurance of touching him from time to time. Since Dot died, his face and voice were the only kind ones Klava knew.

"I'm gonna git my bedroll," Rudy said. "Time to go to sleep. Prob'ly be home tomorrow or the next day. I'll put seed out in the back yard an' you can watch the songbirds like you like to do. You kin watch them for hours, cain't you?"

Rudy spread out his bedroll near the fire and climbed into it. His mind was full of thoughts he knew were nothing but self-pity. He always had to fight self-pity because it was weakness, and he needed to learn to be a stronger man and not give in to emotion. Still, he felt the world was closing in on him, a sensation made all the more terrible because he knew he had no defense against it. He would have to take whatever the world gave him. Klava lay on the ground nearby. As Rudy drifted off to sleep, he knew her eyes were upon him.

The crunch of a footstep on the gravel startled Rudy awake.

He had been having a dreamless sleep and it took him a moment to remember where he was. He rolled over in his bedroll and saw Klava standing over him. She was smiling expectantly, and she had a smear of red around her mouth. She was holding something in her good hand. Something stringy, tattered and red. Rudy sat up to get a better look in the dying firelight. The object Klava was dragging on the ground was an arm.

Rudy jumped to his feet.

"Klava what have you done?"

She seemed to have forgotten she held the arm. She dropped it to the ground.

Rudy grabbed the arm and threw it into the fire. Then he gathered a handful of dried leaves from the edge of the turnout and dumped them onto the flames. The fire billowed upward.

"Klava! What did you do? You killed that old man? Was him, wasn't it? You went up that road and killed him! You thought I would... We gotta git outta here. Pronto!"

Rudy found his canteen and a dirty shirt in the back seat of the Hudson. He doused the shirt with water and washed the blood from Klava's face and hand. She touched his bald head. He threw the bloody shirt into the fire. He led Klava back to the trailer and locked her in. Then, by the revived firelight, he changed the flat tire.

The highway was nearly empty. It was 2:18 a.m. and except for an occasional over-the-road truck, there was no one else on the road. Rudy was frantic. He couldn't focus on a single thought: Did the old man live alone? Did he have neighbors? How soon would he be missed? Had anyone seen Rudy drive the trailer up that road? How would he protect Klava?

Rudy suddenly realized the speedometer was reading 85 miles per hour. He slowed. There were always state patrolmen on this stretch of highway. He didn't want to get pulled over. In another forty minutes, he crossed the state line into Oklahoma. By late that day, he should be home in Ste. Odile.

By five p.m. he was back in Ste. Odile County. He pulled onto an old access road long abandoned by Osage Lead Company that wandered off into the oak and cedar woods. He sat there in the Hudson, occasionally checking on Klava, until dark.

Rudy's block of Gentian Street had only one streetlight, situated at the northwest end, far from Rudy's house. His end of the block was dark, except for Cat Merton's porchlight across the street. He pulled the Hudson into his driveway and back behind his house.

He led Klava into the house through the back door. When they were home, she mostly stayed in an empty rear room which had a view of the back yard and the bird feeder. She spent hours watching the birds feeding from her window. Rudy brought her some raw vegetables and fish that were still in his cooler. She ate ravenously, stroked his arm, mewling quietly and quickly fell into a deep sleep on her blanket on the floor.

Rudy unloaded the car. Klava was snoring heavily. She often slept for twenty-four hours straight when they returned home at the end of the season. He doubted she would awaken before noon the next day.

When the car was unloaded, Rudy sat in his front room in the dark and looked out at the street. There were tears starting to well in his eyes and he was having trouble breathing. This wouldn't do. He had to be stronger or the world would consume him. There were so many thoughts crowding into his mind that he couldn't focus on any of them. All he could think about was how there was nowhere left to hide from his problems, as his dad had told him once, and how desperately he missed and needed Dot. He thought about how he fell so easily into these states of self-pity and how he hated himself for it. He heard a telephone ring in the distance and saw Cat Merton's bedroom light come on across the street. After a few seconds, the light went off.

It rained overnight. Highway 67 north was still a little wet and since it was Sunday morning, almost empty. Cat's little Nash Rambler handled well on the wet road and she agreed to skip church that once so they could get an early start. In a month or so the repo men would come to Rudy's house and take the Hudson and the trailer.

Rudy had put extra birdseed on the ground early that morning. In a few hours, Klava will awaken, he thought, and watch the songbirds feed. She may do this for an hour or more. Then she will notice she is hungry; she will hunt for him, as she always does. She will find the food he left on the countertops in the kitchen, enough to sustain her for a few days. She will hunt for him from one end of the house to the other and realize he is not there. She will wait for him in the dark house after the sun goes down, and when she awakens tomorrow morning, she will still be alone.

Janet, Please

Norman first noticed it at the Founder's Party two weeks before. It was a thought he knew he couldn't have, but one he had predicted and dreaded when he first knew Janet, long before they married. He had tried to keep busy since it appeared, tried to keep his mind preoccupied, so the idea wouldn't eat at him, become an obsession, as he had let happen with other notions so many times in the past. He had to keep his thinking straight. He had a business to run and a father-in-law to keep happy, so he had to overcome distractions and irrelevant personal issues and do what he needed to do. He had to put the realization in the back of his mind, and prohibit it from interfering with his growing success, that he was finding his wife increasingly repellant. He needed to clear his mind of these thoughts and go back to sleep.

Norman had never been a sound sleeper. As a child, he'd had night terrors, and against his pediatrician's advice, had slept in his parents' bed until he was in second grade. His terrors grew worse after his father died. Night after night he needed to be assured by his mother that he was safe, that the mound of clothes on his bedroom chair was not a monster and the creak of the floorboards was not a demon under his bed. He was rarely comforted by her words, though, and all that would soothe him was to follow her back to her bedroom. He never wanted her to hold his hand or touch his shoulder as he made his way with her down the hallway. He felt shame in his fears and his weakness, and her tenderness and understanding made the shame worse. As he slept next to her, he didn't want her embrace or a reassuring hand on his arm. He wanted to be untouched, but not alone.

"The dark can't change things, son," his mother often told him. "Whatever you think you see... the dark can't change things."

Janet never had sleepless nights. In fact, it never took her more than a few minutes to fall asleep. She had begun to snore again. Norman glanced at the alarm clock. The numbers 2:15 glowed red in the dark.

"Janet, please! Roll over on your side!" he barked.

Norman was certain he never snored because he invariably slept on his left side. He had never varied from this position since he was a child. He took comfort in his habits and routines. And now, his sleeping position had the added benefit facing him away from Janet. At 2:22, she was still snoring.

"Janet, please! Roll over on your side!"

There was a confused groan, a complacent sigh off in the darkness, and a rustle of sheets as Janet shifted groggily in bed. Norman thought about sarcastically asking old Una Jewell for a folk remedy to stop the snoring, since Janet placed such absurd, superstitious trust in the old woman's cures.

"I love you, Norman." The words were mumbled in her sleep. In a few moments, she was breathing heavily again.

Norman smiled a little. "I wonder how much you will love me a month from now?" he mumbled quietly. The thought immediately made him a little ashamed of himself. He really didn't want to hurt her or cause her any pain. He just knew he was quickly reaching a point where he couldn't tolerate her anymore. Once her father was gone and the old man had just turned ninety-six, Norman could leave her behind. He would have controlling interest in her family's plastics business. She would be provided for and he could move on with his plans for the company.

The Founder's Party was just the latest incident. Norman's butyrate supplier threw a big summer party for customers at the Marriott every year. This year, for the first time in her life as far as Norman knew, Janet got drunk. It was bad enough she had worn that ridiculous sailor dress. He asked her not to, but somehow, she had got it into her head that Norman secretly liked the dress, in spite of his claims otherwise, so she wore it anyway.

All evening, Norman tried to make conversation with his supplier, his purchaser and his production supervisor, but he watched Janet as she worked her way around the banquet hall and he panicked a little when she ordered a third margarita. She had gained a lot of weight in the last few years: her sweet tooth had only gotten worse as she got older, and her sense of balance seemed to be declining as her body mass increased. He would have to find a way to discreetly take her aside and tell her not to drink anymore.

"Norman *loves* this dress!" he heard her say. She was behind him now talking to a group of women that included Donita, his assistant and two of his saleswomen. "He says he doesn't love it because it makes me look young. Younger than him, but I've seen how he looks at me in it. He's just like a little boy! You know how they can't really hide how they feel about something when they want to fool you?"

Norman knew the time was now to take Janet aside. As he turned to face her, she crashed into him in a seismic, flopping embrace. The force threw him backwards onto the dessert table with Janet on top of him. He cut his ear on the edge of the table, and with her weight on him, he could not breathe for several seconds.

When she saw what she had done, she burst into tears. She blubbered helplessly as he picked himself up, gathered her coat and purse, and drove her home.

"I just wanted to give you a big hug," she sobbed. "I wanted to surprise you with a big hug! You haven't let me hug you for six years. For six years you haven't..." She pawed at him contritely. Her touch made him shiver and disgusted him a little. He refused to reassure her immediately. Whenever she embarrassed him in public, he never forgave her right away.

"Janet, please," he said. "I want you to leave me alone and go to bed. I don't want to talk about this." She reached for him again, but he brushed her hand away.

"But I..."

"Please!"

Janet liked to say she *knew* Norman loved her, knew it even if he didn't know or admit it to himself. She said this to him the very day she met Una Jewell and first asked for her help, as she told Norman later.

The old woman had come to the back door one afternoon in early summer. She was malnourished and exhausted. She asked for kitchen work but told Janet that she had been directed there by voices in the ether who told her she was needed by the household. Janet's Pomeranian, Mayzie, barked nonstop at the old woman and nipped her leg several times. Una kicked at the dog twice, but Janet didn't seem to notice. Always superstitious, Janet was curious about Una's voices, and being soft-hearted, she gave the old woman the apartment above the carriage house at the end of their drive.

In explaining Una's presence to Norman that night, Janet said she could see that the old woman's strength was gone, and she couldn't imagine being old, alone and penniless in the world. Janet helped Una up to the apartment and into a chair by the front window overlooking the drive. Mayzie nipped and barked at Una the entire time, and Janet admitted to Norman she did very little to calm the dog down and keep her away. Janet left the little dog barking outside when she went back to the kitchen to make Una a sandwich. Suddenly, the barking stopped, and Janet assumed Mayzie had found a squirrel or lizard to chase.

There was no sign of the dog when Janet brought a ham sandwich and a glass of lemonade back to Una, who was still sitting by the window in her front room.

"I have no fambly anymore," Una said in a weak and breaking voice, and in an accent Janet could not identify. "I want to be honest wif you, since you a kind person. I come up from the Bayou Chene. From the Atchafalaya. I run for it or the Guilrys would have kilted me. Bad fambly. I was a *traiteur* and a *metamorphé*, and I put a chicken head hex on one of them. Judd. First, I make him become the evil thing, the monster he really was inside. I change him so the whole world can see. But he didn't last too long after that. He die, and they come for me. I want you to know this before you take me in..."

"Oh my," Janet said. "Well, that is so interesting. I bet you have some stories to tell! None of that matters to me. Judge not lest ye be judged. There's two sides to every story, as they say. You just rest and when you're better, we'll find some work for you to do here!"

"I thank you, Missus. I thank you! *Beaucoup... beaucoup!*"

Janet sat with Una until the old lady dozed off in the chair. Janet whistled and called for Mayzie as she walked back to the kitchen, but the little dog was nowhere to be found.

The next morning, as Norman was backing his new truck out of the driveway, he felt a little jolt and heard a muffled crunch as he rolled over something. He got out of the truck. His left rear tire had crushed the head and front legs of an animal he could not identify. It was smooth-skinned and wet and looked something like a large Hellbender salamander, but the tail was too short, and it appeared to have fur around its neck.

"What the holy Hell?" he mumbled. He pulled the truck up a bit, scraped up the carcass with a shovel and dumped it in a trash can. Norman had never seen anything like the creature before. He assumed that his tire smashed its head and front legs in such a way that its normal morphology was unrecognizable. As he got back into the truck, he noticed Una standing at her apartment window, looking down at him. She seemed to smile a little, and nodded, then disappeared back into her room. Norman was glad he removed the creature before Janet saw it. It was too early in the morning for her hysterics.

That evening, Janet invited Una to have dinner with them. Norman objected to this but didn't say anything. Things would be difficult for his wife soon. He felt he could indulge her a little.

"Did Mayzie ever come back?" Norman said as Janet served her tuna casserole.

"Dog won't be back, Missus," Una said. "I got a feelin' of it. Sorry, but I feel that dog ain't comin' back." Norman thought he saw the same expression on the old woman's face he had seen that morning.

"How do you know that... Una?" Norman asked. "How do you know the dog won't be back?"

Una looked at Norman coldly and fixedly. After a few moments of her gaze, he looked away from her, toward Janet.

"I am given to know," Una said. "And as a *metamorphè* I knows the means of changes of things to a more suitable form. More befitting a form to the true nature of the thing. Those ugly on the inside can be made ugly on the outside. That's what they brings on theyself, when I am near. Those thet has strength inside like you wife here, can be made to show strength on the outside."

"Well, I'm sure I don't know what you're talking about, or what that has to do with the dog..." Norman smiled. "But... very interesting, I'm sure. Janet tells me you're sort of a wildcrafter? An herbalist?"

"Oh yes she is," Janet nodded. "I just find that so interesting. I would love to know more, to see if any of that really *works*!"

"I think you already know my opinion, Janet," Norman said. "My grandma was an herbalist out on the Saline Creek. So many smells I remember as a kid out at her place. I was always interested to visit her and see what she was up to. Scared me a little though. Even at seven or eight, I was pretty sure it was nonsense, but maybe not *completely* sure!

No offense, ladies!"

Una was still staring at Norman and continued to do so until he left the dining room. Norman needed to put all thoughts of Una and Janet and his business problems out of his mind and get some sleep, even if it were just an hour or two.

Norman rolled over in his bed. The dial on the alarm clock read 2:45.

His mind was getting too active now and he knew he may never go back to sleep. Nothing unusual. He had lots of nights like this.

A few days after she took Una in, Janet gave the old woman a few light housework duties to do and had her working in the yard and garden, weeding and trimming on days when it wasn't too hot.

Last Friday, Norman got home late. It had been a rough week. He had lost a big automotive component account to Kreitz Compounding in Frankfurt, and an afternoon-long meeting with his sales staff and purchaser had convinced him that they couldn't undercut Kreitz's price to get the business back without eliminating the third shift of production.

Norman was sitting at the dining table going over the minutes of the meeting when Janet walked quietly into the room. Even though it was a warm night, she was wearing her flannel nightgown that read SOMETIMES I WAKE UP CRABBY. SOMETIMES I LET HIM SLEEP LATE on the front. She seemed tentative and a little embarrassed.

"I have some little jars in the kitchen. Tiny little jars. Had marmalade and jelly samples in them." She did not look at him as she spoke.

"Janet, please. I'm busy here."

"Una is going to help us. Help us get close again."

"We never were that close, Janet. It's not who I am. You know that."

"I know you don't believe in these things, but I think it's worth a try. If we give Una some secretions..."

"*Secretions?*"

"Secretions...which I have done already: body secretions and skin flakes, she can help us. She can make a philtre that will make you... make us close again. She swears she can. She says I must demand my happiness. Demand it in this marriage."

"Janet, go to bed. That's nonsense. Disgusting nonsense and I won't be a party to it. And I think we have done all we need to for Una Jewell. Give her a few days, and then get her out of here. Send her to the women's shelter or Harbor Light. I don't want her around here anymore."

This morning, Saturday, as he was reorganizing his garage and painting the garden tool shed, he noticed a smell, a sour, nauseating odor following him around. In one of the extra pockets of his painter's overalls, he found a sachet of asafetida and henbane and other things, things he had seen and smelled at his grandmother's house when he was a child, all stuffed into a small cloth pouch.

Disgusted, Norman didn't speak to Janet for the rest of the afternoon. He only relented after hours of her whimpering and remorse because she was making herself sick and her self-abasement became irritating to the point of distraction. He forgave her on the condition that she remove Una Jewell from the carriage house by noon the next day. When Janet put her hand on his shoulder in gratitude and mewled for a reassuring embrace, Norman's whole body shuddered.

The clock read 3:15.

"This night is never going to end," Norman thought. Janet's breathing had become loud enough to be distracting again. He tried to think of business. He knew his company's contract with North American Digital was also in jeopardy from Kreitz, and that account would be their next target. He had to come up with a pricing strategy.

Norman awoke suddenly with the sensation of falling. He was still on his left side. He wondered how long he had slept. The clock read 3:43. The smell of asafetida was in the room and he wondered if it would ever leave the house. Maybe it was time for him to move out. He could rent a town house overlooking the river and leave all this behind. Best to wait until his father-in-law was gone. It wouldn't be long now. Norman heard movement behind him.

"I'm on my path, Norman," Janet said. Her voice was a coarse whisper. "I love you, Norman."

"I know you do, Janet. I know."

Gradually, Norman became aware that the whole room seemed to be full of and resounding with Janet's breathing, and that her breath was on the back of his head and neck, and that it was stale and voluminous, making his hair wave like a wheat field in the wind.

"Janet, please."

The smell of the asafetida was starting to make him sick. It was the smell he hated most when he visited his grandmother's house so long ago. But the smell, he remembered, should be gone. He had washed down all the furniture that afternoon and washed all the bedclothes.

"I love you, Norman. My path is only to love you. You must accept this, Una says. I must demand it of you. Una says..."

Norman could feel her body against his back, but it was cold and huge and unyielding. It seemed to extend beyond his both at the head and feet. Then he remembered that as of last month, they had twin beds.

"...And I demand it..."

"Janet, what are you doing in my bed...?"

Something like an arm fell over him, but it was huge and heavy, nearly as heavy, it seemed to him in that instant, as his whole body. He remembered his mother telling him that the dark can't change things.

"I love you Norman."

"Yes... I know... Janet... please..."

The Eel King

Experimental Log 37, begun this 21st day of November, 1896, by Sirach Kingdom Treves, Ph.D., M.D.

I have just returned from the shop of Schiller the coppersmith and he finally understood what it is I want him to fabricate. His English is spotty and my German worse, but I sat with him for an hour pouring over my sketches, and I am confident he can make the cuirass of 'honeycombed' cell chambers with all the details I require. He said it would be ready in a month. If it proves effective, which I am certain it will, I will patent it under the name Dr. Treves' Therapeutic Cuirass.

Treves closed his logbook. It occurred to him that he should expand his thinking. If the therapeutic cuirass worked on Emlyn's torso, it would, of course, work on any part of the body, if he could expand the principle into an entire suit of honeycombed chambers. The cuirass would be the experimental model. If his process proved successful, Treves would redesign its application.

Treves thought, as he often did since conceiving this device, how delighted his young son Isambard, so curious about nature and all mechanical things, would be to see it finished. Since the boy's mother had taken him and returned to live with her parents in St. Louis, Treves rarely had the resources to bring him by train down to Ste. Odile to visit.

"Your condition is known as *cutaneous larva migrans*," Treves told Emlyn in September. "It is an infestation of parasitic worms just under the skin. Fortunately for you, I am not only your physician, but I am also a theoretician and researcher. I have had a notion about treatment of parasitic skin conditions since my days at Carthesian University."

"I have heard of your 'research', Dr. Treves," Emlyn sniffed. "You have been a vivisectionist."

"There was a time, yes..."

"As an animal lover, I am appalled. I am only here because you are reputed to be the one physician hereabouts who can treat this condition quickly. Otherwise, I would not resort to your practice."

"My estranged wife agrees with you, Emlyn. This work cost me my marriage and my connection to my young son, my Isambard, yet I persist. It is *that* important to me, to humanity. So, animal research is essential. It is your animals who have infected you with this parasite. You have a houseful of cats and dogs, and a few monkeys and goats and things, I am told. It is from them that this pestilence proceeds."

Treves removed his magnifier from his lab coat pocket and examined the tiny red ridges clustered on Emlyn's chest.

"If God created the lower animals for our use," he continued, "as He did all of Creation, then it would seem to me their use, whether it be in vivisection or other experimental work to benefit those of us made in His divine image, would be perfectly Scriptural. To create laws banning clinical vivisection would be, therefore, blasphemous. Animals are very useful to man, but I don't think I have ever made an emotional attachment to one."

"I strive to be like those Oriental holy men who eat no meat and apologize each morning for the bugs they might step on during the day. I strive and fail to emulate them, but I do honor their commitment to the sanctity of all life. Therefore, my objections to you remain, Doctor, but my options are few. My constitution is very weak, as you know... excuse me, I'm dizzy... light-headed..."

"Breathe slowly and deeply, Emlyn. Calm yourself. We don't want another of your fainting spells."

On his first consultation, Emlyn had fainted twice in Treves' office. Treves attributed it to his patient's mind closing down to cope with his skin misery, and to his excitable nature.

"I have a treatment in mind, Emlyn," Treves went on. "It is all perfectly natural. It uses no chemicals, except for a cocaine solution injected by hypodermic syringe to numb the skin. Otherwise, there are no chemicals concocted by man, but rather a reimagined function of one of God's creatures. It is a more natural application of the sort I think our Maker intends and approves of."

"Anything," Emlyn had become glassy-eyed. "Anything that works."

"It may involve some pain in the treatment, hence the cocaine solution. And there may be some scarring, but it will remove these parasites. My method requires 'attacking' all areas of the infestation simultaneously. This is essential, I think. Do it quicky, get it all treated at once. If we did it a small section at a time, I think, quite frankly, that you may renege on your commitment to this. It won't be a pleasant few moments, but when it is done, you will be cured. You must only endure the brief ordeal of the treatment. Then, if you persist in surrounding yourself with pets... that will be your choice."

"Anything. Anything ethical, I mean. I mean I don't want you testing this on... a pig or something. Just on me."

"I need to develop a device to make it work. It is a device I have designed already. It makes the simultaneous and instantaneous treatment possible. The contraption has only to be fabricated. That will take some capital from you."

"Whatever you need." Emlyn scratched and rubbed his stomach and chest, both bloody under his clothes from days of inflammation.

Treves thought Schiller might ask for a hundred dollars or so to make the cuirass and a framework for it. Therefore, Treves asked

Emlyn for, and was eagerly given, two thousand dollars. Aside from his medical services, Treves felt he was owed something for conceiving and engineering his device. Since Emlyn was in such abject misery and didn't quibble in the least about the fee, Treves felt justified, after some consideration, in charging his client so much.

The cuirass was to be fabricated from copper to cover the general area of an adult male torso. It contained a honeycomb design of oval openings, or cells, each about three and a half inches across and containing a leather adjustment strap within. The cuirass was fitted with bolts to attach it to an adjustable framework, which would be mounted in a tank of water. The top of the framework was hinged to a proximity clutch which, by means of a foot pedal, controlled the position of the cuirass relative to the flesh of the patient. It would be necessary, as the treatment progressed, to slowly advance the cuirass and its active components toward the subject's skin.

Experimental Log 37, 23 November, 1896

The Active Components. Somehow most of them survived. Anguilla anguilla, *the European eel, born in salt water but lives in brackish or fresh water. Serpent-like, muscular of body, the color of fetid mud, voracious. Ravenous eaters of worms and parasites. Perfect species for this experiment. I was fortunate to learn of the Bremen Hatchery in Baton Rouge which breeds the species, among many other species of fish (for future reference!). More fortunate still that sixteen of the twenty I purchased survived the shipment. Each of these appear to average between two and three feet in length, having little variation in girth. They are a perfect size for my purposes. I have now but to wait for Schiller to construct the cuirass.*

Schiller delivered the cuirass to Treves' office on December 15, ahead of schedule. It was exactly correspondent to the specifications given him. Treves hadn't heard from Emlyn for a few days. He decided to walk the few blocks to Emlyn's large house on Chartres Street and give him the good news.

Treves had walked past Emlyn's mansion many times on his evening constitutionals, but had never been inside. It was an impressive house. One of the largest in Ste. Odile, but in an advanced stage of dilapidation. It was of an indeterminant, even incoherent architectural style. It was brick, stone, rotting timber, and terra cotta, with a slate roof, missing many shingles, and several spindly, teetering chimneys, looking down onto Chartres Street from an elevation of fifty or more feet.

As Treves approached the front granite steps, he could hear Emlyn's dogs barking inside. The barking intensified as Treves knocked on the massive but splitting walnut door.

"Insufferable pests," Treves grumbled.

After several minutes' knocking, the door had not been opened and the dogs' barking had started to subside a bit. Treves tried the doorknob and found the door unlocked. He stepped inside. Four tiny white lapdogs scurried toward him, barking excitedly, tails wagging. They swarmed around his feet, each seeming desperate for his attention. The deep resonant barks of larger dogs reverberated down the large staircase from the second floor.

The entry way of the house, the staircase, parlors, and dining room which Treves could see from where he stood were opulent, bizarrely decorated, and filthy. A creature Treves recognized as a lemur sat perched on the dining room chandelier some forty feet away, watching him with some suspicion which quickly dissolved into indifference. Three of the little dogs writhed and skittered around Treves' legs, panting excitedly. The fourth, a dingy white, and looking older than the others, kept its distance as if it were too low in the hierarchy to command immediate access to this visitor. This older dog wagged his tail more tentatively than the others. He seemed to have a slight film over his left eye. A crash in the north parlor startled the three younger dogs. A cat, jumping onto a bookcase, had knocked a glass vase to the floor. The three younger dogs trooped off immediately to investigate.

The older dog approached Treves slowly and submissively, hoping for a pat on the head. Treves did not accommodate. He noted the irregularity with the dog's left eye, and it reminded him of an experiment in trepanation he had been considering for several years.

"Emlyn!" he called. "It's Treves. Are you here?"

The large dogs barked again upstairs.

"Emlyn?"

A massive red dog which Treves recognized as a European mastiff, and a smaller brown and black Staffordshire appeared at the top of the staircase. The red dog barked urgently, and the smaller one joined in. Treves had more than a little trepidation about approaching these animals, but as he watched them, it seemed to him that they were urging him up the stairs.

He climbed the stairs at an even pace, watching the dogs all the way. At the top, the animals bounded down the hallway and into a large, marble-lined bathroom.

The bathroom was opulent yet filthy, like the rest of the house. Against the opposite wall from the door, an enormous marble bathtub sat on an elevated stone platform. Emlyn was sitting in the tub, slouched forward, his nose and mouth nearly submerged. He appeared to be unconscious.

"Emlyn!" Treves shouted. He rushed to the tub and drew his patient's shoulders backward, lifting his face away from the water. "Emlyn! Emlyn wake up!"

Emlyn's eyes fluttered open. "It's too much… too much for me!" he muttered.

The dirty little white dog had followed Treves up the stairs. He sat in the bathroom doorway. Treves patted Emlyn's cheeks gently, until his patient fully opened his eyes.

"Lying here in your bath like Marat before his murder," Treves said. "You could have drowned. It's a very good thing I came along. We've got to do something about these fainting spells of yours."

"The bath soothes me," Emlyn gurgled. "Soothes my inflammation and makes it bearable. There is so much that oppresses me. It's overwhelming, and I black out..."

The little dog in the doorway yapped once for attention. Emlyn glanced toward him.

"Robespierre!" he smiled. "There you are. Such a good boy to come see about me."

"I think he just followed me up the stairs to be petted," Treves said. "Why did you name him Robespierre? Is he a revolutionary among your pets?"

"No," Emlyn smiled. "He is pockmarked and ugly. Only that. Pockmarked and ugly."

"He is fortunate you were not put off by his appearance. Most people would drown a dog like that. Right after its birth. Runts and cripples usually can't expect such accommodation."

"I could never..."

"If you really want the best for him, I think I have a procedure which can fix his eye. It looks like he is losing vision on the left. I think I can make him as fit as the healthy pups. I can fix it, I think. At least I have a theory about that."

"You wouldn't hurt him?"

"Never."

Treves found a dingy, ragged towel and helped Emlyn stand in the tub. Emlyn's infestation was inflamed and raw-looking. Treves wrapped the towel snugly around his patient's waist.

"Looks as though you have more than you can manage here," Treves said.

"Yes. I have no housekeeper or gardener, or accountant. I am not managing things well. My condition supersedes everything, though to be honest, I have never done very well with... things. My father predicted as much. He knew it would take far less than this to overwhelm me."

"Sorry to say it but he wasn't far off the mark, it seems."

"... made a provision in his will that if I used any portion of my inheritance to build shelters or veterinary hospitals or to in any way aid and succor animals, my birthright would be forfeit."

"Wise man. Your resources would be better spent alleviating human ills, not animal ones! I am your doctor, Emlyn, and also your friend."

"Indeed?"

"I can help not only with your medical condition, but also... your life. I can manage things for you. Discipline and order are what are needed here. If I can help you in these areas, too, I feel I must."

Emlyn sat in a dilapidated chair near the bathtub. His expression was amused, incredulous. Robespierre skittered across the marble floor and jumped onto Emlyn's lap.

"Really, Doctor? I am surprised to hear we are friends. As you know I have expressed misgivings about your research, and by extension... your character."

"Unfairly, in my opinion. Even medical ethicists benefit from the type of research I have done. All for the greater good. And I have always been honest with you as a patient and *friend*, and have had your recovery as my first and foremost goal. Knowledge is often painfully acquired. It is naïve to think otherwise. If I gain knowledge to ease human suffering, then yes, I allow myself leeway in how I gain that knowledge. And if my research relieves your suffering, I should think you would be a bit more understanding. Relieving misery is why I am here.

"I came to tell you the cuirass is ready to use. We can proceed with your treatment as quickly as ever you wish."

"It's ready?" Emlyn closed his eyes and Treves though he might faint again. "Then perhaps all of this is almost over, if... if I can endure the treatment. Thank you, Doctor Treves." Emlyn sighed an exhausted sigh. "Yes, yes... you have been a friend!"

Experimental Log 37, 20 December, 1896

Emlyn comes for treatment today. I filled the treatment tank with water two days ago to give the water temperature time to stabilize. I mapped which honeycomb cells in the cuirass needed to be filled to correspond with the areas of inflammation on Emlyn's chest and stomach. Filling these cells occupied most of a day.

The eels I purchased, Anguilla anguilla, *have remained healthy in their holding tank, but are ravenous. I have fed them sparingly to keep their appetites sharp and make them effective components of the treatment I propose. They are muscular and vigorous, and it was with enormous difficulty that I held and secured them in the needed cells of the cuirass, and aligned all their mouths to the exact same depth on the contact barrier, an imaginary limit I assumed was needed for all contact across the surface of the flesh to be equal. In all, eleven of these writhing creatures were required. Now it only remains to convince Emlyn to proceed with the treatment.*

Emlyn has agreed to let me manage his affairs. He trusts me. And I don't intend to give him any reason not to do so. I was looking over his financial records last night, and unless there is anything I have yet to discover, he is enormously wealthy. His father was a lumber man. Apparently, in this part of the country, hardwoods are a gold mine. Emlyn has signed a directive allowing me to set my own salary for the services I am providing. I feel I can fairly and honestly compensate myself to a level that will eliminate the financial limits of my researches. This is for the greater good, and the right thing to do. And with resources at my disposal, I will see my Isambard more often. His mother can hardly refuse, if I reveal to her the incentive of greater financial support, and a guarantee of an outstanding education, such as I had. I can now hope to send my son to Carthesian and give him opportunities in life I could not have provided before now. If he becomes a man of commitment and curiosity, as I think he will, he may even continue the work I have done, and be strong enough to do the researches necessary to benefit a disapproving and sadly ungrateful humanity.

God has laid this opportunity at my doorstep, for a great purpose. I will not fail to take this advantage.

Addendum:

Emlyn allowed me to bring his little dog, Robespierre, to the lab for treatment (experimental) of the deterioration of vision in the left eye. As Munk demonstrated, vision in dogs is localized in the occipital cortical region of the brain. He found the same is true in monkeys. One can extrapolate that this may also apply to great apes, and possibly humans as well. I can learn much from this operation, I think. I have trepanned a dog before with great success. I look forward to this investigation after the eel treatment business is resolved. I will of course need to keep the dog conscious to gauge its responses to the process.

Treves had prepared six syringes with cocaine solution. Emlyn looked at them in horror. His revulsion doubled when he investigated the treatment tank and saw the Therapeutic Cuirass and the eleven writhing eels fixed into cells in the cuirass, their undulating mouths extending three inches out the inner surface.

"Oh, Treves! What have you got me into?" Emlyn looked faint.

"I explained the entire process to you at length. This will relieve your suffering. The injections will numb you. You knew what to expect."

"Yes... but looking at all this. It looks like... insanity." Emlyn braced himself against a stone wall.

"This pedal," Treves placed his foot on the pedal at the bottom of the exterior framework, "is the proximity clutch. I will stand here and with pressure from my foot, control the depth of the access the creatures have to your flesh. They will eagerly eat away the parasites as I advance the clutch. You will feel some tugging and pulling but no pain... as I hypothesize."

"Why eels? Why did it have to be eels?"

"To be honest, they are voracious when it comes to worms such as these, and their long bodies make it easier to secure them in the honeycomb cells. Try putting a perch in there... it won't work!"

"Why do you have shackles at the top of this framework?"

"The involuntary impulse will be to push away the cuirass. Your hands *must* be restrained."

"No... no."

"Emlyn, I have worked hard to gain your trust. Have I gained your trust? If the procedure is too much for you, I will stop it. You know I have your best interests at heart."

"I... don't know what to think."

"Then let me be the example. A researcher who experiments on himself has a fool for a patient, but... this is a matter of trust and reassurance, so... let me show you how simple it will be!" Treves removed his lab coat and his shirt. He climbed a small ladder at the near end of the water tank and slid into the water. The eels began to thrash excitedly.

"All right, now come and affix my wrists in the shackles."

"I'm sure that isn't necessary, Treves."

"I insist. I want every step of the process to be transparent to you."

Emlyn did as Treves asked. He had some difficulty understanding the mechanism of the shackles.

"Now," Treves went on, "release the safety catch on the proximity clutch. It is that brass pin you see." Emlyn did this. "The clutch has three stops," Treves continued. "Each positions the cuirass a little closer to the subject. This is needed as the eels progress in their work."

The eels were thrashing and writhing insanely, churning the water, sloshing much of it out onto the floor.

"Now Emlyn, I want you to press the clutch with your foot just to see how the mechanism works. You needn't engage it all the way to the first stop. I just want you to see how it is controlled."

Emlyn's eyes had become glassy. He steadied himself against the framework of the mechanism. He placed his foot on the proximity clutch.

From a room adjoining the cellar laboratory, at the foot of the stairs, Emlyn heard a tiny yapping sound. "Robespierre?" he said. "Is that Robespierre?"

"Keep your mind on the task at hand, Emlyn."

Treves suddenly questioned the wisdom of this demonstration.

"Where is my dog?" Emlyn sounded delirious. "Have you locked him away somewhere? I *wondered* where he was when I arrived."

"Please reengage the safety catch, Emlyn."

"You have confined him. You intend to do some hideous vivisection on him... don't you?" Emlyn's head drooped. He collapsed on the spot, onto the proximity clutch, forcing it well against the third stop.

Treves noted how oddly dispassionate he was as tatters of lacy flesh, *his* flesh, fluttered off into the roiling water. However, his terror grew as the water reddened and he accepted that the frantic mouths, prematurely crushed against his torso, had nowhere to go to save themselves, but forward.

Demiurge

Journal of Dr. Isambard Kingdom Treves.
December 10, 1922

Aurore has not yet fully come out of the sedative. Her breathing is steady. I can see her on the table from where I sit. She has not stirred, but she breathes.

How would I forgive myself if she does not survive this? She would never blame me if the worst happens, but the rest of the village will. Her father will. I will!

She stood by me in spite of everything. I hope this was not just a sense of duty in her, as I have always been so grateful, and I must say, *surprised* at her devotion to me. How have I deserved it? So many of us came back from the war as lesser men, or changed men, physically and spiritually, and I am one of these. It was the end of illusion and naiveté for us, especially those of us who entered the action thinking there were rules of behavior and civility alive in humanity, even in the struggle for survival and dominance. The gas attacks, the trenches, the mud and death were elements not even our nightmares could muster five years ago. Now, they *are* our nightmares.

Add to this, the disgrace of my court-martial and dishonorable discharge, and I find most days that I am not the man I was before I went to France. I am unlikely to ever be that person again, or to hold him in high regard even if I could be. I still don't know what that means for the future, Aurore's and mine.

As Brunel, for whom I was named, was an engineer of steel and iron, so I strive to be an engineer of bone, flesh, and mind, if I do my work correctly and God allows it. And if He does allow it, the recent horrors may have been for some purpose, if the work I have started bears fruit, and a stronger, more perfected mankind may walk the earth!

As I have relived my father's disgrace, I will redouble his restitution and mine. I will erase the humiliation of my dear Aurore, and at last, deserve her—at least in the opinion of Mr. Chabrol, her disapproving father.

Later

The adjustment period continues. I still have much pain where my eye was, as though it were still in its socket and pierced by the rough splinter. I wear the prosthetic spectacles Aurore had made for me when I go out in public, with its artificial, staring eye, unnaturally blue and rimmed by spiky eyelashes. I can tell when people look at me that it does not hide my freakishness, but only redefines it. I feel their discomfort. I am the Polyphemus of Rouen Street.

And I no longer try to stop the pain. To dull it is artificial. The pain reminds me not only that I am alive, but that my work is unfinished. I welcome the pain. I have survived the apocalypse and been reborn from it. The pain is the reminder of that: it helps me focus on the task ahead and the role I have set for myself.

I must reimagine the Demiurge, the mythic creator-force of the world. When I was very young, my father told me the fable adapted by Christians from the Greeks, of how God modeled creation, but the spirit called Demiurge perfected it, calibrated it. This is how my father saw himself and his work, and how I see mine: perfecting the failings and sometimes deadly mistakes of our evolution. It is only for moments like this, of clarity and purpose, my dear Aurore notwithstanding, that I *stay* alive.

She continues to rest quietly. I was alarmed at how long it took her to begin to recover from the ether yesterday, to bestir her limbs and facial muscles at all: this after I had such difficulty putting her under its influence.

I got the appendix out just in time. It was near the point of bursting, and it would have been a catastrophe if the toxins had spread throughout her abdomen and put her at risk of peritonitis. Such a pointless vestigial organ, the appendix! It serves no function but a destructive one, when it goes wrong.

Humankind, as originally designed by the Creator, had some need for the organ, but that need is lost in the fading memory of time, as are so many other components of the human body which now impede the efficiency of its daily functions. I have jars of these troublesome and unnecessary organs in my study, saved from my surgeries: Tonsils, spleens, appendixes, displayed with the bones, ecorches, and the skull of a child with two faces—all things I have collected over the years. Curiosities all, objects whose only worth is their study by medical students. If my word carried any weight in the government of this land, I would order the appendix routinely removed from every child at puberty to avoid future complications.

Since my surgery has dwindled to nothing, I have been giving Aurore all my attention, and Miss Zollhern has not left her side. Chabrol was here for four hours yesterday. He was much opposed to me doing the operation here in this small village office, and pressed Aurore to let him bring her to the hospital at Bonne Terre, but she was adamant. After she showed movement last evening, a fire at the limeworks called Chabrol away. It apparently was quite serious, because he has not been back yet this morning.

Dec. 12, 1922

The fire at the limeworks was extensive, but Chabrol has a policy with The Phenix, so he is insured against loss. Since that worry has been removed from his mind, he can focus more of his attention on my care and treatment of his daughter. If Aurore and I are still to have a future together, I need to be amicable with the man, but most days this seems impossible. I knew a classmate of his had become a high functionary in the War Department; and Colonel Thorne, as he is known now, has mailed Chabrol transcripts of my court martial proceedings at his request, as Aurore told me last week. My complaints to the War Department, both my telegram and telephone call about this breach of confidentiality, have been thus far ignored.

Soon, Chabrol will receive that parcel, and he will know the story. Not the whole of it, just the official Army version. Then it will be up to me to defend myself to him if I am to ever marry Aurore with his blessing. And she craves his blessing, more now I think, than she would have before the death of her mother.

There is much pain in my eye today, but I can endure it. I think about the battle at Fismette and my wounding every day. It was the beginning of my clarity, my urgency. I had not stopped the bleeding in Gorman's side when the grenade came through the cottage window. It clattered into the corner near me and didn't impress my brain as a completely real object, yet I knew I must shield Gorman's body.

Even the explosion was unreal. There was little pain from the concussion at first, then a pressure in the area of my left eye. I noticed, almost casually, that none of the other five men returning fire in the room had been harmed.

Only then came the pain. The splinter pierced through my left eye and its orbit, and lodged there, just short of exiting my head. I fell against the rear parlor wall. Estes, who had assisted me in surgeries in the past, helped me to a sitting position. He told me to sit still while he tried to extract the splinter.

"No, compress Gorman's wound or he'll be dead in two minutes," I told him. Estes did as I said. I stood and looked at myself in a small mirror hanging on the parlor wall. My wound was horrific, but I looked at it dispassionately and with curiosity, as though it were someone else's face which I must treat, not mine.

Pulling the splinter out was like a blast of fire in my skull.

I immediately looked at myself in the mirror again. As ugly as the wound was, I felt no passion as I looked, only scientific interest, medical detachment. The moment of pulling the splinter out was unlike any moment in my memory, like no other moment of consciousness I had ever experienced in my lifetime. I couldn't take my gaze from it: the horror and beauty of the wound, or remove from my mind the newly reconsidered fact of what an organic machine we are.

And just then, I saw what my father had seen before me: that there is a way to make humans more than they are born to be, to quickly fix atavisms which evolution is so slow to repair. If I ever doubted it before, I now understood how it is possible and necessary to make patients stronger, more resilient, more attuned to the universe around them. But in another moment, a pain like I had never felt hit me and I thought I might lose consciousness. I fumbled through my medical case and found a 3/8 curved needle and a small bottle of alcohol. I splashed the liquid against my burning wound. I stood again in front of the mirror, and in two searing passes, I stitched the gash at my temple. I put a sterile pad against my ruined eye and held it in place with a bandage as best I could manage.

For a few moments, all I could think about was what I had just done. I felt somehow a momentary domination of nature, a godlike command of my own wellbeing, and an awe of my power, which I never felt or imagined before. Machine gun fire shattered the wall above me, but I was indifferent to it, as if I knew it could not harm me. I knew it could not, because I did not *will* it or *allow* it.

After a moment, I was aware of Estes pulling my sleeve.

"Get on the floor, Major!" he screamed. I fell across him, but he maintained pressure on Gorman's wound. My head spun and I thought again I would lose consciousness, but the sensation passed in a few seconds. Looking at the position of the wound in Gorman's abdomen and the rate of blood flow, I knew he must have a gash in the renal artery.

"We have to get him into the hallway away from the gunfire," I said. As Estes crawled past me and grasped Gorman's shoulders, dragging him out of the front room, I compressed the wound as best I could, sliding myself along the floor awkwardly to maintain pressure.

Thankfully, Gorman was unconscious. There was enough light in the hallway of the cottage for me to work. I was light-headed and waves of pain and nausea alternately washed over me. Estes crawled back into the front room for my bag. Gorman's breathing was very faint and stopped altogether every few seconds.

I washed my 3/8 needle with alcohol. My vision blurred and cleared erratically. I removed the bloody gauze Estes had packed onto Gorman's wound and dark blood immediately welled up, obscuring my view inside. With the blunt end of a scalpel, I was able to find and lift the left renal artery and locate the nick in it. I quickly stitched it just as Gorman began to stir.

"He's coming to," Estes said.

"We're done," I said. As the blood flow stopped, I could see Gorman's spleen behind the artery. I noticed a pronounced splenomegaly. "His spleen is enlarged," I said. I tried to focus on the organ, but my vision blurred. I thought I could make out a dark mass on its lower edge. "It's a tumor," I said. "Cancer."

Estes looked into the wound as Gorman began to move. He held

Gorman's shoulders more tightly. "I don't know," he said. "It doesn't look like a tumor to me."

Gorman began to twitch and his eyelids fluttered.

"My God, he's waking up!" Estes said. "I'll get the ether from the front room!"

"No, hold him down!" I shouted. "If I don't get the spleen out, he'll be dead in three months. I can't hold him still myself."

"Maybe you should close him up and do the surgery later..." Estes said.

"He won't be strong enough for another surgery for weeks," I said. "Might be too late then. This could metastasize."

A gurgle arose in Gorman's throat. His eyes opened suddenly. He gasped and coughed out a spray of blood. He screamed.

Estes started to rise from the floor. "I'm getting the ether!" he said.

"Hold him still!" I shouted. In an instant, I had severed the organ and removed it. Gorman shuddered, spat a small mist of blood and lay still.

"He's dead," Estes whispered.

After the action at Fismette, Estes reported this incident to Lieutenant Allen, who reported it to Colonel Rickarts. Estes' accusation was that I performed an experimental surgery on an enlisted man, and did so without use of a sedative or anesthetic agent. The court-martial proceedings started in November, and on the second day of testimony, my father's conviction in 1899 for performing vivisection on Thibault was entered into evidence. Then, my fate was sealed.

My defense was that in my diminished capacity, having just sustained a severe wound myself, I judged an essentially superfluous organ to be cancerous and in need of removal, and judged this act to be in the long-term best interests of a weakened patient. It was dismissed. Instead, it was decided that reckless and experimental surgery is in my nature, and I was found guilty.

The story of this disgrace has remained unknown to Aurore and the rest of the town. That will change when Chabrol receives the packet from his friend in the War Department.

The wound in my eye and temple healed slowly over the weeks following the battle. Having been relieved of duty and awaiting transport home, I treated the injury myself, re-stitching the sutures and cutting out a spot of infection at the sphenoid. I learned to accept the pain, to absorb it as part of a process of self-perfection, which it seemed to me then would be necessary if I were to presume any mastery over the flesh and to extend this view to other people who would submit to my treatment.

Dec. 13

Aurore's fever has not broken. Miss Zollhern has kept cool compresses on her forehead since late this afternoon, but her temperature has not fallen below 103. Aurore cannot sustain a fever for long. I may insist to Chabrol that we move her to St. Louis tomorrow.

At eleven p.m. I told Miss Zollhern to go home and rest. She nodded gratefully. "That's the last of the ether, Doctor. Should I order more right away?"

"In the next day or so. There's no urgent need."

"I heard Belle DuFour talking to the butcher this morning," she said as I helped her on with her coat. "She said Ludovico Gui has escaped from the prison at Chester."

"Escaped?" It was a name I hoped to never hear again.

"Yes. She said he crossed the river, though I don't know how anyone can say that for sure. I hope he doesn't come here!"

But I expect that is exactly what Gui intends to do. I didn't mention it to Miss Zollhern, but I had a letter from Gui not a week ago. He fears his stomach tumor is back, and the warden intends to deny him surgery.

On August 14, 1920, Ludovico Gui robbed the Southwest Bank in East St. Louis. He shot a teller in the spine when he lunged at him, paralyzing the fellow: a man raising three small daughters alone. Gui had been diagnosed with stomach cancer a month before and was desperate for money for the surgery. In growing pain, he escaped down the River Road in a stolen car and took the ferry below Prairie du Rocher across the river to Ste. Odile.

Quite by happenstance he found my practice as he drove through town. I had not performed a surgery since my release from the army. I knew nothing of his crime or his flight from the law when I saved his life that night. He was not two hours on the recovery table when Sheriff Brouchard and his deputy knocked on my door. They had seen the reported stolen car on Rouen Street outside my office. They called an ambulance from Bonne Terre and returned Gui, still unconscious, back to the state police to await trial in Illinois.

And now, I was sure he was heading my way again.

Later

I dozed for a while. I awoke around midnight hearing Aurore gasping for breath in the recovery room. I ran to her side. Her tongue was nearly blocking her air passage. I carefully clamped a tongue compress onto her jaw. Her temperature was still high: 102 degrees. I replaced the damp towel on her forehead.

I had not meant to fall asleep. I knew I must be vigilant. She might have died if I had not awakened. I knew I must stay awake all night... until midmorning the next day, when Miss Zollhern would return.

My mind wandered, lost in a fog of exhaustion. I sat in my desk chair and pushed off my left shoe. A lesion on my heel that had been developing over the last few months was irritated and aching.

I watched Aurore breathing fitfully in the next room. Why hadn't she recovered consciousness yet? What if I had miscalculated and caused her some sort of brain damage, or whatever infection that was causing her fever overtook her and killed her? I should not have trusted to my own ability where she is concerned. Not when *she* is concerned! I should have insisted we go on to the hospital, though there was no way of knowing if the appendix would have burst by then.

I thought of the mistakes I had made in my professional life. Too many mistakes. Maybe I had been wrong about Gorman. Maybe he would have lived if I had not operated. Maybe I should not have removed Fletcher Leslie's arm after Fismette. I had doubts at the time that the infection was as bad as I at first suspected. In battle conditions, one's judgments must be made quickly, and often without the benefit of all vital information. Surely, I had caused unnecessary suffering and death in my professional decisions.

But these things are unavoidable in the course or war and the attempts to save lives. My goal, like my father's was, is the greater good, to avoid suffering and early death through engineering the flesh beyond its evolutionary meanderings and inefficiencies. That is what I have tried to do, and my father before me.

The dull, persistent pain in my foot suddenly and irrationally irritated me. I looked at the lesion on my left heel, red and swollen. I was angered at the annoyance of it, the distraction. And pain is *such* a distraction, a weakness we yield to! I arose from my chair and walked into my operating room. In a drawer I found a sterile scalpel. I sat on the edge of a small bench against the wall and with three exigent, searing slices, I cut the growth from my foot.

The pain of it seemed irrelevant compared to the exhilaration I felt, the same exhilaration I knew when I treated my wounded eye. That sense of mastery over myself and by extension, Aurore and her recovery, was both intoxicating and familiar. And something else: I felt in some sense *cleansed* by the act, as I had that day in battle. Validated as though I had proven again my fealty to my own purpose, and forgiven, by this pain, of harm I may have inadvertently done when treating others.

I wrapped the wound in gauze and tied a bandage around it. The sharp fire of the wound was far greater than the dull ache of the lesion, but I felt invigorated by it. I hobbled to the sink and washed my hands. I was suddenly sleepier than I have ever been in my life, but I knew I must not rest. I must not be weak. I must watch over Aurore. I must *not* sleep.

I splashed cold water onto my face. Just then, I heard a car door slam on the street outside. I braced myself. My locked front doorknob rattled as someone tried to turn it.

Then there was a knock. I paused a moment, then walked to the door.

"Doctor Treves..." a voice called weakly through the door. "It's Gui. Ludovico Gui. Please open the door, sir."

I unlocked and opened the door. Gui collapsed against me. He was deathly pale and thin. Although it was freezing outside, his prison clothes were drenched in perspiration. One tire on the curb, a flatbed truck he must have stolen, was parked opposite my front door. I helped him inside.

"I wish you hadn't come here, Gui," I said. "I don't need trouble like this."

"Warden will let me die," he whispered. "He said so. He laughs about it. I need you to operate. I will go back to prison after that. I am not trying to escape... just survive."

I helped him into the operating room. He collapsed onto the chair near the door. "The pain is almost constant now. I have no strength... no strength left."

"I'll call an ambulance," I said. "We'll get you to Bonne Terre."

"I can't make it," he gasped. "I can't take another step. You must operate now."

I knelt down beside him and lifted his chin to look directly at me. "Gui, I have no ether. I used the last of it on my fiancée. I can't put you under. I can't operate on you."

Gui's eyes were watery and yellow. As he looked at me, the life in them seemed to be fading. "You must do it, Doctor. Ether or no. I must endure it or die. You must do it... please." He crumpled against me. He was barely conscious.

I carried him to the operating table. I lay him on his back and unbuttoned his shirt. I washed his upper abdomen first with soap and water, then with alcohol. He winced under the pressure. I wondered how he could endure the incision.

I applied the straps on the table across his arms, chest, hips, and legs. I slipped on a sterile smock and operating gloves and removed three scalpels and two separators from the bath and placed them on the tray near the table. I felt oddly, almost shamefully, excited about what I had to do.

"The incision is coming, Ludovico," I said. "Brace yourself." I made a quick four-inch incision just under the thoracic cage. He gasped and whimpered a little and made a gurgling sound. His body shivered, but other than that he lay still.

I cut through the abdominals and exposed the stomach. I screwed a separator into place to keep the wound open.

Gui was nearly unconscious now. He was breathing shallowly but steadily, quivering every few moments. I thought of the state of mind he must be in at that moment: the place where pain takes you from the unendurable to the endurable, a place where you observe your own suffering from a distance, almost from another dimension. The scar of my previous surgery was apparent on the stomach wall. I cut just below the scar and opened the stomach.

The tumor inside was widespread and very advanced. The stomach was nearly consumed and nonfunctional. Gui would not live but a few more days, it was apparent, with this unsalvageable organ. There was no hope for him.

I remembered reading a story in *The Lancet* before the war of a similar case treated by a surgeon in Siam. He sectioned the stomach at the top and bottom, removed it and connected the esophagus directly to the large bowel. At the time of publication, the patient was still alive.

I watched the dying man breathing shallowly on the table. There was little likelihood of survival for him beyond that experimental procedure. In a moment, I had done it. I removed the diseased organ and sutured the esophagus and bowel together. In another twenty minutes, I had closed all the wounds.

Exhausted, I removed my smock and gloves and collapsed onto the bench. I was so sleepy I didn't see how I could remain awake for another minute. I knew I should check on Aurore. I just needed to rest for a moment.

Just as my body started to slip into relaxation, over a length of time I could not guess, a startling awareness came over me. Gui was not breathing. I ran to his side, nearly falling when my injured foot gave way.

Gui was dead. He appeared to have been dead for some time, for his body temperature had noticeably dropped. I looked at his peaceful, sunken face for many minutes. It seemed to grow more ashen as I looked at it, more corpse-like. The dead look so profoundly different from the living. A deep sigh came from me, from the deepest part of my body, that emotional toll that must be paid by those who try to save lives and fail. It was a feeling I had encountered many times, that I must avoid self-reproach and self-hatred and accept death and loss as part of the surgical effort or leave the profession and my research behind me.

I returned to my bench and sat. I would have to call the sheriff soon. In an hour or so. Or not until daybreak. I needed a few minutes' rest. I had never felt so exhausted since that day at Fismette.

I heard a dog barking on Rouen Street, and another dog answering him. It was morning. I had fallen asleep. I was startled to see Gui on the table, rigid and pale. I remembered his knock on my door, his surgery.

I stood and looked into the recovery room at Aurore. I could not tell if she was breathing or not. I went to her side.

She was cold and rigid. She must have died soon after Gui. I had killed her! Killed my Aurore! I collapsed to my knees beside her bed. I couldn't breathe. I couldn't draw breath in past the gurgling wail I heard escaping from me.

Later

The sheriff and the coroner are gone. Gui's body has been removed back to Chester. Chabrol does not want an autopsy. He is satisfied that his daughter has died as a result of my poor treatment, professional incompetence and the experimental nature of my practice. He is filing charges against me and has removed Aurore to Fabian's for preparation for burial.

And how can I dispute this? What successes can I claim to contradict him? I think I am truly deserving of anything Chabrol can muster against me. Aurore is dead only because I could not keep a vigil over her. I could not keep awake for another hour. I try to strengthen the flesh, and I have no more control over my own than that. I could not keep my eye open.

But that is a weakness I can solve. Simply and quickly. I can remain awake from now on. Awake and vigilant. A scalpel I didn't use on Gui is still on the tray.

A slice above and a slice below, a few seconds of pain looking at my hated face in the mirror, and I will not block out the light or the world again.

Oblivion

Principia Morgan was proud to be named after Isaac Newton's famous mathematical treatise. Inadvertently, of course. Her mother admitted she didn't remember where she had first heard the name, but it sounded like the name of a Roman goddess, so she and her late husband decided it would be more than fitting for their daughter. Principia and her mother arose every morning by three to prepare a midday meal for the students Principia taught at LaMotte Crossing School. This morning, they were cutting bacon, turnips, carrots, and onions for a soup Principia would finish later in the morning. Her mother had started a pot of stock the day before, letting it simmer most of the night.

"I hope your pump's not frozen at the school," Hattie said. "If it is and it snows like the almanac says, you'll have to melt enough snow for about a gallon..."

"I know, Mother. No snow yet. Just because the almanac says..."

"Your father swore by that almanac. And he was right most of the time, too. Stoke your fire fierce then let it die down and get good and hot. Heat up these vegetables and bacon in a skillet. Too bad all we had was bacon. Add the water to the stock 'til you've got your gallon. Cook it all slow."

"I brought in plenty of firewood yesterday. I'll get it stoked up well when I get to school." Principia felt her face tighten a little when her mother mentioned her father. He had been dead two years, but Hattie still mentioned him once or more every day. Principia knew what her mother was trying to do, what she needed to do for Principia's sake, so she no longer asked her to stop mentioning him.

"All right, dear, I have put everything in jars and we'll put it all in the rucksack, and you're ready to go," Hattie seemed to be speaking to the air, not her daughter. There was no need to say these things out loud. Their morning routine rarely varied.

Hattie insisted on pronouncing her daughter's name *Prin-SIP-ea* rather than *Prin-CHIP-ea* as it would be in Latin. Principia no longer mentioned this, either. Her mother lived her life at peace with certain facts, and it was important to the household to keep this arrangement in place. As she packed the rucksack with the jars, Principia remembered that last night had been another night of visitation, as she had come to call them.

A few weeks after her father's death, after he swallowed lye then cut his own throat with his straight razor, either out of agony or because the lye didn't work quickly enough, Principia was awakened in her room by a presence. As a child, she had come to expect there would be nights her father would come into her room. In the dead of night, she would awaken and find his dark form standing over her.

"You are growing, Principia," he would say. "Your body is changing. If I don't massage your legs you will have pain. Growing pains. Terrible pains. I would take that pain onto myself rather than see you suffer, if I could. This will help more than you know. And I do so love this togetherness with you. Being together." One night two years before, it was December 14, Principia said no.

"I don't want you in my room, Father," she said. "I don't want you to touch me like that anymore. This is the sin of Lot and I won't have it!"

"You are far too precious to me to allow you to feel any pain," he said and tried to lie next to her in her bed. She rolled onto the floor and screamed. Her copy of *Middlemarch*, which she had been reading for the last few days, was under the bed. She grasped it and began hitting her father's arms, face and head with it. Her mother ran into the room. She refused to look at her husband, as if, it seemed to Principia, to do so would verify what she had refused to see since her daughter's young childhood. Hattie led her sobbing daughter into the front room to comfort her. Late the next afternoon, sitting on a frozen log behind their barn, Principia's father killed himself.

Soon after this, late at night, when she could not manage a deep sleep, Principia began to have visitations. Last night, as had happened twice before, she awoke to feel a hand on her leg. The first two times, she saw nothing when she opened her eyes, but last night she saw a shadow standing over her, a form darker than the darkness of her room, like a tear in the familiar world that surrounded her. At the top of the form, a smudge of light flickered for a moment like a displaced soul, and then vanished. And whether the words were actual and alive in the room or only inside her mind, she heard her father's voice say: "I love you. I want to always be with you. Together."

She never mentioned these visitations to her mother because she knew that in a state of half-sleep, the mind could play tricks, and being superstitious, Hattie would be upset.

"I think I'm going to hitch the wagon today," Principia said as she pulled on her winter coat and wrapped her scarf around her neck and head.

"Poor old Jimmy!" Hattie said. "Out in that freezing barn all night."

Principia kissed her mother goodbye, and hitching the rucksack over her shoulder, went out into the cold. Jimmy was a fourteen-year-old draft horse Principia's father had bought from Luther Quay four years ago. In the barn, Principia filled the feedbag with oats and hooked it over Jimmy's ears. While he ate, she drew the buckboard up to him and hitched it. She dropped the rucksack in the back.

"I'm sorry to hitch the wagon today Jimmy," Principia said, "but I may have children to cart home later, if the weather turns."

Removing the feedbag, she climbed onto the buckboard seat and coaxed Jimmy out onto the dim road. The moon was full but veiled and indistinct behind a scrim of clouds. The sky was uniform, gray and full of snow. It pressed down on the landscape, giving the impression of short distance and definite space from above. Simultaneously, it spread across the earth, compressing the far hills that disappeared into darkness and diffused moonlight many miles to the west toward the village of Oubli and Lesterton beyond.

After only a few minutes on the rough road, the snow began to fall. The snowflakes were small and sparse, and Principia hoped they would remain so and stop quickly. By the time she reached the Saline Bridge, a mile on, the snowfall had become heavier and the flakes larger. Principia thought of her first memory of the bridge. She was no more than three or four years old and she and her parents were in the wagon, travelling to visit her Aunt Rae in Oubli for Easter dinner. It was also the first time she remembered her father telling her he loved her.

The bridge was icy, and repairs that needed to be made in warmer weather had never been done. Principia slowed Jimmy and decided to proceed across the bridge as slowly as possible.

"I love you, child," she remembered her father saying as they crossed all those years ago. His hand was on her knee as she sat between her parents.

"You climb back on into the wagon," Hattie said, helping her daughter over the seat back. "Seat ain't wide enough for three abreast."

Jimmy stepped cautiously onto the icy planks. The Saline Bridge was barely the width of the buckboard, and in the darkness, Principia thought the old horse might lose his footing. Halfway across she heard a splitting sound and Jimmy's left front hoof went through the bridge floor. The horse fell precariously against the rail. He pulled his leg out of the break and limped slowly across the bridge to the other side. Principia stopped him and climbed down from the seat to look at his wound. In the darkness, she saw a gash on the long pastern above the hoof. Blood, black in the diffused moonlight, flowed down the first joint and over the hoof.

"Oh, Jimmy," Principia said, "I'm so sorry. I'd take you home, but I have to get to school. It's just two more miles. I'll bind you up then. That's all we could do for you at home. Hopefully, that will take care of you." She climbed back into the seat.

The old horse limped noticeably and seemed to struggle up the hill overlooking the Lesterton valley. The snow was falling a little heavier now. The schoolhouse was somewhere down in the darkness halfway across the valley floor. Beyond that, Principia saw a single spot of light from what must have been the village of Oubli.

"Mostly downhill from here, old boy," Principia said. "I think this snow will let up soon."

The wind picked up a little as the wagon moved down the gradual hill into the valley. Jimmy's limp was less pronounced than it had been at first, and Principia hoped that meant his wound was superficial. She was just starting to see steam rise from the old horse's back as his huge body warmed from exertion. Principia felt colder. She thought she had not dressed warmly enough this morning. She looked forward to getting to school and stoking up the fire in the iron stove. She watched the spot of light across the valley at Oubli and wondered that there would be anyone else up at this time on such a cold morning. A gust of wind blew past her face just as the wagon creaked and the sounds together almost sounded like a phrase: *always with you* whispered in her ear. She felt the distant light and the rhythm of falling snow had mesmerized her. "I'd better pay attention to the road," she thought.

Principia wondered if Peter Browne would come to school early to help her. He was a boy of fourteen whom had not started his schooling until a year ago. She was only four years older than him, but he seemed very much like a child to her. He was still on the McGuffey Eclectic First Reader with the younger children and was struggling. The earlier the better to start with language skills, Principia had noticed. She'd been taught this at Harris Teacher's College and seen it for herself since she had been given her post at LaMotte Crossing School. She had taken special pains with Peter, and had quickly noticed signs of his shy infatuation with her.

After harvest this year, when school had started again, Principia asked Peter if he would like to stay after school a while and she would read to him. He eagerly agreed. She began with her favorite, *Sonnets from The Portuguese*. At first, Peter seemed confused and restless, but after a few days he became noticeably more interested. He began asking questions and one afternoon suddenly seemed to understand that these florid, labyrinthine ways of talking were just saying things that, in simpler language, were familiar to him. Principia had picked a second book which she felt would interest the boy more immediately, that she intended to start that afternoon: *The Hunchback of Notre Dame*.

Within another half-mile, Jimmy had begun limping more noticeably again. He snorted and shook his head occasionally as he walked, and Principia could tell he was in pain. The fallow fields of the abandoned Du Vet farm were entirely snow-covered. On the far side of those, she could see the dark schoolhouse and shed in the glade beyond the bend in the road and the tiny spot of light from Oubli off in the distance behind them.

As she approached the school, Principia saw a dark figure sitting on the front step, rise and shake the settled snow off himself. It was Peter Browne. He was wearing his threadbare sack coat with several layers under it, and his woolen cap bound to his head with a thin scarf. He looked frozen through.

"Peter!" Principia called, "You shouldn't be here so early. You're a block of ice!"

"I knew you'd need help this morning Miss Morgan. I'm allright."
He noticed Jimmy's hobbling step. "Looks like Jimmy's been lamed."

"Poor old fellow! His hoof went through the bridge. Since you're
here, can you unhitch him and see to him in the shed? Clean his leg
and bind it?"

"Yes, Miss Morgan," Peter unhitched Jimmy and led him back to the
shed.

Principia retrieved her rucksack from the wagon and unlocked the
schoolhouse door. It was freezing inside. She lay the rucksack on the
floor near the stove and placed two kerosene lamps on her desk. She
put kindling and hardwood logs into the stove and found her box of
matches on the shelf behind it. Soon she had a fire going and she
closed the stove door. She lit the kerosene lamps. She found her
enameled pot in the corner cabinet and took it outside to the pump.
Luckily the water was flowing. She filled the pot and brought it back
inside. She dumped her beef broth into another pot and placed it on
the stovetop. The mantel clock key was in her desk drawer. She found
it and wound the Seth Thomas clock on the shelf next to the western
window. Five fifteen a.m. The snow had let up, somewhat. The tiny
light was still visible off in Oubli.

Peter came in the front door and stomped the snow off his feet.

"I don't think Jimmy has got a broke bone," he said.

"*Broken* bone," Principia corrected. "Well that's good. I'm glad to
hear that."

"Broken. Think he cut a blood-vein though. He bled a lot. I had a
hard time stoppin' it. He ain't a-gonna want to walk, Miss."

"He *won't* want to walk."

"Walkin' will just open up the cut again. He'll be contrary for a day
or two, at least."

"I can leave him here overnight," Principia said. "Make sure there's
hay and liquid water for him out there."

"I done it already, Miss Morgan. Anything else you need help with?"

"No, Peter. Thank you. You might look at your reader for a while.
Practice sounding out your words." The boy nodded and sat at his
place on the front row bench. His reader was in his desk in front of
him. "How is your father these days, Peter?" Principia continued.

The boy shrugged. "He got full as a tick last night and fell off the
ladder in the barn a-tryin' to pull a bale down. Hurt his wrist pretty
good. He pretty much give up on Sons of Temperance."

Principia thought of correcting Peter's "give", but she just smiled at
him. "Sorry to hear that," she said.

Principia swept and tidied the schoolroom while Peter poured over
his lesson. As the sun was coming up, she put her vegetables and bacon
in a skillet on the stovetop. By seven a.m. the sky was still dark and
snow was still falling a little. A horse snorted outside, and a wagon
could be heard pulling up to the front door. Most mornings, Caber
McClendon brought his son Walter, aged eight, and most of the other

children who attended LaMotte Crossing School.

The front door opened and Caber, a farmer of about forty entered, followed by his son, as well as Virginia Spencer, age fourteen, Norma Vernet, age eleven, Jasper and Helen Dumas, nine-year-old twins, and Lucy Strickland and Solana Marais, both age six.

"Good morning, Mr. McClendon," Principia smiled. "I didn't know if everyone would make it in today."

"Morning Miss Morgan," McClendon nodded, helping Lucy and Solana remove their coats. "Aw, it ain't too bad out there. Snow pretty much stopped. I take the almanac with a grain of salt. I think we'll be all right today."

"I think my mother has that same almanac and swears by it! Thank you again for delivering everyone."

"You bet. See you this evenin'. Walter, you help out Miss Morgan now, if she needs somethin'." McClendon went out the door, closing it firmly behind him.

"Everybody hang your coats and wraps on your pegs," Principia said to the slow-moving children. "Then take your places. Clean off your slates and we'll get started soon. If you are too cold, you may keep your coats on." She scraped the vegetables she had been simmering into the pot of broth and placed a lid on it.

In the mornings, Principia usually started the younger children, Lucy, Solana and Walter, along with Peter who was struggling, on simple reading, while Virginia, Norma and the Dumas twins practiced their cursive, followed by reading and arithmetic. She saved history and geography for the afternoons, when she knew the children's logical faculties might be tiring.

Peter's early-morning reading had benefited him, and he read aloud more comfortably today than he had the previous few days. Lucy and Solana were quick learners and were doing very well, and Walter was coming along slowly and steadily. Principia checked her pot of soup every half-hour or so. Glancing out the western window she noticed that the snow had started falling again. The day was dark and gray, and she thought she would keep the children indoors at their recess time. She put more oak logs in the stove. She had not been able to warm herself all morning. She shivered as if icy fingers were scuttling along the back of her neck.

At recess time, Peter went out to the shed to check on Jimmy while the younger children played jackstraws and checkers or looked at the few picture books Principia had purchased herself for the school. At eleven thirty, Principia removed nine wooden bowls from the cupboard and, filling each with her soup, placed one in front of each student. She filled a bowl for herself and took it to her desk and ate.

Lucy and Solana wouldn't eat their soup. That was not unusual. Peter ate both children's meal and collected the bowls, taking them outside, with Walter's help, to rinse off at the pump. When the boys came back inside, they were snow-covered.

"Really comin' down out there, Miss Morgan," Peter said. Principia glanced out the window. The wind had picked up and the snow was falling so heavily, drifts were starting to form against the shed.

"Oh my," she said. "This is not what we want to see." She stepped outside the front door and scanned the dim sky from east to west. *I hope this blows over,* she thought. She wondered if she should walk the children home before conditions got worse. Hitching the wagon was not possible now with Jimmy's injury. She thought it was premature to decide. She would wait a while longer. She was very eager to be beginning *Hunchback* with Peter. She didn't want to disappoint him.

After the children had finished eating, Principia removed her pot of soup from the stove. She set it in the snow outside the front door and thought it would make the next day's lunch, too. She had promised Virginia, Norma, Jasper, and Helen that they could have a spelling bee that afternoon. She decided to only spend twenty minutes or so on this activity. She'd noticed in the last few weeks that Helen had a difficult time directing her attention at an activity for much longer than that.

As Principia was preparing to start these four on their geography lesson and return to the younger ones and their numbers, she glanced outside. The snowfall had increased and had buried about six inches of the wagon wheels. A soft pillow of snow had accumulated on the wagon seat just since lunchtime. Principia felt a twinge of fear inside her. In another hour or two the road would be impassable. In the terrible blizzard of two years before, in her last year at her position, Mrs. Newcomer, the teacher Principia had replaced, and her class had been trapped in this building for three days under the drifts. There wasn't enough food or firewood in the schoolhouse for that now. Principia knew she would have to get the children out.

She wondered where she should take them. LaMotte and her own home were about three miles to the east but most of the road was uphill, and that would be a difficult walk for the younger children. As far as she knew, none of the family homes were nearer than hers. Principia stepped out the front door. She looked to the east and to the west. The small spot of light was still visible in Oubli to the west. It was all level ground or slightly downhill from here. That would be easier, and it was no further away than LaMotte.

"Peter, come here please," she called.

The boy ran to her side.

"Get your coat and wraps on. We have to get the children out. Into town, I think, down to Oubli."

"Yes, Miss Morgan. I think that's a good idea."

"There's a coil of rope out in the shed. Get it for me and make sure Jimmy has enough to eat for a few days."

The boy nodded, pulled on his coat and ran out to the shed.

Principia directed the children to tidy up their spaces and get their coats on.

"We are going for a walk." she said.

When Peter returned with the rope, Principia gathered the children around her.

"This is a little unusual," she smiled. "We have to walk a few miles and the snow is coming down pretty hard, I don't want anyone to get lost. Peter and I are going to tie everyone together and we will all walk in a line down to Oubli."

"I'm cold, Miss Morgan," Lucy said. "It's too hard to walk through snow."

"It will only get harder the longer we wait," Principia said, touching the child's hair. "We can still tell where the road is. We don't want to get snowed in where nobody can get to us for a few days. I don't want to get snowed in here for three days...does anyone?" She pulled on her coat.

"No," the children said in unison.

Peter began tying the rope around the waists of the younger children, then the older ones, and finally himself. Principia tied it around herself and cut off the excess rope with the penknife she kept in her desk drawer. On a clean slate on her desktop she wrote: *Gone to Oubli*.

"Is everyone ready? She said.

"Yes, Miss Morgan."

When all the children were outside, Principia locked the school door. She hung her slate with its message on a nail on the door. She led the children out onto the road. It was still snowing heavily, and Principia felt she needed to get everyone to Oubli in an hour or an hour and a half before the road became impassable. The younger children were catching the fluffy snowflakes in their mouths.

"We will have to walk as quickly as we can," Principia started walking to the west, leading her small caravan behind her. "But tell me if we are moving too fast. There is a house over in Oubli with a light inside, since early this morning. That's where we are going."

Lucy and Solana both slipped in the snow and as they steadied themselves back on their feet, seemed on the verge of tears. Principia wondered if leading the children out this way was the wisest thing to do. She'd also read of teachers and their students getting trapped in their schoolrooms in Nebraska and Kansas, and she didn't want that to happen to her class.

She realized she had no sense of how long they had been walking, but guessed it must have been more than a half-hour. She could no longer feel her fingers or feet.

"I'm too cold!" Solana complained.

"We're all cold," Virginia said. She often tried to help Principia with the younger children. "That's why we have to walk fast. The sooner we get to that house the sooner we will be warm again!"

"Thank you, Virginia," Principia smiled.

In the heavy snowfall, the road ahead of them had become a soft groove pressed into the white landscape. It was early afternoon, but the sky had never brightened much. Principia still saw the spot of light ahead, though now it seemed placed higher in the distant village than it had before.

"Miss Morgan," Peter spoke up behind her. "you know it's a split in the road up yonder?"

"Yes, Peter."

"Left side goes up a steep hill and the right side over the low-water bridge."

"Yes."

"Right side would be easier for these kids but you gotta go about a quarter mile past the fork to know if it's open or not. Be hard on them, the little 'uns, to hafta double-back."

"Yes, it would."

"I can go on ahead and check?"

"I don't know Peter. I don't want to send you on alone in these conditions."

"I'll be all right. They're all about half-froze already. Don't want them to have to cover the same ground twict."

Principia frowned through the flakes at him. There was no doubt or uncertainty in his face.

"I shouldn't let you out of my sight. I know I shouldn't, but you're right. We have to keep this walk as short as possible. Alright then, but please hurry and be careful!"

Peter nodded, untied himself and ran ahead of them on the road. In a few hundred feet Principia lost sight of him in the snowfall. She looked behind her to see Virginia comforting Solana and Lucy. Lucy was crying.

"My hands and feet are so cold!" Lucy said.

"I know," Virginia said. She and Helen were rubbing the two little girls' hands and faces to warm them. Principia's eyes were watering from the cold. Fear stabbed through her. Should she have kept the children at the school? What if she couldn't get them to Oubli? They could all die on the road. She gathered them all in a circle.

"I know we're all cold," she said. "We have just a bit farther to go and we'll be warm. Just a bit farther. Peter has gone ahead to see if the bridge is clear and we can get through. He's waiting for us up ahead. We have to get to him, all right?"

"Yes Miss Morgan," the children mumbled.

The snow was now nearly as high as the knees of the younger girls, and walking through it was exhausting them. Through the snowfall, Principia could see the fork in the road. In the gloom, a dark figure stood watching them approach. Principia waved.

"Peter!" she shouted. No response. The figure looked taller than Peter. It didn't move. She felt a shiver run up her neck. The rope tying everyone together jerked. Principia looked behind her. Walter had fallen. When she looked back at the road ahead, the dark figure was gone.

"Peter!" she shouted. "*Peter!*" The fields and woods were dead and silent around them.

"Where is Peter, Miss Morgan?" It was Walter's voice. He sounded weak, as if he were speaking a thought rather than asking a question.

"Up ahead somewhere. I just saw him, I think. He's probably waiting for us on the other side of the bridge."

"Up ahead somewhere," Walter repeated.

Principia could see the remnants of Peter's footprints in the snow ahead of them. They were quickly being lost and becoming vaguer by the moment in the ongoing downfall. In another few feet the footprints seemed to be gone. She could not see any impression of them anywhere.

"*Peter!*" The wind picked up a little and the drifts were quickly covering the road. She thought of waiting at this spot a while to see if Peter returned. Looking behind her, Walter was looking confused, and Solana and Lucy were still crying. Principia knew she had to get the children to shelter immediately. She walked forward to the bridge. Soon the younger children would not be able to walk at all. She started to cry. There was no sense or feeling inside her that Peter was alive anywhere in the world.

There was a small rise just beyond the bridge. The village of Oubli should be visible from there. If anything were still visible. Solana and Lucy had stopped crying. Walter sat in the snow and seemed to be in a daze. The rest of the children sat or collapsed onto the ground.

"I don't see how we can go any farther, Miss," Virginia said. "These little ones are done..."

"You stay here, all of you," Principia said. She untied the rope from her waist. "I can see the town from just ahead, right up here." Principia hurried through the drift to the top of the hillock. She stared as deeply and far as she could into the reaches of the dark day. There was no sign of the village, no sign of it at all. No light beacon in a window to be seen. It occurred to her suddenly that the light had never been there. The village, she remembered, is only visible beyond the Saline Ridge another half-mile away. It was not Oubli she had been seeing all day. But just above her, just at the height of a man, she saw the small light again. The light hovered, it flickered a moment like a displaced soul, then vanished into the dark smudge of a standing form within the wall of falling snow beyond the edge of the road.

The wind swirled around her head as the children behind her settled in quietly. Huddled on the ground together, the snow was starting to drift over them. They were no longer lost or frightened or in danger. Now they were quiet, and still, and accepting sleep. The wind swirled around Principia's head again and her tears froze on her cheek as she heard the word the wind formed, and repeated:

Together... together.

Porphyria

Viktor closed the elevator cage door in disgust. His friend, Sandor Bessenyei, could not look at him. Sandor was pale and covered with perspiration from the fever he'd had all morning. He collapsed against the side of the cage as it made its way slowly up the mine headframe to the surface.

"I am sorry," Sandor mumbled. "I am too sick. *Èn vagyok a beteg.* I am too sick to work anymore."

"*Èn vagyok az egyetlen barátja.* I am your only friend here," Viktor said. "It would seem you could try a little longer. Not everyone has money to live on. Some of us have to work. If you feel better a month from now, they won't hire you back, you know? You quit now and you're done for in the mines, and no one else will hire Hungarians in this place. When your money runs out, you're finished. In the meanwhile, I'm down in this pit with nobody to talk to."

"My money will soon be gone," Sandor said. "Regardless of that, I cannot work anymore. My strength has left me for good, I think."

Sandor felt ashamed, though he tried to hide a little smile. There was something very predictable but oddly innocent about Viktor's resentful nature. Sandor knew Viktor would see his illness as abandonment and a personal inconvenience. Back in Budapest, Viktor had been an academic, a professor of Elizabethan literature at St Stephen's until he was terminated for being "impossibly disagreeable". When the war started in 1914, he feared conscription into the Army. He responded to a recruitment advertisement for able-bodied men to come to America and take jobs in the mines of the Osage Lead Company, asking Sandor, his only real friend, to come with him.

To the disbelief of his family, Sandor agreed because he knew his friend expected it, depended upon it. His health had never been robust, and though he quickly regretted his decision, he swore to God in Viktor's presence to never go back on his word. Sandor's wife had died of peritonitis the year before, the very week they had started reading Shakespeare out loud to each other in English. His grieving period was a short one, and knowing his friend could not function in the world alone, Sandor sold his rare books and documents shop and made the long and difficult trip with Viktor to the village of Ste. Odile on the banks of the Mississippi.

Sandor looked at Viktor meekly with eyes that were, by the minute, growing increasingly sensitive and watery, as the elevator cage climbed up the mineshaft toward the afternoon daylight. Last winter his teeth had begun to discolor and his gums to recede from them, as the doctor predicted. Doctor Treves had examined Sandor four months ago and told him he had porphyria, a disease of the blood. He told Sandor he would crave blood to compensate for the deficiency in his own. He said that he would become weak and be unable to tolerate sunlight, that exposure to it would blister and scar his skin, and that soon he may expect to start having hallucinations.

"I am sorry, my friend," Sandor said. "I really can't help it. God is my witness, I am too sick to continue loading ore by hand. I was never really strong enough for this. I can't score-out in a single shift anymore. *Kívánom, hogy soha nem volt íde.*"

"Speak English! I, too, wish I had never come here," Viktor nodded. "But here we are. I suppose you are blaming me for this."

They'd never had the elevator cage to themselves before. This was the first time they had ever left work after shift change. Viktor had waited for Sandor in the staging area underground as he spoke to the shift boss in his office and collected his final wages. By that time, the early shift had finished and gone home for the day and the second shift had taken over, blasting tunnel to the west and southwest. With a war raging in Europe, the demand for lead had never been higher.

At the surface, Viktor opened the cage door and the two men stepped out into the sunlight. Sandor squinted and shaded his eyes with his hand. He twitched in pain a few times, as he had done more and more recently, in a manner that seemed to irritate Viktor.

Sandor was careful not to pity himself in his situation. He did pity his friend though. Viktor had no love for himself and seemed to be naively angry at the rest of humanity because of it. Sandor knew how completely Viktor had come to depend upon him, even if Viktor himself didn't know. Very soon after his wife's death, Sandor became Viktor's only unassailable human contact in the world, and he accepted this as a responsibility he must uphold.

The volume Sandor had prized above all others in his bookshop in Budapest was a late sixteenth century copy of Tyndale's translation of the Bible. The first time Sandor opened the book, his eye was drawn to Cain's disavowal in Genesis: "Am I my brother's keeper?" Sandor knew the phrase first appeared in Tyndale's translation, and when he opened the book, coincidentally, a second and third time to the same passage, and then dreamt about it that night, he was certain he was receiving a directive for his life and thinking. He spoke with Father Bartok at St Emeric's, who confirmed that Sandor had been given signs. That was why he had agreed to come to America and to take difficult and unpleasant work.

It worried Sandor that he could not make his companion understand how sick he was, and that he must inevitably leave this friendless man alone in a foreign place which, after two years, he had made no effort to adjust to. To press these facts upon Viktor would anger and upset him, and Sandor could not decide if he should insist to his own satisfaction that his friend understood what his doctors had foreseen or not continue to bring it up.

It was Saturday afternoon, the end of the work week. The two men walked east into town toward Tranquille House on Rouen Street, where they were boarders. From Sunday night until Saturday afternoon, they shared a room there. After their shift on Saturday, they gathered their things and boarded the train for a seventeen-mile trip west to LaMotte where Viktor had a room. Sandor's tiny house was a mile further, in the woods near Gibson Cemetery.

There were seven buildings on the muddy main street of LaMotte and only five of them were still in use. As the men approached Viktor's boarding house, a dilapidated brick building with a collapsing porch roof, Mrs. Hobbs, the landlady, came out the front screen door.

"There you are, Mr. Suba." Mrs. Hobbs was a woman of forty who looked twenty years older. Four of her front teeth were missing. "I reckon you heard the news?"

"I heard no news, Mrs. Hobbs," Viktor said.

"Well, then, I'll tell you. America's a-gettin' into the war. Your European war. Now we been dragged into it."

Viktor and Sandor looked at each other. Sandor thought it best to hide their elation from Mrs. Hobbs.

"I see," Viktor said. "I know it isn't good news to you, Mrs. Hobbs, but it will certainly end the war faster."

"What do we care how fast a war in Europe ends? It ain't our war!"

"Certainly," Sandor said. "We are sorry for that. Politics is an unhappy business."

"That ain't the half of it!" Mrs. Hobbs seemed determined to stoke her own rage. "It's gonna be a conscription. A draft. And you fellas, you foreigners, ain't a-gonna be in it. Our American boys hafta go fight your damned war while you Hunkies get to stay here a-workin' just as safe and sound as you please! I know you two come here to get out of it, now we gotta do your fightin' for you!"

"This great country loves the people of Europe..." Sandor began. His voice was weak.

"Well, it got nothin' to do with love," Mrs. Hobbs interrupted. "I don't love you people and I don't know nobody who does."

"I know it's just politics and national interests," Viktor said. He looked disapprovingly at Sandor. He knew Mrs. Hobbs well enough to know she resented anyone telling her how she felt or should feel about anything. "I don't know why my friend said that!"

Sandor smiled. "Love isn't something you know about, Viktor! We are upsetting you, Mrs. Hobbs. I will leave you both here. I am exhausted. I hope your son is improved."

Mrs. Hobbs' nine year old son, Vernon, had been sick for several weeks, coughing and pale, as had several other children at his school.

"You never mind about Vernon!" Mrs. Hobbs snapped. "I ain't the only one around here thinks you know more about these sick kids than any of us!" She turned suddenly and walked back to her house. Sandor watched her walk away, dumbfounded.

"What did she mean by that?" Sandor asked, but Viktor had turned away from him and was following Mrs. Hobbs back into the boarding house.

Sandor always enjoyed the walk from the train depot out to his property west of LaMotte on Saturday afternoons after work. The road out of the small town was a dirt path maintained by the county out into the oak woods, where it ended at an old logging road which wound past Sandor's small frame house. The house bordered the old Gibson Cemetery, and had been built for the caretaker just before the beginning of the Civil War. The cemetery had been abandoned for at least fifty years, and now, like Sandor's clapboard home, was nearly lost in the hardwood forest.

As Sandor had grown sicker, his appetite had changed and become limited. As he unlocked his peeling front door, he thought he might make himself a stuffed pepper or cabbage roll for a light dinner. He still had some Csabai sausage in his pantry, though what he really wanted, as he realized more and more lately, was raw, bloody meat.

Since Dr. Treves told him he would crave blood as an effect of his illness, he had hungered for little else. He remembered having no particular taste for it before Treves diagnosed him, and he wondered if he was merely being influenced by the suggestion. "You are suffering from an anemia," Treves said, "and your body will naturally want to replace, from other sources, what it has lost."

Days ago, he had left a lamb chop wrapped in brown paper in his ice box. The ice was nearly gone, and the chop was no longer frozen. He removed it and placed it in his sink. When it reached room temperature, he would eat it raw. There was a half-bottle of wine in his pantry. He found a clean coffee cup in his cupboard and filled it half full.

Sandor sat at his small kitchen table and thought about his friend. The pain in Sandor's joints and mouth and skin was almost constant, yet he still thought mostly about the suffering of Viktor, loveless and alone in the world, except for their exasperating and one-sided friendship.

Unlike Viktor, Sandor had experienced love. He knew what it meant to love another person completely, to the point of self-sacrifice and complete immersion in the happiness of the other. When his wife Eva, finally died of her peritonitis a year before he left Hungary, though his loss was great, he was overwhelmed with gratitude that her suffering was done, and knew his relief was an expression of his love for her, and therefore right and just. He celebrated her passing with a high mass, followed in the evening by a glass of red wine and a special meal, a *pörkölt*, and he suspected that his neighbors on Hruza Street thought he was either insane or evil. He didn't expect anyone else to understand how grateful he was. He kept his grief a private and moderate thing, as Eva would have wanted.

Viktor had only had two brief flirtations in all the years Sandor had known him. Each lasted until they became an inconvenience to him and he stopped investing the little effort he was willing to attempt, and the women lost interest. Viktor was teaching *King Lear* in his last semester at the university, and Sandor told his wife it was a sad irony that Regan's description of her aging father: "He hath always but slightly known himself," did not inspire personal insight in his friend.

After the sun went down, Sandor stepped out onto his porch. In the twilight and in the dark, away from the sunlight that seared his festering skin, he felt a little more comfortable. He sat on his front step and sipped from his cup of red wine until his stomach started to burn. Tree frogs burred in the woods all around him and whippoorwills called to each other from the southwest and northeast. He thought how wonderful it was that these creatures could carry on their natural lives and tendencies despite human destruction and influence in the world. He felt he had entered a new phase of life: the last phase. His working years were over. He was destined to die in a strange land. Away from home, surrounded by unfriendly and disapproving strangers who resented him and his countrymen. He would live in this small wooden house, a hermit in the woods, until his health failed or his money ran out. Either or both would come soon enough. It made his heart ache to think of leaving his friend here alone.

He wondered what suffering his disease would bring. Dr. Treves had given him no chance of recovery, and he knew the longer he lived, the worse the pain would become. It would be bad for him to live too much longer. If he only had the strength to end his own life, he could avoid a long and torturous decline. But he believed, he *knew*, as Hamlet did, that suicide is the gravest of mortal sins and if he committed such an act, he would never be reunited with his Eva in the next world. He felt a tear well painfully in his eye, and suddenly he craved blood, the blood that seemed to calm him more and more as his disease progressed. He remembered the lamb he had left in his sink.

He went back into the house and tore the paper off the lamb chop. He bit into it, savoring its bloody piquancy. There was a hint of decay in its smell, but he bit into it again and again until it was gone. He wiped the blood from his chin with a towel hanging over the back of his kitchen chair.

A loud crash and a spray of glass behind him in the front room caused his legs to collapse. Looking behind him, he saw a damp mossy rock on his front room floor surrounded by glass shards. He heard the laughter of children out in the dark. Sandor got unsteadily to his feet and opened his front door. Three boys stood thirty feet away at the edge of the cemetery.

"Vernon Hobbs died!" one of the boys called. "And everybody knows you did it!"

"Everbody knows!" the other two boys repeated.

"You little hooligans!" Sandor shouted. "I'll get the sheriff on you! His wife is one of us!"

"You kilt Vernon," the first boy continued, "and Boyer in Ste. Odile and them three kids in Lesterton, 'cause you're a vampire!"

"A *vampire*!" the other boys echoed.

It took Sandor a moment to realize he had heard the boys right. "What nonsense!" he said. "Who put such nonsense in your superstitious heads?"

"Everbody knows!" the first boy went on. "Vampires is from Hungry and you're from Hungry. You're pasty and long-toothed and you cain't come out in the daylight. And kids is gettin' sick and dyin'."

"You ignorant yokels," Sandor interrupted. "Superstitious fools! You think you can cure sickness by putting knives under a bed or running chickens over people. You have to use medicine and go to the doctor!"

"Got a present for you!" the first boy said as he heaved a long string of bulbous shapes onto Sandor's porch. It hit the dry boards with a dull *thunk*, and flakes of skin floated down, jarred loose by the impact. It was a string of garlic. The boys ran off into the darkness, toward LaMotte.

Sandor kicked the garlic off the porch. He stood for a few moments looking in the direction the boys had run. He knew they were repeating things they had heard their parents saying. He had seen mob violence before, back in Budapest. He had seen a mob drive Jews out of the neighborhood, and later hang a homosexual man who was suspected of killing a boy. Sandor knew that fearful, superstitious people needed scapegoats for their problems, and now he had come into their focus. To defend himself against these suspicions would be futile. In the morning, he would cover himself against the sun as best he could and take the train to Ste. Odile to see the sheriff.

Sandor went back inside and swept up the broken glass as best he could. He sat on his single kitchen chair. The fearsome and painful but essentially peaceful death he foresaw for himself an hour ago was impossible now. He knew these people would never leave him alone to die in the dignity of isolation. He thought again about taking his own life, but knew, for his late wife's sake, it was out of the question. He suddenly craved the comfort of more raw, bloody meat. That would calm him down, but his icebox was empty.

A branch snapped outside in the dark. Sandor found his butcher knife in his sink and faced his front door. A footstep on his porch sent a stab of fear through his stomach, and he thought, *What will become of poor Viktor when I am gone?*

The front door opened slowly, and Viktor stepped in, breathing heavily and out of breath. He was holding a large burlap sack.

"Viktor!" Sandor whispered. "What is it? What has happened?"

"The worst," Viktor said quietly. "Mrs. Hobbs son died, and she has ordered me out of her house."

"I heard. Some boys came here..."

"I have no home, but now none of us do. No Hungarian is safe here anymore."

"What do you mean?"

"In Burley's Tavern in Lesterton today some Hungarians were drunk and boasting about how they could not be drafted into the Army, how they would stay behind while the Americans went off to the war. They boasted they would stay behind and take all the mine jobs and take care of all the abandoned wives, too."

"Oh," Sandor whispered. "Such stupidity in the world."

"A fight broke out, then a riot," Viktor sat on the kitchen chair and put the burlap sack on the table with a metallic clang. "They burned most of the Hungarian homes and loaded the families on a boxcar bound for St. Louis. Five Hungarians have been killed. So far. The word is they... the mob, will be heading out this way, to Ste. Odile, by morning. Maybe a hundred men. They want us all dead or gone."

"My friend, you must stay with me," Sandor said. "We will make our way to Ste. Odile early tomorrow. The sheriff, his wife is Hungarian..."

"I am so sorry I brought you here," Viktor interrupted. "For my own selfish reasons, I brought you here with me. A man so full of love as you are..." Viktor reached into the burlap sack and withdrew a straight razor, a bucket, and a heavy old revolver. He laid the things side by side on the tabletop.

"My God, Viktor!" Sandor said. "What is all this?"

"The gun is empty," Viktor said. "As you know, the company store will not sell cartridges to Hungarians. Hold it in your hand when the mob comes. Hold it up and they will shoot you. Quick and painless. Over in an instant. I told Mrs. Hobbs, that yes, you were what they say you are, and you are responsible for the children. They will be here sometime tomorrow when the train comes, and your suffering will be over. I wanted to be certain your suffering would be over."

"Viktor..."

"I would like to think I have learned something from you, though it may not seem so." Viktor set the bucket on the floor under his left arm. In an instant, he took the razor and slashed his left wrist. Sandor shuddered in horror as his friend lowered his bleeding arm over the bucket.

"No Viktor! Let me bind it!"

"Leave it alone, Sandor." Viktor smiled. "When Mrs. Hobbs threw me out of her house and told me the news, all I thought of was your wellbeing and how I could deliver you from this. It was a surprise to me, a revelation, that these were my thoughts at a time like this, but I of course knew it was only your influence. Only you! I thank you for that... that I hardly know myself at this moment. This will calm you as you wait for them. The blood will calm you, as you have said... as you wait for the mob." Viktor looked down at the quickly filling bucket and smiled a fading smile. "Thank you for never abandoning me."

Sandor felt his friend's forehead. It was already cooling to the touch.

Viktor's expression had become bland and peaceful and unmistakably benevolent. Sandor smiled a mirthless, emotional smile, and was grateful to have deserved such charity, if he truly did deserve it: to have had such a friend, in a harsh and unwelcoming world.

The Radium Girls

Even though it had been five years since the surgeons removed most of Rettie's jaw, she knew her sister Lestoria still had difficulty understanding her when she spoke. Rettie's lower lip and chin and much of her tongue were gone, and Lestoria had to watch her face patiently as she tried to form her words, to understand them, because Rettie hated to repeat herself. At least once a week, to Rettie's annoyance, Lestoria mentioned she felt lucky that her radium sickness had only caused a large goiter to form on her chin and throat. Her tongue and lips were intact, and most of the time she could speak clearly enough to be understood.

"Willy Schmidt is a bully!" Rettie said. "Bullies deserve a little humiliation now and again. Bring them down a peg or two, as they say."

Lestoria shrugged. Rettie hated when she was trying to make a point on a subject she felt very strongly about, and Lestoria's response was to shrug. Rettie saw this as a brush-off: a condescension.

Lestoria looked at her sister wearily. "I'm not sure I heard you right, Rettie. Bullies deserve what?"

"Bullies deserve humiliation. Humiliation. Don't they?"

"Oh, I wish you would stop doing that Rettie!" Lestoria shook her head. "I wish you would stop saying things that are... provocative or... controversial and then say, 'don't they', or 'wouldn't they', like of course the whole world lines up with you! You say it as though it's not a question but a... a... statement of what everyone believes! If you just said it as a question, not a *statement* like that, it wouldn't be so irritating! I don't always agree with you. I don't know what bullies deserve."

"Well, let me tell you then," Rettie said. "They deserve humiliation."

Lestoria shrugged again.

"Leaving us at Dr. Treves' office like that with no way to get home! He knows how we hate to go out in the town, how we hate to be seen! To leave us there to make our own way home. He knew we didn't have cab fare! It was humiliating and terrifying. He wanted to humiliate us, so I want to do the same to him."

"He's a drunkard, Rettie. He was drunk when he dropped us off. He's thoughtless and addle-brained, like all drunkards. With that moonshine they all drink now, since Prohibition, it's no wonder! It's so much worse than the legal liquor they used to drink. Father was that way too, a drunkard, and so was Chet, if we want to speak frankly."

"Don't you talk about Chet like that!" Rettie scolded. She had been especially close to their dead brother, or at least that's what she remembered, even though it was Lestoria who actually cared for him. Chet and Willy Schmidt were childhood friends and had been in the same unit in the War, the 1st Infantry Division under General Bullard, and seen action at Cantigny and in the Argonne. When Willy froze on the unit's advance out of a trench, Chet had gone back to get him. Chet calmed and reassured his terrified friend. As he pushed Willy over the top, a German shell exploded thirty feet away, and a piece of shrapnel severed Chet's spine.

Back home, Chet lingered for nearly three years before he died, never telling the story of Willy's cowardice to anyone but his sisters. Chet had told his sisters he had seen Willy try to be brave, to not disgrace his unit, but as much as he tried, he could not overcome the fear that gripped him more than the other men. That fear was more basic and irrational in Willy, and Chet knew his friend couldn't help himself. Chet worried more than anyone when Willy started drinking while they were still in France. He knew it was Willy's way of numbing the shame he felt in himself, and he knew Willy would drink as long as he felt the shame.

It was Willy who got the sisters their jobs at the United States Radium Factory in Orange, New Jersey after the war. Willy was an old college friend of the owner's nephew, and the girls were anxious and grateful to have jobs offered to them on the East Coast so far from home and so near New York City. They never expected, coming from a small, out-of-the-way place like Ste. Odile, to ever have such an adventure.

Like so many of the girls who worked at the factory, painting luminous numbers on the clock faces with radium, that miracle substance which, according to so many magazine and billboard advertisements, ensured health and vitality, they pointed their paintbrushes by passing them through their lips, and like so many other girls, got cancers of the mouth, lips, and jaw as a result. After many horrible surgeries and their hideous disfigurements, Rettie and Lestoria returned home to Ste. Odile and resolved to live out their days as hermits, hiding themselves in their rented house, never stepping outside except in their fenced back garden or veiled for infrequent trips to see Dr. Treves and other doctors in town.

Rettie sat by the parlor window, loudly sipping coffee from a china cup.

"It's Willy's fault we're monsters. It's his fault our lives are ruined!" she said.

Lestoria sighed. She was tired of having this talk.

"No one knew about the radium," she said. "Willy was doing us a kindness by getting us the jobs. No one knew what would happen. And... if the lawsuit works out, we may be a little more secure... If it works out. I don't consider my life to be ruined. Where there's life, there's hope. And I don't think of myself as a monster. I wish you would quit calling us that."

"Willy wanted us out of town!" Rettie snapped. "He wondered how much Chet had told us. He wanted us away from Ste. Odile! Monsters and old maids! That's what we are, and it can all be laid at the doorstep of Willy Schmidt! And now he tells me he is raising our rent by a dollar a week! Is this place, is this palace at 244 Mal Ardents worth seven dollars a week? Our little savings won't last!"

"It's 422 Mal Ardents. You always do that. Yes, I think it's a fair price. And I wish you'd get this notion about Willy out of your head. He isn't bad. He's just a... weakling. His problems are all a weakness of character, not malice." Lestoria closed her eyes, as she often did when she had a headache.

Rettie could see that her outburst had exhausted her sister. Lestoria's blood pressure had been running dangerously high for a year, and Dr. Treves and others told Rettie to not distress Lestoria or upset her excessively for fear of making the condition worse, or even fatal. Both sisters agreed they wanted nothing more of the world than confinement in their own home, away from the leers and revulsion of the world outside. Rettie was terrified at the thought of losing her sister and living out a long and cloistered life alone. She must do a better job of not upsetting Lestoria, she knew.

Still, Rettie had enough regard for herself to know she could not let insult, ill-use or bullying pass with no response or reaction. She and her sister were Delaportes. Their family had once been the second largest landowners in Ste. Odile County. Their grandfather had been mayor for two terms before he drank himself to death in 1902.

The Schmidts, on the other hand, had only come to Ste. Odile fifty or sixty years earlier. They were part of a wave of Germans who swept into the area at that time, gradually displacing and outnumbering the original old French families. The Schmidts had made their money in leather-tanning and winemaking and later real estate, buying, among many others, the house Rettie and Lestoria occupied now. Although Willy gave them the place at what Lestoria considered a good price, he made demands of them. He refused to pay for repairs Rettie wanted, calling them frivolous and unnecessary, and he wouldn't pay for yardwork, insisting that if they weren't determined to live as hermits, they were able-bodied enough to do the work themselves.

Willy did take them to see the several doctors in town they visited, when it suited him to do so. But the last trip to see Dr. Treves, the surgeon, was, for Rettie, the last straw. Willy smelled of alcohol when he picked them up. The sisters were both in their best flowered dresses and their heads were covered in lacy veils and hats, as they always were when they went out. Willy dropped them at the doctor's office, telling them he would be back for them in an hour. He was meeting a friend at Herve's, a speakeasy near the river.

An hour and a half later, Willy had still not returned for them. Dr. Treves offered to give Rettie and Lestoria a lift home, but they declined, not wanting to trouble him. So, the doctor closed his office and went home, leaving the sisters sitting on the bench outside his front door. After another hour of waiting, it became clear to them they would have to walk the seven blocks from Dr. Treves' office on Rouen Street to their house on Mal Ardents.

The sun was going down. The two walked tentatively, arm in arm, hoping they would not meet anyone on the street. Constantinople Street was one of two main thoroughfares through the town. Lestoria suggested if they went a little out of their way, over to Gentian, then north to Mal Ardents, they would be likely to encounter fewer people.

"If we just walk quickly and quietly, no one will notice us," she said.

Gentian was nearly empty. A dog tied to a clothesline barked at them from a back yard. As they crossed Endymion, they heard a sound they both dreaded: the sound of children playing nearby.

On the east side of the street stood the rear wall of the grounds of the old Academy of Perpetua, once a girl's school and later an orphanage, but now empty and deteriorating. A portion of the brick-and-stone wall had collapsed years before, revealing the small gothic Reliquary Chapel inside. As they approached the breach in the wall, the sisters could see three young boys, none older than about ten, throwing rocks and bits of broken masonry at the stained glass windows of the chapel. Lestoria held Rettie's arm tightly.

"Don't say anything to them, Rettie!" she said. "Damage is done. Let's just keep walking."

"Nonsense!" Rettie said. "That's sacred ground! Hey! You boys stop that! That's a *church* you're desecrating! Stop it or I'll get the sheriff!"

The boys stopped and looked at the sisters.

"It ain't a church no more," the tallest one said. "Just a old building!"

"It's consecrated!" Rettie insisted. "It's *not* just a building!"

"You can't tell us what to do," another boy said. "We don't have to mind you. You talk funny."

"How come you got your heads covered up like that?" the tall boy said.

Lestoria pulled on her sister's arm. "Let's go!" she said. "Come *on!*"

Rettie seemed to suddenly understand her sister's sense of urgency. The two began to walk more quickly north toward home. The boys ran out onto the sidewalk behind the sisters.

"Are you them Radium Girls?" The tall boy said. "Them sisters? The ugly ones?"

Rettie and Lestoria ignored him and picked up their walking pace. The tall boy ran up behind them and, grabbing both their veils at once, yanked them off. Rettie's hat was pinned to her hair, so her head was twitched backward painfully. Their veils and their flowered hats fell to the sidewalk. Lestoria kept walking but Rettie stopped and gathered their accessories from the ground.

The tall boy seemed dumbstruck for a moment. "It *is* you!" he said. He laughed a little. "You're worser than they say! You ort to never come outside! You're monsters!"

"You're the monsters!" Rettie said. "The three of you!" Her voice quivered and there were tears in her eyes. The boys picked up bits of rubble from the collapsed wall and began throwing pieces of broken bricks and masonry at the sisters. Rettie and Lestoria scurried away as quickly as they could in their Sunday shoes, shielding the backs of their heads with their hands as they went. In a half block they were out of range. Rettie thanked God the boys didn't chase them.

By the time they got home, Lestoria was drenched in sweat, trembling, and lightheaded. She complained of a headache and collapsed on the sofa. Rettie got her sister a damp cloth for her forehead and a glass of lemonade.

"I'm calling the sheriff!" Rettie realized she was sobbing. "That's assault, pure and simple, what those awful boys did! That's what the world thinks of us. How dare he call us monsters! They threw rocks at us!"

"Let it drop," Lestoria sighed. "It's how boys act. Forget about it."

"This is Willy Schmidt's doing," Rettie mumbled. "A bully showing us how helpless we are without him! He just thinks he has complete control over us, doesn't he?"

Lestoria looked at her sister wearily. "He's a drunkard. A drunkard has no more sense of responsibility than a tom cat." She turned over to face the back of the sofa. "I never want to leave this house again," she said.

It was just then Rettie decided to teach Willy a lesson.

The problem was, the sisters *were* very much dependent on Willy, so whatever Rettie decided to do, she would have to look innocent of any plot against him. They couldn't afford to be put out of the house or lose their rides to see doctors, and such. And there was no use trying to involve Lestoria: she would have no part in such a thing.

The next morning, Rettie climbed the pull-down ladder into the attic to find a box she had placed there when they moved in. It contained a few of Chet's personal things, including some letters he had received from his old friends from the 1st Infantry. If she remembered right, one of them lived up in St. Louis, about sixty miles north.

She found the worn, cardboard box where she had left it, on top of a rafter toward the east side of the house. Inside, at the bottom, were a few torn envelopes. On one she read a neatly written return address:

Walter Dye
1267 Chouteau Ave
St. Louis

Early in the afternoon, after lunch and while Lestoria was napping, Rettie sat at her desk in the front room and composed a letter:

Dear Mr. Dye:

I am Rettie Delaporte, the sister of your lately departed comrade-in-arms, Chet Delaporte. Thank you for the card you sent on Chet's death. He suffered greatly in his last years, thanks to another, less heroic fellow soldier. I am speaking, of course, about Willy Schmidt. Willy's cowardice, freezing in fear as your unit was advancing at Cantigny that day and my brother's attempt to retrieve him, resulted in the injury which robbed Chet of the use of his legs and eventually killed him. To add insult to injury, Willy got my sister and myself jobs at the Radium Factory, which resulted in our radium poisoning and disfigurement. Now he is our landlord, and he charges us too much rent and refuses to fix things. He is, in my opinion, a coward and a bully who has singlehandedly devastated my entire family. He is a man who seems to pay no price for his misdeeds, yet the Delaportes have paid a terrible price.

I think it is high time he had some sense of what others think of him and his failures as a man and a soldier. It is my goal, perhaps a petty one in your estimation, to have some small sense of satisfaction, some small sense of justice regarding this man who has so negatively affected our lives. I know Willy was not well thought of in your unit during the War, but I wasn't sure how much you knew of his complicity in Chet's injury and death.

I am not speaking of anything too injurious or drastic. I will be satisfied if any illusion he may still have about any high or even adequate opinion others have of him is dispelled for good. Since my sister and I are still somewhat at his mercy, it must be something he does not suspect our involvement in. The first idea that occurred to me, was that he learns that you and your comrades know him to be the coward that he is. I wondered if you might inform him somehow, by letter or telephone, that his years-long charade has fooled no one? Is this too much to ask? Am I a petty, venal person to suggest it?

Sincerely,
Rettie Delaporte

Rettie finished the letter in time to send it off in the afternoon mail. She quickly regretted the whole idea as childish and beneath her. But the letter was sent. She would see what sort of reply it generated.

By the end of the week she had a response.

Miss Delaporte:

I was surprised and happy to get your letter. As someone who lived with Willy Schmidt for most of a year, I don't think you are out of line feeling the way you do and wanting some sense of justice. I would feel the same. An idea came to me before I finished reading your note. I just read a book a few months ago about a coward in the English Army whose old friends each send him a white feather to shame him. Beside me, there are two other men in St.

Louis who were in our unit in France. I suggested to them that we tell Willy we are having a special dinner to commemorate our wartime experiences and invite him to come. After the dinner, each of us will present him with a white feather to show him exactly how we all felt about him. It is an understatement to say the fellows were all keen on the idea. Schmidt had no friends in our unit, except Chet, and nobody was fooled about how Chet's injury was anyone's fault but Willy's, even though your brother wanted his friend to think otherwise. If you like my idea, I would hope you and your sister would come along too. In that way, you can represent the spirit of your brave brother.

I would like to do this on the evening of August 24 at my house at 7 o'clock. You have my address. Please let me know what you think.

Your Friend,
Walter Dye

Rettie sat in her desk chair, nearly overwhelmed with a sense of relief, and vindication. She was right to conceive of this plan after all. She quickly scribbled an acceptance of the invitation, then poured herself a cup of coffee and sat at the kitchen table to consider how she would convince her sister and Willy to make the long drive to St. Louis.

When Lestoria woke from her nap, she was unenthusiastic about the prospect of a long car trip.

"Oh, Rett, I don't have the energy for that. Can't you go without me?"

"It's only right that you come," Rettie insisted. "We will represent the memory of our brother. We should *both* go... shouldn't we? I want you to come with me."

That evening Rettie, called Willy.

"Well, as I see it Willy, you *have* to come. Walter Dye specifically contacted me for the purpose of finding you. It's going to be your old comrades-in-arms and he wants to remember and commemorate the service and sacrifice of Chet and the others in your unit who have passed on."

"Oh, I never liked Walter Dye. A busybody and a know-it-all. And I know he never liked me. None of those guys liked me much. From the first, they didn't. I tried to get on their good side, but no dice..."

Rettie could tell Willy was a little drunk. "Walter must remember you in a better light than you think."

"Well, I guess it's one way to spend an evening, if you want. Not looking forward to that drive. August twenty-fourth, you said? Hmm. All right. Remind me a few days before. I'll pick you up at four thirty that day. Make sure you're ready!"

Lestoria barely slept the night before the trip. It had been a hot night and she'd had headaches and cold-sweats, which meant Rettie, concerned for her sister's wellbeing, was up most of the night too.

"I'm not sure I'm up to this Rettie," Lestoria mumbled, sipping her coffee the next morning.

"I knew you were going to say that, and I don't want to hear it! It will do you a world of good to get out, change your routine. You'll thank me tomorrow. Won't you?"

Willy arrived forty minutes late. He pulled up in front of the house and blew his horn, as he always did when he picked the sisters up.

"So rude!" Rettie clucked. "He may as well have been raised in a barnyard! Let's go, Lestoria!"

Rettie took her sister's arm and helped her out the front door. It was a little less hot outside than in the house. A dark bank of clouds hung over the western hills of Ste. Odile County and there was a smell of rain in the air. It had been breezy in the morning, but all was ominously still now. Rettie hated when breezes blew her veil and revealed glimpses of her face. She held the end of the veil down against her chest to prevent this. She preferred still, hot days to refreshing breezes. She opened the rear driver-side door of Willy's Dodge, and helped her sister get situated inside. Rettie got in the passenger side and noticed that Willy already smelled of alcohol.

"Well, better late than never," Rettie scolded. "I hope we can get there in less than two hours. I hate being late."

"Aw, we'll get there in plenty of time. We'll get there when we get there. You got the address?"

"No!" Rettie said sarcastically. "I have no idea where we're going. I'm just going to guess and hope everything turns out all right! Of course I have the address! Would I set out to find a place without the address? It's 2671 Chouteau Avenue. I memorized it."

"I don't know why in the world we'd want to commemorate something we'd all just as soon forget," Willy mumbled. "Those guys never liked me anyway. I tried to make them like me...."

Highway 67, a two lane highway, ran either alongside or near the river all the way north to St. Louis and through many small towns that seemed to Rettie to be nothing more than wide spots in the road: a gas station, a post office, and maybe a diner or feed store was all most of them amounted to. It was early evening and the towns of Belgique and Pompeii we already shuttered and dark.

Crystal City, forty minutes up the highway, was a larger, busier town. As Willy stopped at the first intersection, Rettie could see at least two more intersections ahead. She felt a little exhilarated as they drove past a nice-looking restaurant, to see couples and families going inside to enjoy, what she imagined, and hoped for their sakes, would be a good meal. Roast beef? Chicken or fish? It would be lovely, she thought, to be able to go to an elegant restaurant, or just a nice one, and order a delicious meal prepared by real, professional cooks.

At the last intersection in town before the highway twisted along out into the darkening fields and woods of the flood plain, Rettie noticed a flashing neon sign atop the doorway of a well-kept clapboard building. CLUB ALGIERS, DINING AND DANCING, the sign said. The building was surrounded by a large parking lot, which was full of roadsters and sedans. Beautifully dressed women, sequined, in fur stoles and pearls accompanied by dapper, clean-shaven men in double-breasted suits and two-toned shoes were sliding out of the cars and making their way toward the large, orange front door.

Rettie was glad the traffic light was red so that she could watch the scene a little longer.

"Look how they are all dressed," she said, almost to herself. "It's a good-sized town, but I wouldn't expect anything so elegant."

Willy removed his flask from his vest pocket and drank. "Speakeasy," he said. "They come all the way from St. Louis to go to that place."

Neither Rettie nor Lestoria had ever had a very serious boyfriend in their lives, and certainly none who would have ever taken them to such a place. Rettie tried to imagine what such an evening out would be like. The anticipation of it would be thrilling: deciding what to wear, shoes, accessories, the trip to the beauty shop for hair and nails, the sitting in the parlor waiting for the young man to arrive. It would all be so exhilarating!

But Rettie and her sister would never have such an evening. Monsters never had an elegant evening out, she thought. And thanks to Willy Schmidt, they were monsters. The traffic signal changed to green and Willy eased the Dodge forward, north, into the darkness.

As they left town, it started to rain a little and Rettie wondered about the ladies just arriving at the Club Algiers and their beautiful dresses. Any gentleman, any *true* gentleman picking up a lady on an evening like this, when rain was expected, would surely bring an umbrella with him.

As they drove further north, Willy sipped more and more from his flask.

"Willy, if you get drunk you could kill us all!" Rettie snapped.

"Leave him alone," Lestoria said. Her voice was weak. She seemed to Rettie to be tired and listless. She had been napping through much of the drive and had shown no interest in the speakeasy or any of the towns or scenery they passed.

In another forty-five minutes, they were inside the St. Louis city limits. They began passing through dense neighborhoods of one-and two-story brick houses, churches, and what had once been taverns. The further north they went, they began to see hoboes and vagrants in nearly every block.

"Look at the houses... how closely they're all packed together," Rettie said. "How can people live so packed together like this? And all the vagrants! Seedy customers, aren't they? I don't like the looks of those seedy customers. Men and women both!"

"They're just people down on their luck," Lestoria admonished.

"Bums and ne'er-do-wells!" Willy slurred. He took another drink. "Cut your throat for the price of a sandwich. I don't know why we're coming all the way up here for this..."

At Chouteau Avenue, Willy turned west.

"You said 2671?" he said. "We're close to that now. This doesn't look right."

"Yes, I did!" Rettie's tone was sharp with disapproval. "You're drunk Willy! Drunk again! What an impression you're going to make on your old friends! And you must have the address wrong. This whole area is a railroad yard."

"I had a few swigs," Willy said. "I needed it. I don't know why I agreed to this. Them guys never liked me."

For as far as Rettie could see along the north side of the dark avenue, there were train yards, turntables, and train sheds. On the south side of the street were factories and mechanic shops. There were no automobiles closer than three or four blocks ahead of them. A trolley approached from the west. Dark figures of a few men stood here and there on the corners, but there were no houses anywhere to be seen. Some of the vagrants shouted things at them: obscenities or demands for money. A stab of fear and disorientation seized Rettie's body.

"You drunken fool!" she shouted. "You've gotten us lost. I gave you the address."

"You said 2671," Willy protested. "That should be in this block."

Irritated, Rettie dug into her purse for the slip of paper on which she had written the address. She found it folded in the bottom. Under the passing light of a streetlamp, she looked at it. She gasped a little when she saw what she had written: 1267 Chouteau. She had jumbled the address numbers in her memory.

"I found the address you gave me!" Willy insisted. "I didn't want to do this. I only did it because you wanted to. I know you need a night out because you never get one, but I didn't want to do this. I'm trying to find the place, even though..." He turned to look at Rettie in the back seat. Rettie could see the fear in his face, a terror and fear that were beginning to form themselves into tears. Rettie realized that look had always been on Willy's face. Always, as long as she had known him. She was suddenly ashamed of herself.

"Willy," she almost whispered. "You're right. This isn't a thing we should do tonight. Not if it bothers you, or... you're afraid. Stop the car. Let's just go back home. I'm sorry to have suggested this."

Willy looked back at her again, puzzled but relieved. As he did, the Dodge swerved toward the approaching trolley.

"Willy, look out!" Rettie screamed.

Willy pulled the steering wheel sharply to the right. The car jumped the granite curb with a terrible jolt. In an unreal moment of violence and shock and a spray of breaking glass, the Dodge crashed into a limestone retaining wall below the railroad turntable. Rettie was thrown into the front seat, her head smashing against the dashboard.

She didn't move for a moment. As she tried to right herself and determine how hurt she was, she felt a sharp pain in her neck, and she could see her right hand was pushed back at an unnatural angle. Her wrist and hand were broken. Willy lay still next to her, against the steering wheel. His head was covered in blood, and in many seconds of looking at him as she tried to collect herself and determine if she could move, she did not see him breathe.

After a moment, Rettie sat upright. She looked back over the broken seat and saw her sister lying still against her door, but breathing.

"Lestoria!" Rettie screamed. "Thank God you're alive! Oh, my dear!"

Lestoria said nothing. Rettie painfully climbed back next to her. She lifted her sister's veil and looked in her own purse for a handkerchief. There was much blood on Lestoria's forehead and temple to wipe away. Rettie looked deeply into her sister's face. Lestoria's eyes were looking in different directions, and the flesh above the left eye sagged. Distorted and gnarled as it now was above her blistered and distended jaw goiter, it was no longer the face of her sister and only companion. Lestoria's twisted wet lips moved a little but said nothing.

"Lestoria!" Rettie screamed. "Lestoria...!"

At the corner of the block nearby, four hoboes had seen the terrible accident. One of them laughed a little laugh and clapped his hands together. The four looked at each other with excitement, then looked eagerly back toward the steaming and shattered wreckage. Now, as Rettie watched them, as she held the bottom of her veil against her chest with her unbroken hand, they approached the car.

Immurement

I am forgetting so much. So many aspects of the outside, sinful world are becoming vaguer and lost to me. I know it is the month of December and this is the Year of our Lord, 1348. And I know I have been immured in this cell for two years and five months.

My father's wish to place me in the cloister of the Sisters of Perpetua possibly saved my life. Was it God's will? Months after he did so, the plague, still devastating the world even now, swept through Alsace and my village of Riquewihr. I was saved, as were my Sisters in Christ, yet the devastation of the land is so enormous, word has come that His Holiness Pope Clement VI may decide we are of more use out in the world, operating orphanages, teaching and caring for the sick. Whatever decision His Holiness comes to, by the grace of God, it will not affect me. I will never leave this cell.

There were Flagellants on the road below yesterday morning. Or maybe it was the day before. They passed by a year ago or more, on the way to Riquewihr and Zellenberg. I could not see them through the oilette or my narrow *meurtriere* on the adjacent wall, but I could hear them. There were many voices, maybe one hundred, praying, "Save us, save us," as they walked. I was at prayer, my *terce*, when they passed.

Since she considered this important information to be conveyed and not idle gossip, Sister Monica broke her partial silence as she pushed my supper through the oilette, to tell me that the group meant to meet at the Upper Gate at Riquewihr that evening to scourge themselves and encourage the town to beg for God's forgiveness and deliverance from the pestilence. She also said the Jews Belshom and Milhaud had been found guilty of poisoning the well of a vintner who owed them money, and thereby bringing the plague to the town. They were to be burned alive that night.

I suppose they are dead now. I have known them since I was a child. They had many business dealings with my father and loaned him money in the drought. They were kind to me and objected when my father decided to send me to Perpetua's, even as a student, an oblate. I think they knew he meant to leave me here.

One wonders why the Jews seem to suffer less in the plague. The Church and the townspeople see evil agency and witchcraft at work. I have not seen anything of the world. I went on pilgrimage to Mont Ste. Odile when I was a child. I have been to Strasbourg once and to Zellenberg and of course, Riquewihr, so I haven't seen much of the

Jews. But it seems to me, a people who mix but slightly with the masses and keep their own company would be little exposed to the miasma bringing death to the land. But I am nothing, and may not question the wisdom of the Church.

It is impossible to keep this cell warm. Sister Monica pushes a few sticks and beech and maple faggots as she can gather through the oilette for me to burn. I freeze on my cot all night and offer my discomfort up to Jesus as a gift, humble as it is. My fingers are numb at my rosary and my nose and feet frozen as I repeat the psalms. But, I must thank Our Lord for this opportunity to offer up my suffering to Him.

My acceptance of my fate must be complete and my prayers constant and sincere. I am fighting a battle within my own heart for control of my soul and physical body, as I have done my whole life. I have tried to please my Father in Heaven, in as much as I have failed to please my father on earth.

He was known as Yvain of Andlau as a younger man. My grandfather was a cooper in that town and was training my father in the trade when he slipped out of the family home one night at age twelve or thirteen to make his way to Riquewihr. He was in hopes of apprenticing himself to a vintner, the profession he actually wanted to follow. Father was very fortunate. He was taken in and employed by Hypollite Ledoc, who operated the largest vineyard in the region. By the time father was eighteen, he was running the business, and when old Ledoc died, he made father his sole heir. Father also inherited Lodoc's large house near the North Gate, and that is where I was born.

Mother was born and raised in Zellenberg, and she always told me she thought she had a vocation. Her greatest wish was to join the cloister at Perpetua's and give her life to God. But when she met my father, she was overtaken by a strange obsession with him. She even felt the influence of the Evil One, she said, and when she abandoned her desire to serve God and married, what happiness she felt was tempered with no small portion of shame.

She seemed tormented by this choice all her life. When my brother was born, she saw her difficulties in the birth as punishment for taking the wrong path in her life. She felt she was being called to account. She died the day after the birth.

Soon I began to feel that mother had been right about the Evil One. I began to have visions of the demon in my room at night. I saw him emerge from the wall of my bedchamber and hold me against the mattress. I felt him pressing my body against himself whilst I resisted as much as I could, given that my arms and legs were nearly paralyzed and could barely move. I prayed night and day to be relieved of this torment.

I told Father of my struggles. Never loving or affectionate, my dilemma made him shun me all the more, to my great sorrow. So overwhelming was my wish to please Father, that there were moments when I almost lost sight of my growing love of God and the fearful encroachments of evil I was beginning to see everywhere. On the day I turned eleven years old, I was overcome by a great fever and sickness. For several days I laid in my bed in a delirium, being cared for by Isabel, the housekeeper. In a vision, I saw the Evil One moving across my dark chamber in a mist. The nearly black figure seemed to seep from the timbers of the ceiling in several places at once, then congeal into one dimensionless form. At length, as Isabel slept at my bedside, the demon vanished before my eyes. Soon, the irresistible sensation overtook me, that the malignant spirit had entered and now resided in my body.

My sickness persisted for another week or more. The fever of my body was now compounded by a contagion of soul. I felt unclean, *contaminated*. I could feel the evil form moving within me, writhing under my skin, oppressing my lungs, heart, and guts. For weeks, it seemed, I couldn't eat, sleep or rest.

Father didn't believe me. He thought it to be merely female hysteria, as I was coming of age. I started to wail and whimper in pain and distraction, almost constantly, even though most of the time, I was unaware I was doing it. Soon Father would not allow me into his presence. He made me eat my meals alone and spend every evening at prayer locked in my bedchamber. This hurt me greatly. I felt that I was such a disappointment to him. I cannot account for why. He never returned the devotion I gave him.

One evening while reading in the Book of Judith of the fate of Holofernes, a tremendous pain seized my right forearm. I felt movement within the arm, I thought. At first there were pinpricks, then a mass which felt as if it were the size of my fist, that seemed to want to move from wrist to elbow. I pulled back my sleeve. I wasn't sure I could see the movement under my skin that I was feeling, but I recognized, unmistakably, that the flesh of the forearm had turned a dead-looking greenish-gray.

The next day, Father acted on an idea he'd had for some time, and committed me, with a large gift in gold, as a novice at Perpetua's. I had already been an oblate for a year, and so my transition to a new life was not a terribly difficult one. The routine of my day changed little. More prayer, but only slightly more. My greatest regret was knowing that my father preferred to live his life without me. I wanted only to live in his presence, with his approval. I prayed my new life would please him.

I feel I adjusted well. The silence, the routine, the cloister suited me. Abbess quickly took to me. She had favored me as an oblate, and did so as a novice. She put me in the vegetable gardens in the mornings and as one of the copyists in the afternoons, whose sisterly task had been, for many years past, to copy the writings of the great Benedictine theologians at work in their monastery at Ribeauville. I soon felt less vexed by the evil spirit that I still believed lived within me. I sensed it was still there, but subdued, and neutralized.

In a year's time, I had finished my novitiate. I was certain that Father and the rest of my household would be so proud of the knowledge that I had become a Bride of Christ. When the day of my vows arrived, I was filled with a pride that was, to my mind, nearly sinful. High mass was celebrated, the ceremony performed, and I received my black veil. Instead of solemnity and spiritual elation, my heart sank and felt empty, because my father and brother were not there. The only member of my household to witness my crossing over to this sacred, spiritual life, was Isabel, the housekeeper.

I found myself weeping at prayer for the next week or more. It was sinful to let my own prideful sadness interfere with my prayers, my offering to Christ. After all, what did it matter how the world and those close to me regarded my spiritual life? All that matters is that I made that choice and that I have a personal covenant with God. To value anything more would be prideful; indeed, and a sin.

The ugly transformation I saw on my forearm had never completely faded. It had diminished considerably as I neared my ceremony, but had seemed to slowly return in the weeks after. One evening—it has been nearly three years now—the community was at Vespers. As we were singing the *Magnificat,* a strange sensation overtook me. I felt somehow as if my very entrails were being displaced, moved from their normal positions within me. I felt as though my guts were suffocating and I needed to rip open my belly to let them breathe. I started to whimper and cry out, or so Sister Monica and Abbess told me. I have no memory of it, nor of being carried to my bedchamber and watched over for the rest of the night. Abbess ordered me to stay in my bed until the next morning; until Canon Trincant, an old friend of Father's, came, in the afternoon, to question me and pray over me. I overheard Canon speaking with Abbess outside my door. He told her he was certain I was under the influence of the Evil One, and he recommended that my vows be invalidated, and I be sent home to my family. My presence in a holy place, he said, was blasphemy.

Abbess never mentioned this suggestion to me. She never acted on it, either. Two mornings later, I was back at my duties in the vegetable garden. I saw Canon Trincant approach up the hill from town. With him was another man whom I recognized as old Mignot, a master stonemason from Riquewihr. I could not hear their conversation from my position in the garden, but I saw them walk to the hillside behind the chapel, talk for several minutes, pointing and gesticulating all the while, until Mignot nodded, shook the Canon's hand, and the two men made their way back down to the road below.

The following Monday, Mignot returned early in the morning. With him were men with mattocks and picks and spades. They gathered at the spot where Canon and Mignot had talked and began digging out the hillside. Soon after, dressed building stone started arriving by oxcart and construction began. None of the sisters seemed to know what was being built, and Abbess gave no indication, but when I saw that the stonemasons were forming a garderobe, and that the new building had no door, I knew, and I realized to my horror, that the workmen were building my living tomb.

Abbess said nothing at first. When she looked at me, which I noticed she did several times, it was sorrowfully, I thought, but she made no mention of the cell being built or its purpose. In a few weeks, the cell was finished. One morning afterwards, before prayer, Abbess sent for me.

"I have been well-pleased with your growth in spirit since you have joined us here, Sister Clytie," she said.

"Thank you, Abbess. I know this is where Our Lord wants me to be. I have no doubt of it."

"Nor do I, child. I know your vocation is true. It has been a source of great pain for Canon and myself to witness what has been happening to you."

I nodded and blinked away the tears that were forming in my eyes.

"I am pained," Abbess continued, "so very pained to see it happening to one so pure and true. But this is the way of the Evil One. And Canon, too, grieves. This has touched him. He has prayed over it."

"I am so sorry to be such a worry to yourself and Canon, Abbess."

"It isn't your doing, child. You are a victim."

"Yes, Abbess."

"Still, there is our community of Sisters to consider."

I nodded again but could say nothing.

"Canon has told your father he must remove you from our community. Your father has said it is not his wish to do so. He feels, with what is happening to you, it is best for all if you are removed from society altogether."

"But there is the Rite of..."

"Monseigneur Krueger, the exorcist, died at Colmar last month. Plague. In this time of pestilence, there is no one to replace him."

"Father doesn't want me cleansed," I whispered. "He wants me removed. The cell on the hillside is for me, is it not, Abbess?"

"Just so. Canon says you must be removed as soon as can be. Your father made a large contribution to our cloister and to the Church of the Ramparts. The Canon and the bishop are both in support of this decision."

I crossed myself. "It is obviously God's will, then." I said.

It is now two years and five months since.

How great a piety must one have to live this immured life? Am I strong enough and faithful enough to endure it for years to come? I must be!

The days and the weeks press on. I know I must take solace in prayer and contemplation, but it distresses me to admit in my heart that these things do not comfort me as they should. The walls around me press in. It is but a few arm-lengths from one wall to its opposite, yet this cell is all of Creation to me.

Sometimes I feel I am suffocating in it and I gasp for breath. Some days the walls and ceiling seem closer to me, more oppressive than they were the day before. As I pray the rosary, I become distracted, in warmer weather, watching ants and beetles coming in and going out the oilette. Those tiny, insensible creatures have more freedom than I, a being in God's image, who has devoted her life to Him.

And the silence is a bottomless lake in which I am drowning. From the distance, sounds of birds or livestock or the rustling of a breeze do waft in. I hear people on the road from time to time, and if Sister Monica has some bit of news she feels I must have, she makes an exception to her vow of partial silence to tell me. But in the main, these sounds are but evidence of a distant world to which I am not connected. They do nothing but make my loneliness, my isolation more severe.

And the Evil One vexes me. I feel the movement of... something within my body. There are times when I feel I must explode for an inability to contain the mass inside me. I have fainted three or four times and awakened with memory of a dream. They are always dreams of violence and destruction, and on my awakening, I see that I have acted on the dream and destroyed my table, my chair, and broken my crucifix! Where can the terrible strength to do this come from, except the Evil One? Why am I so oppressed? How can I endure this, locked away alone in this cell with no hope of succor?

Prayer is my only solace. Prayer. Yet prayer seems to me now like a hollow whisper, ignored before it is uttered, spat across the emptiness of life. It seems no more effective than that. But... I know I must not succumb to such thoughts. This is the victory of the Evil One. The victory. His victory. Unclean and vile!

Evening. Sister Monica brought me fish for my evening meal, and coarse bread. My hunger was not satisfied, but there would be no miracle of loaves and fishes for me. Sister also said the pestilence has struck hard again in Zellenberg and Ribeauville in the last few days. It is feared it is making its way, with renewed strength, toward Riquewihr and our enclave.

"People of means are starting to abandon the villages," Sister Monica whispered. "It is safer in the north. I heard your father may be one of them. And the Bishop... the Bishop may give us dispensation to move away with them. Until the pestilence is passed."

"All but me," I responded. "Walled in. Disconnected from community and death, as Canon said. All but *me*."

"But surely, under the circumstances, Sister Clytie, you can be freed? Who will feed you? Workmen could be brought up from the village..."

"The provision of my father's gift was I am never to be freed and incur the displeasure of Our Lord and the advocacy of the Evil One. By the demon within me, I am condemned."

Sister Monica's voice quavered with emotion. "I will bring you dried fish and fruits and vegetables as I can. Enough to store and sustain you until the pestilence has left the region."

"Thank you, Sister. God bless you."

I awoke this evening on the floor. I remember hearing the movement of carts on the road this afternoon. People abandoning the village. That's the last thing I remember before losing consciousness. As I arose from the floor, I realized my knuckles were bloody and my arms and hands completely discolored now: gray-green and knotted with muscle and sinew. I noticed bloody marks on the wall next to the oilette, and vaguely remembered hitting the wall with my fists as if to break free of my prison. I remembered believing I saw a door in the wall with a dark figure standing on its threshold, inviting me to pass through. Then I realized there was no door, and I flew into a rage.

I thought of my father's old cat, Rodrigo. I remembered how he slept most days in a window of our house overlooking the North Gate. Once or twice a day, he would awaken and sit at the front door. I thought of how his mind must work, to live only from moment to moment and have no thought of the future and its possible travails, to be distracted by the flitting of a fly or a reflection of sunlight on a wall, to fix the entirety of his awareness on such tiny stimuli, and be content. I thought of how, at any given moment, as he sat by the door, the totality of his desire and happiness amounted to nothing more than being let outside. The simplest of needs, the humblest of requests of another being. In its fulfillment: *happiness.*

This simple happiness is where my mind wanders more and more frequently. How will I live when there are no sounds at all coming up the hillside? When I know the villages along the mountainsides and across the wide Alsacian valley are empty? Cows, sheep, people gone? Even now, of course, I can have no contact with anyone except Sister Monica. Still, there is some comfort in knowing that people are nearby whether I can interact with them or not. Soon, I will have no companionship but the parasite which lives within me.

Though sometimes, I think I catch movement scuttering across my cell too quickly and indistinctly for me to clearly see. It is either the Evil One or his familiars, I think. I *think.* Or it is nothing but my increasingly diseased perceptions. I look at the oilette and wonder if it has always been on that wall, or if it has moved. I look at the walls surrounding me and know they are closer than they were a few days ago. As I suspected before. Closer. They are surely closing in on me.

Morning. I am awakened by the carts. The endless sound of carts abandoning the village. Then I remember. I remember. Last evening. The terrible events of last evening. My father came. I remembered this as I sit up from my position on the floor. *My father came!* I notice a small gold ring on the floor near me. My father came last night... Unlikely as that was to ever happen, he came to my cell.

"I am leaving the village," he said through the oilette. "I do not know for how long."

"Father... Father..."

"I sometimes have regrets for putting you in this cell, though I know it was the right thing to do. The Evil One is in you, and those around you deserve aid and protection from you."

"All I wanted was to please you. I want to live in our house again to be near you and prove that I can overcome this test the Lord has given me. Given *us. Our family!*"

"No. I am satisfied I have done the right thing. You must accept your life here to protect others. It is God's will, I am certain of it."

"It *isn't*. I don't believe Our Lord's only plan for me is in this cell. I can spread the word about the work of the Evil One in this world."

Father stooped to look at me as best he could through the oilette. "Look at you. You're a monster now. You are lost to darkness and a servant of demons. You are transformed. This could only happen if it were God's will."

I wept. "Then why did you come?"

He removed a small gold ring from his leather purse at his waist. "Your mother wanted you to have this. I meant to give it to you years ago. As I am going and may not see you again, I wanted you to have it..."

He held it up for me to see just outside the oilette. In an instant, I thought of how I had tried to please him since childhood and wanted nothing more than to live with him as his devoted daughter. An impulse came over me so quickly that I could not consider or weigh it in my mind. In a tiny particle of a second, I had reached through the oilette, and had grasped him by both wrists. Then all was darkness until just now.

Standing, I realize the floor is discolored. I step back and nearly stumble across a pliant mass behind me. Father is there. His arms are bloody and his shoulders splintered and compressed as if forced through a space much too small to accommodate them. His head is crushed. Flattened at the back and the face sheared off as if planed through the narrow oilette. He is growing slowly rigid, and the blood darkening my floor is all but dried. I will gather him up and put him on my cot. There he will remain. I do not foresee a reason, or expect any inclination overcoming me, to move him.

Oxen snort and mewl under their burdens on the road below as the villagers, with the means to do so, press on up the hills away from Riquewihr. There, from the high hillsides and mountaintops overlooking the wide and beneficent plain below, they will watch and wait for the end of this pestilence, for the subsidence of the capricious anger of God.

Consecration

Everything had died in the summer. The corn and sorghum withered in the drought. Cattle died of thirst and sun. Charmaine's mother, Elaine Aubin, coughed blood until she died in early July. Charmaine herself felt her childhood die that same month when she decided, at thirteen, her schooling was over and she should work in Great-Uncle Joseph's store, the Ste. Odile Feed and Dry Goods. He was aged and no longer able to do all the work anymore, and as her last living relation, he had taken her in.

As her mother's life faded away in their sweltering upstairs bedroom at Phrygia House orphanage, she told Charmaine to pray to the Virgin Mary for guidance. As a child of the cook, Sister Celeste, the Mother Superior, told Charmaine she could keep their room and finish her education after her mother was gone, if she wished to continue her duties as a helper in the kitchen. Just before the funeral, Charmaine did pray, and it was then that the Virgin told her she must change the course of her life, and that her Uncle Joseph needed her. On the afternoon of the burial, she spoke to Sister Celeste:

"It is very generous of you, to let me stay," she said. "I have prayed to the Virgin. I know I wish to serve our Lord and live in the image of His Holy Mother Mary. I am very sure that in time I will want to do these things as one of your sisters. I know I want to join the Sisters of Perpetua someday. For now, though, I must think of the needs of my Uncle Joseph in his last years. He always helped Mother and me when he could, and he has offered to take me in if I can help him with the store."

"The Order will be blessed by your vocation, Miss Charmaine Aubin, and I do believe you have one," Sister Celeste said. "I have known you since you were an infant and your mother first came to work for us. I know you will always do the right thing." She smiled as the girl found Uncle Joseph in the crowd, took his arm, and the two of them walked toward the Endymion Road and the outskirts of town.

Charmaine's mother, Elaine, always had a special affection for her Uncle Joseph. He was the older brother of Jeanne, her own mother. As a child and young man, Joseph had been very close to his twin sister Marie. Marie had died forty-five years earlier under circumstances no one in the family would discuss. Charmaine suspected there was some sort of disgrace attached to the death, but her mother told her to never mention the subject to Uncle Joseph.

Uncle Joseph lived in an old house on Bucephalus Street in town.

Three times a week, a woman looked in on him to make sure he was eating as he should and to clean his house. On days when he felt strong enough, he walked to Endymion Street and then west out of town until it became a county road, to his feed store. Charmaine decided she would live in the store's back room. She had never lived alone before, but she was excited about the prospect. She thought it made sense to stay on the premises to keep an eye on things, and Uncle Joseph eventually agreed. And, after living her entire life with her mother in one small room at the orphanage, she couldn't accept the idea of living in her uncle's tiny, cluttered house, where she would have little privacy. Despite her initial fears of living alone, she was thrilled at the thought of finally having a private place of her own.

In her first week of working at the store, Uncle Joseph taught Charmaine how to make change from the cash register, count out and balance the cash drawer in the evenings, prepare the bank deposit, inventory and order feed and dry goods, and keep track of everything in a ledger. She easily learned everything Uncle Joseph taught her, and he was pleased enough with her progress that by the second week he began arriving at the store later in the mornings and walking home earlier in the evenings. It was soon obvious to Charmaine that the main reason her uncle came out to the store at all was for her conversation and companionship. She could see great affection for her in his face.

At first Charmaine looked forward to closing the store every day at four in the afternoon. She enjoyed the thought of evenings on her own, of making herself a light dinner then reading in her Adirondack chair just outside the front door until dark, or on an old glider out back near the bank of the Little Saline Creek. Last year, as her mother declined, she had read Jane Austen's *Pride and Prejudice,* and a scene toward the end had always stayed with her: the disgraced Mr. Wickham approaches Elizabeth hidden in a copse reading a letter from her aunt. Wickham says: "I am afraid I interrupt your solitary ramble, my dear sister?"

Charmaine wondered at the luxury of having a "solitary ramble", of having the time and isolation to read or draw or pursue her own thoughts and imagination in writing, or however she wished. She'd had very little time like that while her mother was alive. But now, living on her own, she had her evenings. When she moved into the back of the store, she had brought her novels and entomology books, an empty notebook which she intended to fill with stories and poetry, and a half-empty notebook which she had used for English assignments in school. In this one, she meant to record her observations on nature, especially the life cycles of the insects that lived on the creek bank and alluvial areas nearby.

At first, she was excited about the possibilities of these activities. For the first week she designated time for her rosary, for reading, (she was halfway through *The Age of Innocence*) and for drawing. She tried writing poetry just before she went to bed, but found it stimulated her mind too much and she had difficulty getting to sleep. But she was soon aware that the feeling of excitement had somehow been replaced with one of anxiety, of fear of the silence and emptiness of her evenings and a sense of vulnerable isolation that became worse as she considered going to bed each night. She added more prayers to the Virgin to her nightly routine, but they didn't seem to help. She reminded herself that she must be grateful for her new privacy and freedom. She just needed time to adjust to her solitary life.

As she lay on her cot at night, Charmaine found that the odd sounds and creaks of the old store, which had been built of logs in the 1880s when Uncle Joseph was a young man, got more mysterious and unnerving the longer she lived there. One night, as she was just drifting off to sleep, she was startled awake by a skittering sound on the floor under her cot. She just caught a glimpse of movement in the darkness, which headed toward the store and the seed bags kept there.

"Rats," she whispered. She decided to get dressed and sit up for the rest of the night.

Two days later, Uncle Joseph brought a large yellow cat to the store. Charmaine named her Hecate because the Greek goddess had once assumed the form of a cat to escape the monster Typhon. That very night Hecate killed a rat and left it on the floor beside Charmaine's cot. Charmaine stepped on the soft, still warm carcass in the dark when she got up to see if she had locked the front door. A shudder of disgust and fear swept over her. She dragged the rug on which the dead rat laid outside the back door. The next morning, she wrapped the carcass in the rug and buried it on the creek bank.

It wasn't unusual for an entire day to pass at the store without Charmaine seeing a single customer. On a wet Wednesday morning a month after she moved in, she decided the intermittent rain would keep the customers away all day. She had already said her morning's rosary, but she thought, given the opportunity, maybe she was intended to say another. She never used working hours for writing or drawing or reading. That was Uncle Joseph's time and to use it for herself wouldn't be proper. But praying, she thought, could surely never be inappropriate.

"I offer these prayers to the Blessed Virgin that I may be more like Her and Her Holy Son in my everyday life," she said as she knelt behind the counter. As she started her second Hail Mary, she heard the front door open behind her. She stood and was startled to see a tall man in black standing in the doorway. The man was very thin and was wearing something like an old Inverness cape despite the extreme heat of the day. His entire head and face were wrapped in gauze bandages. Two openings were left in the wrappings: one for his right eye and one for his mouth. Sprigs of long, gray hair sprouted out from between the bandages here and there, and on top of his head he wore a dusty silk top-hat.

Charmaine gasped weakly at his appearance. The man seemed to smile a little smile under his bandages.

"I am so sorry to startle you like this, young woman," he said. His voice was deep but wet-sounding and slightly garbled. "I know I present an unusual and to some, unsettling appearance."

"I am sorry to seem..."

"Perfectly understandable," the man continued. "My clothes are many decades out of style, and I am afflicted by a degenerative condition of the skin and always keep my face wrapped when I go out. I am an odd sight to see, I know."

Charmaine noticed he was wearing leather gloves. No part of his skin was visible except for the pink swelling of his lips and a dark, violet area around his eye.

"I am sorry to have reacted so," she said. "I am used to seeing farmers and tradesmen and people like that here..."

"Yes," he interrupted. "I lived here once. Very long ago. I travel through sometimes. I was atypical here back then and continue to be so now!"

Charmaine nodded and smiled shyly. "Is... there something I can help you with?"

He looked at her intently in a way that added to her discomfort.

"What would be your name, young woman, if you don't mind in my asking?"

"I am Charmaine Aubin. This is my Uncle Joseph's store. I am helping him here."

"That is most commendable. I have a secret to tell you, Charmaine. I noticed you the day you moved in. I saw you had books and notebooks and I thought: 'What an intelligent and excellently interesting young woman she must be.'"

Charmaine grew more uneasy. She wished Uncle Joseph were there, but it was still early, and he usually came later in the morning.

"You saw me?" Charmaine said. "But how? I don't remember seeing anyone."

"One with my physical peculiarities learns ways to remain unseen!" Again, he seemed to smile. "It is because you are intelligent and... interesting, that I knew you alone among your companions, among any friends you may have, would appreciate a special gift."

"Gift?"

The man placed a heavy golden coin on the counter.

"A Roman aureus," he said. "Nearly two thousand years old. Think of the history it has seen. Think. I *know* you will!"

"Sir, I can't accept such a gift! You are a stranger to me..." Charmaine was astonished. When she raised her eyes to repeat her protest, the man was gone.

She picked up the coin and examined it. It was exquisitely heavy and worn. On one side of the coin was the profile image of a man. She could barely make out the words: SEPTIMUS SEVERUS. On the reverse was the image of an eagle between two standards and the inscription: XIV GEMMINA MARTIA VICTRIX. Why would a stranger leave her such a gift? She heard a step on the wooden walk outside the front door and quickly slipped the coin into her apron pocket.

Uncle Joseph stood in the threshold for several seconds, watching down the road, as the stranger walked away. His face was flushed when he stepped inside and looked at her. He was breathless.

"Charmaine! Who was that?"

"I don't know, Uncle. He just stopped in here to talk and when I looked up, he was gone. I've never seen him before."

"What did he say to you?"

"Just that he saw me move in here," Charmaine said, "and that he thought I must be very... smart. Very intelligent. I am glad you're early today, Uncle. He was an odd character!"

"What did he look like?"

"His face was bandaged, but as you could see, he was tall and thin."

Uncle Joseph's expression darkened.

"He didn't tell you his name?"

"No."

"Did he leave anything with you? Any sort of gift?"

Charmaine was ashamed at how quickly and easily she lied.

"No."

Uncle Joseph sat in an old ladderback chair near the counter. He still seemed to be exhausted from his walk there.

"I can't be sure. It seems so unlikely, it's been so long ago," he said. "In any event, you cannot stay here alone at night anymore. I won't risk it. I won't put you at risk, child."

"What is it Uncle Joseph? What's wrong?"

"You may not be safe here alone at night. There was a time here when young girls and women were not safe in Ste. Odile. We thought that was long past us, but I can't be sure."

"Are you talking about the *Homme de Cauchemar*? That bogeyman mother told me about?"

"Yes, child," Uncle Joseph nodded. "Orien Bastide. A name your family knew too well at one time.

Charmaine was confused. "But mother said Madam Montes killed him. Old Anatolia."

"There was never any proof of it. I always thought we shouldn't assume."

"I don't understand. You think that man might have been Bastide?"

Uncle Joseph was distracted. He said nothing for a moment.

"You'll be all right here until dark. I am going to walk back into town and borrow Mrs. Zell's truck. Then, we're going to load your things and some of this furniture for you. You will stay at my house for a while. Until I know."

"But Uncle Joseph, I think I'm fine here. Probably. I want to stay. This is my own private place. That man was probably not... that was so long ago."

"No. I won't... take that chance." Uncle Joseph waved his hand dismissively and walked out the front door.

Charmaine sadly gathered her few possessions and put them in a wooden crate. She had noticed recently how older people live more fearfully, exaggerating the threat of small things. She knew this was because they felt weaker and more vulnerable in old age. She had to honor Uncle Joseph's wishes, but she felt that in time, she could convince him that she was perfectly safe living at the store alone.

By noon, there had been no customers. Charmaine sat on the front step of the store to listen to the cicadas and watch two robins playing in the dusty road. She was startled when the telephone rang. It was old Mrs. Zell who ran the boarding house next door to Uncle Joseph's house.

"It's terrible, child, *terrible!*"

It always took Charmaine a moment to adjust to Mrs. Zell's odd way of emphasizing certain words in her phrases and actually listen to what the old woman was saying.

"What is it, Mrs. Zell?"

"Just terrible! And I am *so sorry* to be the one to tell you. Joseph was hit by a DeSoto, I'm pretty sure it was a *DeSoto,* walking here a while ago. He *died* ten minutes ago! I'm so *sorry* to have to tell you, Charmaine!"

For a moment Mrs. Zell's words made no sense, but when Charmaine understood and acknowledged what she was being told, she felt oddly unresponsive to it. An hour later, after she closed the store and was walking into town, it finally struck her that Uncle Joseph was *dead*, and she was truly alone in the world.

***

The funeral mass was said at the Church of the Holy Mandilion in Ste. Odile three days later. Several farmer's and their wives attended, as well as other merchants from the town and a few of Joseph's elderly friends whom Charmaine did not know. Charmaine stayed at Uncle Joseph's house that week waiting for the service and admitting creditors to the property who laid claims to furniture and personal items to help satisfy some remaining debts Uncle Joseph had accumulated trying to keep his store open through the terrible Depression the country was struggling through.

The day after the funeral, Charmaine told Mrs. Zell she had to get back out to the store. More creditors were laying claim to certain merchandise and fixtures, and Charmaine was determined to sell whatever was left to try to keep the store operating.

"Joseph would be so *proud* of you trying to *carry on* this way!" Mrs. Zell said.

"I know he truly loved me," Charmaine smiled. "He wanted to protect me from the world. Even silly things."

"Silly things?"

"A strange man came to the store the day Uncle Joseph died. Uncle Joseph just got a glimpse of him as he walked away. He started talking about that Bastide person and the *Homme de Cauchemar*."

"Bastide?" Mrs. Zell's voice was very stern. "*Bastide*?"

"Yes. Silly, I know. Superstition. But Uncle Joseph wanted to protect me from everything."

"What was this *strange man* like?"

"He was tall and slender with odd clothes and a funny old hat. His head was wrapped in bandages."

"And did he *compliment* your intelligence and curiosity?"

"Yes."

"And did he leave you a *gift*? Perhaps an antique *gold coin*?"

Charmaine was shocked that the old woman could have guessed her secret so accurately. She nodded. Mrs. Zell took Charmaine's arm and directed her to sit in a kitchen chair. Mrs. Zell sat across from her.

"I understand why Joseph was *concerned*." She said. "Joseph and your mother never *told* you about Joseph's twin sister, your great-aunt *Marie Delaporte Chardin*."

"No. It was a subject I was told not to ask about or mention to Uncle Joseph."

"Bastide was real. He was the cause of *Marie's* sad end."

"But that was... 1882? How does it affect me now? Mother said Bastide was dead. Killed by Miss Montes long ago."

"Miss Montes is not the *first* woman to think she had rid the *world* of Bastide. There was another, Miss *Perdita*, back in Marie's time. Fitting, that two women should have done it, or *tried*. Bastide managed to survive the first time, maybe he did the *second*, too. In all your *reading*, have you come across an unholy agent, a *demon* known as the incubus?"

"Yes. The bringer of nightmares. The demon of carnality. The attacker of women in their sleep. Yes. I read of it in Ovid or Virgil, I think."

"The *physical* body of Bastide was *host* to such a being. He was of two *natures*. He lived so for nearly *two thousand years*."

Charmaine studied Mrs. Zell's face to make sure the old woman truly believed the statement she had just made.

"Mrs. Zell. Surely this is... nonsense? You can't seriously think..."

"He lived like a baron at the old *Jardin Noir* estate, ruined now. Your great-aunt *Marie*, like many before her, was *attacked* by him. Marie killed her own daughter in a fit of *despair* and hopelessness, to protect the child from such a *horror* in the future. Marie was *hanged* on de Castres Island in front of the whole *town*. That is what *Joseph* feared for you."

Charmaine had always heard stories of the deranged mother who had murdered her own child and was hanged for it, but she never suspected she had any family connection to those horrific events of so long ago. Mrs. Zell said she agreed with Joseph's concern about

Charmaine living alone at the store. The old woman became agitated and nearly fainted when she could not convince Charmaine to stay in town in her boarding house. When Mrs. Zell lay down to rest, Charmaine started to walk back to the store.

It was evening when she started to walk and fully dark when she reached the edge of town. The nearly full moon was rising and by the time the street became a dirt road; the fields, pastures and trees were washed in silvery light. The burring of the tree frogs became louder, denser, as she got further from town, and the calling of the whippoorwills that seemed miles removed, across the illuminated, sheltering countryside when she started out, now sounded no more than an arm's length away.

Less than a mile from the store, she approached the old Lamarcke Farm, which had been abandoned years before she was born. Beyond the dust-covered milkweeds at the edge of the road, the dilapidated farmhouse still stood, although half of the roof and the porch had collapsed in a storm in the spring. Charmaine heard what sounded like a board falling inside the farmhouse and thought there must be a racoon or opossum moving around inside. She remembered she had not said a rosary since yesterday. She had her beads in the pocket of her dress. She took them out, made the sign of the cross, and began to pray.

"*I believe in God the Father Almighty, Creator of Heaven and earth...*"

Another sound came from the old farmhouse, as if something heavy were being pushed across a floor, followed by a chittering animal sound. Charmaine began to walk faster.

"*And in Jesus Christ, His only begotten son, our Lord...*"

There was a sound of splitting wood, and Charmaine could see the front door of the farmhouse pull away slightly from the door frame. Suddenly, a dark form appeared in the moonlit road in front of her. It was the size of a very large cat but shaped like a weasel or otter. It stopped in the road, making the chittering sound she had heard a moment earlier. It seemed to be looking at her. A second creature, identical to the first, emerged in an undulating and fluid motion from the dark bushes and attacked the first one. They then both quickly disappeared into the woods on the opposite side of the road.

Charmaine put her rosary back in her pocket and hurried on toward the store, less than a half-mile away.

Charmaine had put food out for Hecate, her cat, when she left a few days before. When she opened the front door of the store, she was surprised to see most of the food still in its bowl, uneaten next to the counter. The cat didn't come to greet her as usual.

"Kitty, kitty," Charmaine called. "Hecate... kitty, kitty."

No response. Charmaine assumed the cat was out hunting in the woods, as she loved to do. Charmaine decided to get into bed and finish her rosary. She selected a dress she would wear tomorrow when she reopened the store and laid it across a chair. She slipped on her nightgown and sat on the edge of her cot. There was a rosary on her night table, next to her lamp. She lay back on the cot to pray.

A large fly flew up from the unlit far side of the cot and flew past Charmaine's head. She swatted at it, and it disappeared into the shadow from which it had come. She looked over the edge of the cot. The fly landed on a bloody smear of bone and yellow fur on the floor below her.

Charmaine gasped and jumped off the cot. Cautiously, she rounded the foot of her bed and stared into the shadow.

"Hecate!" she whispered.

The smear of fur and bone extended across the floor back toward the rear window Charmaine always left slightly open for the cat to get outside when she wanted. Charmaine could see more bits of bone and flesh in the shadows, and a fragment of jaw with a few teeth visible.

Charmaine was paralyzed with terror for a few moments. Something must have come in the window after Hecate and torn her to pieces. She wondered if this could have been done by the two creatures she had just seen in the road.

Charmaine ran to the window and closed it. Then she found the bucket and some rags and cleaned up the flesh and blood now dried and stuck to the floor.

Afterwards, Charmaine sat up for a while. She felt she wouldn't be able to sleep and she could not concentrate to finish her rosary, so she decided to read from her old textbook, *Insects of North America*, that she had left at her bedside. Each creak and groan the planks of the old building made, which Charmaine had mostly learned to ignore at night, now startled and terrified her. Several times she rechecked the doors and windows to make sure they were secure, and finally, by midnight, she was so exhausted that she thought she might be able to sleep.

As she lay on her cot in the darkness, Charmaine gradually noticed that the night sounds, the tree frogs, the whippoorwills, and the settling of the old building, all seemed to stop at once.

Before she could think too deeply about the oddness of this, she felt a wave of abject relaxation wash over her. She saw herself in some sort of ancient stone fortress surrounded by robed, archaic figures engaged in some sort of ritual, a ritual which seemed to be a response to an impending and pervasive tragedy.

By slow degrees, Charmaine began to ascend from her dream state and become aware of the room around her, though she kept her eyes tightly shut. She felt a presence nearby, in the shadows or possibly at the edge of her bed. She meant to fully open her eyes and sit up, but found she could not move. Somehow, the presence she sensed was no longer at a distance, but on the cot behind her. She felt a pressure against her back from a rough form which seemed to extend beyond hers at head and foot. She thought she heard a voice, a deep, wet growl that may have come from behind her or from inside her own head. It spoke one word as she realized, to her horror, that she was being pushed onto her back: one word that neutralized the prayer she could not make herself say:

"*YOU!*"

***

When Charmaine regained consciousness, what she could see of the sky was gray, and she thought of all the late summer dawns she had seen before her mother died, across the barrier of hills in Ste. Odile. She liked to watch the mist on the wide river in the cool, damp mornings before it burned off and the town began to come to life in the humid sunshine.

She moved her right leg a little, and a terrible pain shot through her thigh and groin. She remembered something horrifying had happened in the night, but she could recall no details, as though her soul, her faith and her image of herself were forbidding her to do so. She knew she was seriously injured. She could see her upper thighs were smeared in blood that had soaked through her gown and dried.

She painfully stood. The room went dark and her head spun. She steadied herself against her chair. She thought she should call Mrs. Zell for help. She moved slowly out of her room toward the front of the store, and as she entered the front room, she saw the ragged end of the telephone cord lying on the floor beneath the old crank telephone. The cord appeared to have been chewed through.

Charmaine thought it odd that she was unsurprised and unmoved by this. She thought she would clean herself and her bed, lie down and rest for as long as her healing took. She knew if she had to, she could recover alone.

No customers or creditors came to the store that day. Charmaine was strangely glad. She didn't want the company or help of men. She didn't want to explain to a man what had happened to her body and how it had changed her perceptions of everything, and how she intended to recover. She wanted her mother or one of the nuns from Phrygia House or Mrs. Zell. If she couldn't have the care and understanding of a woman, she wanted to be left alone.

As the afternoon wore on, she napped on her cot, had a little soup and bread, and realized, to her surprise, that she didn't fear the oncoming night. She sensed somehow that the threat to her was past, and that whatever had violated and damaged her was finished with her now, and would not be back.

She felt feverish in the night but slept well. In the morning, she was rested and able to move around a little easier than the day before. On the fourth day, she awoke feeling a little nauseous, but it passed. That day, a man from Easton Seed came in a truck to take most of the seed corn Uncle Joseph had not yet paid for. Charmaine concealed her injuries from the man, and he seemed to take little notice of her.

Over the next ten days Charmaine awoke nauseous every morning, and her sickness grew worse every day. She often felt the urge to vomit and just managed to get out the back door in time. Late on the twelfth day, she felt tremendous pain and cramping in her lower abdomen. She locked the front door of the store and lay on her cot with a damp cloth on her forehead.

She slept fitfully that night. She dreamt of medieval heretics burning at the stake in a mountain meadow, and of her memory of a dark presence watching her as she slept. Before dawn, the cramping got so severe it was almost unbearable. She thought of saying a rosary, but she would not be able to concentrate long enough to finish it.

"Blessed Virgin," she whispered. "I have always revered you and prayed for your guidance. Please help me now. Help me with this..."

Charmaine could tell she was bleeding again. She rolled herself off her cot onto the floor. She slipped off her nightgown and lay on her right side. She felt another wave of pain, then a twinge of release, expulsion, and she knew the worst of her suffering was over. She lay still for a few moments. She wanted to look at the place where her hip touched the floor, but she could not do it immediately. She propped herself up on her right elbow.

"Dear Blessed Virgin, thank you for delivering me from this pain..."

Charmaine sat up. There was a spot of blood where her hip had been, and a tiny morsel of flesh in the center of it. The tissue twitched a little and then lay still. Tears filled Charmaine's eyes as she understood what had happened.

"How can this be?" she sobbed. "How can this happen... to me?"

She thought of Mrs. Zell. The old woman had been right.

"She will understand and help me with this. Help me put this behind me. Uncle Joseph was right..."

Charmaine slowly stood and washed herself. She did not know what to do with the morsel on the floor. She looked at the dark spot in the moonlight. She dressed herself.

"Surely this little thing has a soul. It was made through no agency of its own. It is innocent, and... beloved of God, and the Holy Virgin."

Charmaine had kept her drawing pencils and erasers in a tobacco tin on her table. She emptied the tin. She sat on the floor next to the bloody spot and wondered why the Virgin had subjected her to this. But she knew she must not question it.

At first, she didn't want to touch the little bit of tissue but then she thought, the end of this small life was a good thing. God did this so that it may not become a profanity. Its death was a blessing from God and the Virgin. She picked up the fetus and lay it in the palm of her hand.

"Still, as a child of God, it needs a blessing, a baptism. It deserves to be consecrated as an innocent and sent into God's presence."

Charmaine walked to the sink at the rear of her room. She wetted her fingers and touched the fetus.

"I baptize thee in the name of the Father, the Son and the Holy

Ghost, Amen. Now may you avoid the pain of Purgatory and be happy for all eternity with God and the Heavenly Hosts."

She placed the fetus into the tobacco tin and closed the lid. She went out the back door into the moonlight. The hoe was leaning against the back steps. She dug a small hole under the large cypress tree. She placed the tin in the hole and covered it with dirt. She knelt beside the spot. Tears returned to her eyes as she prayed the rosary from memory.

Afterwards, she stood. She watched the spot for a few more moments. She thought she would close the store for good and move back into town with Mrs. Zell. Charmaine missed her mother at that moment, more than she had all summer. She needed her mother now. Mrs Zell would understand. Only Mrs. Zell would understand.

Charmaine's gaze had drifted up to the full moon, but something made her look back at the tiny grave at her feet. A small clump of dirt moved, then several more. A small glint of silvery light reflected off something wet on the ground. More granules of earth were disturbed, and Charmaine gasped a little and sobbed at whatever mercies the Virgin would grant or refuse her, and she thought of the agonies of her mother watching at that moment, helpless against the will of Heaven, as the infernal morsel of flesh crawled toward her daughter in the moonlight.

Somnambulist

Diary of Seraphica Thibault
December 4, 1922

Today is the tenth anniversary of my Visitation. The first of three Visitations, I mean. At age ten, sitting on my bed on a frigid day a month after my mother died, I saw St. Michael the Archangel emerge from my wall and tell me to minister to all the black babies of Africa. This being only the most recent of many lesser visions I had at that time, my father committed me to the St. Perpetua Female Infirmary, or asylum south of town, where I spent the next eighteen months. I spoke to the doctors who treated me, of a world which existed unseen near to our own from which my visions came, visions slipping in and out of our world at will. I was diagnosed with female hysteria, as I was approaching womanhood, and when my imaginative tendencies subsided, the kindly sisters released me back to my family. I have functioned reasonably well since then. I have made myself useful and come to understand that I am loved.

In fact, even including that difficult period, I have never counted myself anything but fortunate, before now. Overly imaginative and something of a misfit, but fortunate. Until the end of the Great War four years ago, my family was relatively prosperous, in spite of my father's business reversals. My brother, Urbain, joined the Army against my father's wishes but, thank God, never shipped out of New Jersey before the Armistice was signed. My own Theophile was still too young to enlist in 1918, but I know he would have done so had he been of age. The violent passions of young men will soon no longer vex and worry me. Soon all my daily concerns will be the complaints, irritabilities, diminished health and function of a very old man.

Today is the day he comes for me. And it is the day the five hundred acres transfers to my father, the rich bottom land that was my dowry. The land includes the gravel bar on the River Aux Vases, ice-covered now, where Theophile and I picnicked on my birthday in June. I remember I thought I saw a great water snake in the stream that day, but Theophile showed me it was only an oak branch and laughed at me. Now, all that land belongs to my father to try his hand once again at farming, having failed before, as he failed at running his market in town. I wish I believed he would be more successful at trying again to work the land, and that this awful thing I have agreed to do would be for some purpose.

Louis Dreaux. My husband. I believe I have only seen him four or five times in my life. A widower and hermit, whose wife died under questionable circumstances, and he in the habit of coming into town no more than once every few months. A rather mysterious person. He had a falling out with father once, over seed corn he had bought, if I remember. That was the only time I heard him speak. We were married on Thursday in the parlor of Mr. Politte, the Justice of the Peace. Dreaux rode an old mule into town for the wedding and did not look at me through the ceremony. The kiss he gave me at the end of it was a glancing one, on the cheek. Rather than any affection or interest in completing this union, it almost seemed to me, or at least I imagined it, that he was only fulfilling an unpleasant responsibility.

Theophile and I had talked of having a family someday. The Thibaults and the Arnauds are two of the oldest families in Ste. Odile and have intermarried many times in the last two and a half centuries. He is my fourth cousin, in fact, and we foresaw our marriage as being the culminating union of these two old lines. When he would walk me to my door in the evenings, knowing my imaginative nature, he would then watch my window from across the street until my light was out and he knew I was secure and safe for the night.

Now, Theophile will not even speak to me. I know how he must feel. I only wish I could make him understand how *I* feel. And I have only thought it privately, but my aged husband cannot live forever. Then, as father stipulated in his agreement with Dreaux, and since he has no children, I will inherit his house and all remaining lands and all his animals. Then, perhaps, if he will still have me, Theophile and I can begin our life together. It would be a good start for us, I think. Surely that and the benefit to my family, makes this worth doing?

Dec. 8, evening

I am here. Dreaux arrived to collect me in his dray wagon at about two in the afternoon. He and Father loaded my chifforobe and trunk into the back of it and tied everything down. Not much to carry. Not much of a load for the old mule pulling the wagon. I might have known this old man would not own a truck or an automobile. Sitting on that wagon in the biting wind, I felt numb and nearly frozen by the time we got back to his house. Our house. Dreaux built it himself fifty years ago and added on to it when he was first married. It is a two-and-a-half-story clapboard place, electrified now, deeper than it is wide and needing a coat of paint. There is a large front porch which wraps around the right side, and it sits on a slight prominence above the flood line, in a meadow which gives way to a grassless yard and slopes further down to the bank of the River Aux Vases. It seems to me unfriendly, and in no sense of the word, a home.

Dreaux pulled the wagon up behind the house and stopped.

"Kitchen through the back door," He said, never looking at me. "I put ham and beans on this morning so you'd have somethin' to eat. Go on in. L'Andre's gonna help me get your things inside." As he said this, an old black man roughly my husband's age emerged from a shed attached to the large barn and walked toward us. I went into the kitchen.

The room was sparse but tidy. The linoleum on the floor was worn in some places, torn and patched in others. The smell of the ham and beans filled the house. The covered pot sat on a gas range which looked new. Next to this stood a new Frigidaire refrigerator. I expected my new husband planned for me to make good use of these appliances. Better than burning wood and having an icebox. There were coat hooks on the wall by the back door. I hung my scarf and coat on these. I walked into the dining room which adjoined the kitchen.

The only furnishings in that oddly unwelcoming room were a table of oak planks, two wooden chairs and a sideboard. In a pine-framed fireplace on the wall opposite burned a fire, which was having but a small effect upon the forbidding temperature of the room. Above this hung a very old photograph in an ornate frame of a dour, plump-faced young woman. I took this to be an image of Adele, Dreaux's long-dead wife. A huffing sound to my left directed my attention toward the front room.

As I looked toward the sound, the light from the great front window blinded me a little. I saw a large form on the sofa, dark and substantial, bestir itself and exhale a deep breath. This mass seemed almost liquid on its surface as waves of muscle rolled under the furry flesh. The form resolved itself into a huge mastiff which arose from the sofa and walked aggressively toward me. I could hear the rumble of a growl in his throat. I froze.

"Potiphar!" Dreaux shouted from behind me. "Sit!"

The dog slowed his gait and approached me more tentatively. He sniffed my hand and dress, then sat just next to me in an attitude of vigilance. Dreaux patted the dog's enormous head. "Got nothing to fear from him anymore," he said, "now that he's seen you with me. Now... he'll protect you to the death of him."

I scratched the dog's broad head. He pushed against me a bit, his wet mouth brushing the back of my hand. "That won't be necessary, I hope!" I said. "Good boy. Potiphar! Named for Potiphar of old?"

"Yes, and for his great-great grandfather whose master was an old wildcrafter, or witch, as may be. Old Euphrosine. One pup in every litter since has carried the name."

"I've heard of Euphrosine. My grandmother spoke of her."

A dark look passed over Dreaux's face. "I shouldn't have mentioned her," he said. "A wildcrafter is nothing but a witch and I won't have reference to such dark and un-Christian things in my house. Do not suffer a witch to live."

"Oh, but surely an old woman who mixes medicines and delivers babies can't be called a witch?"

"Enough on the subject!" Dreaux said suddenly. I was a little startled by his vehemence. "We won't talk about dark and un-Christian things here!" He stepped back into the kitchen and fretted about with dishes sitting near the sink and the pot heating on the stove in some imaginary, urgent task. He never looked at me. "Do you want any of this food?" he asked. "I can put it away or throw it out if you have no taste for it."

"I will have some. Let me see my room first. I will put the food away after."

"Our room," Dreaux said. "We are married and will share a room. I won't make a mockery of the sacrament."

I meant to say, "Of course," but only nodded my assent.

Just at that moment, L'Andre pushed through the kitchen door with my trunk. I judged it to be eighty or ninety pounds and L'Andre was struggling with it. As he pulled it across the threshold, he glanced at me for the tiniest part of a second with a look that seemed to imply he had something to tell me. I decided I had imagined it.

Dreaux took the trunk, lifting it easily off the floor. "We'll get the chifforobe in, then tend to the wagon," he said. "I'll take this upstairs." With what seemed like little effort, Dreaux carried the trunk into the front room and up the stairs. I followed him, and Potiphar followed me.

The second floor of the house was freezing and unadorned. At the center of a short hallway was a floor-to-ceiling window which looked out on the sloping meadow and the River Aux Vases below. There were two bedrooms off the hallway, and two other rooms at the end of it near a smaller stairway going up to the attic. The smaller bedroom had an iron bed in it with a straw mattress, a wardrobe, and a tiny window. The master bedroom was twice as large. There was a stove vented out the rear wall, a large Jenny Lind bed, a small dresser and vanity both of which had been pushed into a corner, in my estimation, to make room for my chifforobe.

Dreaux placed my trunk at the foot of the bed. A puff of dust arose from the rough floor when he did this.

"Freezing in here," he said. He pulled open the front of the stove and pushed two oak logs in. Dreaux went downstairs and in another fifteen minutes, he and L'Andre had carried my chifforobe upstairs and placed it against the west wall of the room opposite the bed.

"I'll leave you on your own to unpack," Dreaux said. "If you haven't eaten in an hour, I'm throwing the beans out to the hogs." He went downstairs.

I sat on the edge of my trunk, looking around at the sparse, chilly room. I could see the river from the large window in the hallway. The banks were crusted with ice, but the current still flowed down the center of the stream. Potiphar circled a spot on the bedroom floor, then lay down with a thud. He looked up at me quizzically (I would say) and after a moment, laid his head down on his paws.

"Good boy," I said. My voice quivered. "Good boy. I know we'll be good friends. You'll keep me company." I looked behind me, at the wide, freezing bed and realized I was crying.

Dec. 9, morning

All day yesterday I thought of bedtime. As the sun set, I settled into our bedroom and busied myself with unpacking my trunk and loading my chifforobe.

For an hour or so in the evening, Dreaux and I sat in the parlor near the fire. Dreaux leafed through the *Ste. Odile Seraphim*, mumbling now and then over an obituary or an arrest notice. I would try to respond to his comments, try to engage him in some sort of conversation, but no conversation developed. Potiphar lay at my feet, between my chair and the fire.

"Thinks he's your dog now," Dreaux muttered. "He ain't."

The evening seemed endless. The mantle clock did eventually strike nine. Dreaux folded his newspaper and dropped it on the floor. He stood.

"I go to bed at this time," he said. "Whether you do... it's up to you."

"Of course," I said, rising. Potiphar stood and followed Dreaux to the kitchen door. Dreaux opened the door and let the dog out.

"Suit yourself," he said over his shoulder. "Go ahead. I gotta wait to let the dog back in."

I went upstairs and changed into my sleeping gown behind the screen. I slipped into the freezing bed. I chose the left side because it seemed less used and compressed than the right. Even though the quilt covered me, I still felt cold. I could not stop shivering. After a few moments, I heard Dreaux's footsteps on the stair, accompanied by Potiphar's huffing gallop. My teeth were chattering, and my body was so tense my feet and legs started to cramp. At that moment, I hated my father for all his carelessness and foolishness with money; hated him for what I would have to endure in the next few moments.

Dreaux stepped behind the screen as Potiphar jumped onto the bed and lay next to me. I was on my right side but thought, to show my new husband some small sign of acceptance and accommodation, that I should lie on my back.

"Off! Get off the bed!" Dreaux shouted at the dog. "He's used to sleeping with me."

"I don't really mind, if you..."

"No room for him, too. He's almost as big as you are."

Potiphar reluctantly slid himself off the bed and flopped onto the floor across the bedroom doorway with a thud.

"And so you know," Dreaux continued, "unless you'll be scared or startled, I walk in my sleep. Done it for years. Can't help it... I sleep a troubled sleep and can be very unsettled... just so you know."

"All right," I said.

Dreaux turned out the light and slipped into the bed next to me. He smelled of damp leather and something else: burnt motor oil, I thought. I lay there stiffly and anxiously, awaiting his rough touch and knowing I must somehow welcome it. Moonlight streamed in from the great window across the hallway, extending a cold and ghostly beam across Potiphar's slowly breathing mass and up to the foot of the bed. I lay there for a few moments but Dreaux did not move. After a while, his breathing became deep and rhythmical, and I knew he was asleep.

The old Westminster clock in the dining room chimed every fifteen minutes, and I think I heard every chime all the night long. I may have slept for a few minutes at a time.

Just after the clock struck two fifteen, I opened my eyes and saw Potiphar's great face a few inches from mine. He sniffed me and licked my hand, which extended beyond the edge of the mattress. I sat up and patted his nose.

"Go lie down," I whispered to him. "Go on." He lay down where he stood. As I lay my head back down on my pillow, I heard a low, throaty sound growing behind me. I would have otherwise sworn it was the dog, but Potiphar was motionless on the floor in front of me.

As I settled back down, I glanced behind me, and I was startled to see Dreaux sitting on the edge of the bed.

"Are you all right?" I asked. He made no intelligible answer but a sound like a low growl and mumbled something that could have been a word; it could have been "faithless", but I could not make it out. Potiphar raised his head at the sound and looked toward Dreaux. After a moment, Dreaux lay down again and resumed a steady, deep breathing.

After perhaps another hour, I began to feel drowsy. Just as I felt myself drifting off to sleep, Dreaux twitched suddenly. He moaned loudly as if he were in trying to escape some great terror in a nightmare. He sounded as if he were trying to form words, but the only sound he could utter was a series of grunts and stifled screams. I rolled over in the bed to face him and was shaken to see he was looking at me: staring with a glazed and fixed stare, his head still on the pillow, looking through dead, compassionless eyes as though he were looking at me from some other world back into this one. As I watched him, the features of his face seemed to change and move somehow, one displacing another like a film of oil on a puddle, stirred with a stick. It was a grotesque impression. I wanted to not be seeing it, and could scarcely convince myself I *was* seeing it, but I could not turn my eyes away.

He took a deep breath and then exhaled a slow, gurgling sound that gradually, and to my terror, formed itself into one distinguishable and hateful word: "Whore." That word, *that* merciless, despicable word was more frightening and dreaded than any other he could have said, and hearing it terrified me far more than any other would have.

"Dreaux...?" I said. A growl started to gurgle in his throat. "Dreaux!"

I repeated. I could hear Potiphar whimper on the floor behind me, a sound that had anguish and *familiarity* in it. Before I knew I had done it, I jumped out of the bed. I stepped on Potiphar's tail as I did so, and he yelped a little. I grabbed my dressing gown which lay across the foot of the bed and wrapped it around myself. I went out into the hallway and sat on the cold floor in front of the great window. In a moment, Potiphar had joined me and lay on the floor in front of me. I pushed my freezing feet under the great dog's body to warm them. There, so situated, I resolved to spend the rest of the night.

Of course, I didn't sleep at all after that. Dreaux continued to make desperate moaning sounds from time to time, but after a few hours he settled into a peaceful sleep. I sat in the freezing hallway for hours, sobbing occasionally as I considered the life I had married into. I wondered if I had imagined what I had seen in his face. I *must* have imagined it. I started to drift off to sleep just before dawn, but a rooster crowing startled me fully awake. I stood. Potiphar also stood, stretched and yawned. I thought it best to keep myself busy and my mind as occupied as possible. I went back into the bedroom and dressed as quietly as I could. Dreaux slept on, now snoring loudly. I found that I could not make myself look at him.

Dec. 10

Downstairs, I let Potiphar outside and started a fire in the dining room fireplace. The kitchen was very cold, so I lit two burners on the stove to warm the room a little until I decided what to make for breakfast. I put on a pot of coffee, and I found potatoes under the sink and ham in the refrigerator, along with a half chicken and some of the ham and beans.

I was startled when the back door suddenly opened. L'Andre came inside with a basket with five brown eggs in it. He let Potiphar in behind him.

"Oh, you startled me, L'Andre," I said. "And I'm not myself today."

"Sorry Missus," he said. "I gather the eggs of a morning and feed the lifestocks."

"I'll have coffee in a minute. Do you want some?" I sliced off a strip of fat from the ham and tossed it to Potiphar, who ate it in a quick gulp.

"Well, I would, Missus, if you're offering and if Mr. Dreaux don't mind."

"Freezing outside. Too cold even to snow, as my grandmother used to say. You need something to warm you up. Have you had your breakfast?"

"That I have, Missus."

"How long have you been working for Mr. Dreaux, L'Andre?" I poured some coffee into a stoneware mug and handed it to him.

"Long time. Since... 1901. Twenty-one year." He sipped his coffee.

"So you knew Mrs. Dreaux? The first Mrs. Dreaux, I mean?"

"Oh yes. She didn't treat me too bad. Never gave me coffee like you, though. Sickly woman. Nervous and vaporish. Always trying to please him, get his trust."

"Oh? What happened to her? Consumption? My father told me not to ask about her."

"Yeah, that's best." L'Andre looked at me as he had the day before.

"But what happened to her, L'Andre?"

He sipped his coffee again. "They had they quarrels. He said very bad things to her. Thought bad things... that were wrong. She never give him no reason to grieve, in spite of what he thought. His sleepwalking upset her, too. She took a bad fall. Tripped on the hall rug upstairs and fell through the window up there. Twenty-two feet down on her head. Accident. I'm sure..."

"Them hogs and chickens fed, are they?" Dreaux was standing in the dining room doorway.

"As good as done, Mister." L'Andre said. He placed his half-empty coffee cup on the kitchen table and went out the back door.

"Couldn't you let him finish his coffee?" I said.

"Coulda finished it if he wanted to. I didn't tell him to stop. Didn't tell you what I wanted for breakfast either, so how is it you're down here cookin'?"

I was surprised by this question.

"I... wanted to have it ready when you came down. I didn't want to wake you. You seemed to have had a restless night. Watching you last night... reminded me of nightmares I had as a girl, when I thought another world was pressing in on me."

"There is such a place, I think," Dreaux said, "and that may be where I go to for all I know. Last night was no worse than usual. I have nightmares. Prone to nightmares nearly every night. And then sleepwalking, as I told you." He sat at the kitchen table.

"So last night was *normal*? Last night was a *normal* night? I got no rest at all last night."

"You'll adjust yourself to it. You have no other choice, do you?"

I thought about what he said for a moment and decided to change the subject.

"I'm sorry. You don't want ham and eggs? Grits?" I said.

"I do. The point is, you don't make anything but what I tell you to make. You don't guess. We don't have food to waste."

"Of course not. I was never one to waste food. I am very economical."

"Well, you'd better be, or get used to it. Your father said it of you, and I took him at his word, in spite of how he cheated me on that seed corn..."

I cut several slices of ham and put them on to fry. I poured a cup of coffee and sat it in front of him. He sipped it loudly.

"Changed my mind," he said suddenly. "I don't want grits. I want fried potaters. See, if I hadn't told you, we'd be feedin' them grits to the hogs. And that half chicken in the refrigerator? That's what I want for dinner."

I took two red potatoes from under the sink and started to slice them.

"So, you have restless nights... often?" I said.

"Most nights," he sipped his coffee. "I dread to sleep. If I didn't have to, I wouldn't. It's a fearful place I go to. A black place, fearful and un-Christian. Dark forces I must resist. You're my wife now, I figure you should know."

I was torn between asking him more about these night terrors and doubt as to whether I wanted to know more. He seemed to have said all about it he intended to. I put the potato slices in the skillet with the ham. Potiphar lay at my feet, hoping for more scraps.

"I didn't tell you," Dreaux said, "L'Andre and me will be gone today... until tomorrow. You're by yourself tonight."

"Gone?"

"Have to take the wagon to Bonne Terre to pick up the new fan mill. It's Belcher and Taylor, so they only ship to Dodson's in Bonne Terre around here. Too far to make it back tonight. Too expensive to have them bring it here."

"I'm going to be here alone? If you had a truck... why don't you have a truck?"

"A team works as well for most things. You leave that to me. That's my business. And I heard you and L'Andre talking about Mrs. Dreaux. Don't ask him about her again, you hear me?"

"I do." I said.

After breakfast, Dreaux wrapped his wool scarf around his neck, put on his heavy coat and met L'Andre outside the barn. L'Andre had hitched the team to the wagon. Through the door, I could hear Dreaux speaking harshly to L'Andre: "I told you never to speak to anyone about Adele," he said. "I won't tell you again."

The two of them climbed onto the wagon and slowly drove off.

I felt both relief and apprehension watching my new husband drive away. I was glad to not feel his presence nearby and the attendant duty to defer to him and make conversation with him, but I also felt very sequestered and isolated from family and friends out here alone on a frozen hillside above the River Aux Vases.

I cleared away the dishes and cleaned the kitchen. As I finished drying Dreaux's plate, I heard the sound of a horse snorting: the sound seemed to come from just inside the tree line at the north edge of the large, frost-covered yard. Looking out the window over the sink I could see nothing unusual in the direction of the sound, except a group of crows who flew suddenly out of their cover among some oak trees as if they had been disturbed. I checked the back door to make sure it was locked, though Potiphar showed no sign of agitation.

I went into the front room and locked the door. I looked out the north window toward the trees. I again saw nothing unusual: the crows were settling back onto their branches. I climbed the stairs with Potiphar at my side. In my bedroom, I stoked the fire in the stove and made the bed. When Potiphar jumped upon it and lay down, I smiled at him and didn't object. Sitting at my vanity, I looked at my image in the mirror: I saw a face young and not unattractive. I thought how whatever wit, charms and allure I briefly have in this short life are given to a joyless old man.

Again, I heard, or thought I heard, the snorting of a horse. A stab of fear struck my stomach. Potiphar seemed to take notice too. He sat up and muffled a bark. I hurried out to the window at the north end of the hallway, and there across the cold expanse, I saw Theophile, my former fiancé. Theophile, leading his old dray horse toward the house!

I hurried down the stairs and to the back door. I threw it open and there he stood, the man who, since we were both thirteen, I had promised to spend my life with.

He smiled a little smile at me and then seemed to deliberately lose it. I smiled at him and fought an urge to embrace him.

"What are you doing here?" I said. "I didn't know if I would see you again!" Potiphar sniffed Theophile's hand but made no sign of aggression toward him.

"I didn't know either," Theophile said. "I didn't know if I wanted to see you again, but..."

"I hope you have tried to understand this. It was for my father. I don't know what else I could have done." I looked up the road Dreaux had taken a few minutes before.

"He's gone," Theophile said. "I watched him go."

"You're frozen. Tie your horse there and come in."

We stepped into the kitchen.

"There is still coffee left from breakfast," I said. "Sit and I will get you some."

"Thank you," Theophile nodded, and sat at the kitchen table. "I have been out there for hours. Watching for Dreaux to leave. Your husband."

"But... why?" I placed a cup of coffee in front of him.

"His man, L'Andre, told Deni at Nixon's that they were going to pick up machinery in Bonne Terre today."

"Yes?"

"I hated you for marrying that old man!" He sipped his coffee. "Hated you. But I know why you did it. For your father... to lose everything twice in a lifetime would be such a disgrace. Your brother told me he was at the end of his rope. But all of yesterday I thought about it. I can't stand the thought of you... with him."

"He didn't touch me, if that's what's on your mind."

"He will. He'll get around to it."

"I don't know." I poured myself a cup of coffee. "I think... he may just want someone else in the house with him. I sense something about him. A *terror* of something. But if I'm wrong, he is my legal husband."

I sat across from Theophile at the table. "You know I loved you. I do love you. I just wanted you to understand why I had to do this."

"Yes, yes."

I sipped my coffee. "It was a terrible thing for me to think about... this marriage. But I did it, and so far, I am a wife in name only. It's as bad... or worse than I expected. He is a sleepwalker. He scared the life out of me last night, walking around like a dead person. And I guess my eyes were playing tricks on me... anyway... He talked in his sleep, too. He said hateful things. It's wrong to think about it like this, but facts are facts. The fact is, he's an old man. How long can he last? It isn't bad to say that; it's only the truth. He must know I don't love him and I think these thoughts. Someday, this property will be mine. Then we can..."

"He's as strong as an ox. I looked up his family in the county records at the courthouse. His father died at ninety-one, his mother at ninety-six. He could live for twenty more years!" Theophile looked at me intently for a moment, then looked away. "If his horse trampled him or the wagon rolled over him... that would speed things up!"

"Well, that's neither here nor there, is it? Nothing like that is likely to happen."

"Maybe not likely," he looked at me again, "but they *could* happen, or something like them. He could take a fall down the stairs sleepwalking some night. It depends on how much we want to be together, I suppose...?"

I couldn't believe what I was hearing. "This isn't you talking," I said. "I would have never expected to hear such talk from you. You don't mean what you're saying."

"I do mean it. Our lives were planned. Everything was set before Dreaux came along. He's not going to get in my way... in *our* way."

"This is nonsense! Are you talking about *killing* him? You would kill him to get him out of the way?"

"If it's necessary. I would do whatever is necessary."

"And how would we live with that? How could we live a life together based on something so despicable?"

Theophile looked at me in a way that I can only describe as terrifying.

"There is nothing so terrible to me as the thought of you... with him. Anything else is unimportant."

"I think you should go now. Go home and think about what you are saying. I won't be a party to any such thing."

Theophile's horse snorted outside. Then immediately, another horse snorted. As I moved to look out the back window the door was thrown open. Dreaux burst into the room holding a large mechanic's wrench.

"You're your father's daughter, all right!" he screamed at me. "I knew you'd be up to something like this before long!"

"She's up to nothing at all, old man!" Theophile stood.

"I heard your horse as we pulled away," Dreaux said. "I knew it must be you waiting for your chance to make a fool out of me! And you!" He looked at me hatefully. "Ready to betray the one who saved your family! Now I know what you're made of!" He lunged at me, but Theophile threw his arms around him and the two of them crashed into the wall. Dreaux dropped the wrench and Theophile grabbed it.

"Stop this!" I screamed. "I didn't invite him here."

"No, she didn't," Theophile said. "I watched for you to go, then I surprised her. I just wanted to talk to her. She was my fiancée for two years, until you bought her!"

Dreaux got to his feet. He grabbed the handle of an iron skillet I had left on the stove and swung it wildly at Theophile, striking a glancing blow on his ear and cheek. Theophile fell into the corner. Dreaux ran into the front room and returned with an old single-shot shotgun. He leveled it at Theophile.

"I'm in my rights to shoot you," Dreaux said. "Get out of my house!"

Theophile struggled to get to his feet. His ear was bleeding profusely.

"You're gonna wish you had killed me old man," Theophile said. "I'll be watching you. If you mistreat her... you'll wish you'd killed me." He made his way unsteadily out the back door.

"He only came here to talk to me. We were engaged until my father's setbacks," I said, my voice shaking as I found a cloth and wiped away the blood spatters on the door jamb from Theophile's injury. My feelings were a mix of anger and guilt, even though I knew I had nothing to feel guilty about. "I would be married to him now if not for..."

"All the more reason to keep an eye on him," Dreaux interrupted. "I better never see him in this house again. It'll be reckoning for the both of you! I'll kill you before I let you play the whore and make a fool out of me! I'm watching you, missy!"

He returned his shotgun to the front room closet.

"I never thought for a moment you'd trust me." I said.

Dreaux sent L'Andre to Bonne Terre alone to pick up the seed mill. The rest of the day, he was in the barn and the other outbuildings, making room, I guessed, for his new piece of machinery, and scrapping what parts he could from the old one. I swept the floors and dusted, Potiphar patiently following me from room to room. Having had no sleep the night before, I was soon exhausted. In mid-afternoon, I stoked up the fires upstairs and down and took the half chicken from the refrigerator and prepared it to roast.

At four o'clock, Dreaux came inside and drank a straight shot of whiskey from a bottle he kept in a cabinet next to the stove. His dinner was ready by then.

After dinner, Dreaux stoked the fire in the front room and removed his Bible from the sideboard in the dining room. He returned to his chair by the fire and opened the Bible. "I have to sit up tonight," he said. "It would be bad for me to sleep after what happened today. Bad for you, too."

"Bad for me?"

"I would have bad dreams tonight. Worse than usual, and I would act them out. I don't know what would happen. In fact, it will be bad for a few nights, but I can't stay awake forever. For your sake, I... You can sit here a while if you wish. I am up for the night."

All the rest of the evening, I kept to my room. I read some M. R. James and worked on a scarf I am knitting. Potiphar lay across the bed and every so often would raise his head and look at me, then settle back to sleep again. I thought about the first Mrs. Dreaux and wondered if there was anything unsettling to know about her death. Had Dreaux suspected her, too? Had his somnambulism terrified her? Had her death been an accident, as I was told? I went to bed early and, exhausted from my previous night's insomnia, slept soundly all night.

Dec. 11

Dreaux spent the morning fixing an axle on his hay wagon. In the late afternoon, L'Andre returned with the seed mill, and he and Dreaux removed it to the barn and spent an hour or more setting it up and preparing it for use.

As the sun was setting and I was heating up some succotash for supper, I happened to glance at the tree line, a hundred yards to the north. Just at that moment, I saw Theophile step out of the saplings and look toward the barn, then toward the house! In a second, he disappeared into the woods again.

A sense of dread and fear swept over me. I felt weak and unsteady for a few moments. Theophile said he would be watching Dreaux, but I didn't take him at his word. Knowing him as I do, I should have. What was he planning?

Dreaux said very little as he ate his supper. He nodded off a couple of times as we ate, and I knew he would not be able to stay awake another night. After we had eaten, Dreaux went into the front room and I cleaned the kitchen and washed the dishes, keeping an eye on the spot where I had seen Theophile. I saw no sign he was still out there. I thought surely he could only stand to watch in the freezing cold for so long. I hoped he had gone home.

I went up to bed before Dreaux. I changed into my gown and walked to the small bedroom at the end of the hallway. I looked out the north window but still saw no sign of Theophile out in the dark. I remembered his habit, when we were courting, to watch my window from the unlit street until he knew I was safely in bed. In those days it seemed like a protective act, but, as I watched the dark woods, it seemed jealous and compulsive.

I climbed into my cold bed and pulled the quilt up to my face. Potiphar climbed into the bed next to me. He seemed to fall asleep immediately.

"Silly old boy," I smiled. "You know you're not going to be able to stay there!"

I must've fallen asleep as soon as the bed warmed a little. I had a troubling dream of the first Mrs. Dreaux struggling with her husband, my husband, who appeared to be a faceless specter. In a rage, he threw her from the great window in the hallway. She fell on the back of her head and died instantly. I heard Potiphar whimper, off in some indeterminate distance, and was roused a little as he climbed off the bed. I drifted off again.

After a while I became dimly aware of the dark wall in front of me. Then, suddenly, to my great terror, I felt a hand upon my back!

My body went instantly stiff with fear and for a moment I was unable to move at all. In another second, I threw myself from under the quilt onto the floor. Looking back across the bed, I saw Dreaux, his dead, insensate eyes fixed upon me, as he slowly sat up. He made a growling, gurgling sound. Potiphar whimpered in the doorway and arose from the floor. He did not look directly at Dreaux, but looked at me and seemed riven between the instinct to protect me or run away from the corpse-like somnambulist.

Dreaux arose from the bed and stood silently, staring into the darkness for a moment. A sound grew in his throat and resolved itself into that hateful word: "Whore." Suddenly, he crashed his fist down on the tabletop next to his side of the bed, smashing the wash basin and a lamp. A spray of blood spread across the wallpaper in front of him from his wounded arm, but he took no notice of it. He seemed to be transfixed by a murderous and unquenchable rage. Potiphar yelped and cowered against the great window outside our room. I ran to the small bedroom at the end of the hallway and flashed the light switch on and off twice. I didn't know if Theophile was watching, but if he were, he would surely take this as a signal of distress.

In an instant, I realized that by running into the small bedroom, I had cut myself off from the stairway. I turned and looked back toward our room and saw Dreaux, silhouetted against the great window in the moonlight, blocking my only means of escape. Blood dripped from his right arm, and he uttered a low, wet-sounding growl. Slowly, he walked toward me. I retreated into the small bedroom and slammed the door. As I did, I noticed that Dreaux had removed the doorknob, making the door impossible to lock. In that instant, the door crashed open as Dreaux threw himself against it.

"Whore..." he growled.

"Dreaux!" I screamed. "Louis! Wake up!" I tried to push past him, but he grabbed my wrist and held it like a vise. In another second, I heard Potiphar bark, and Dreaux pitched forward violently as the great dog pounced upon him from behind. As Dreaux fell to the floor with Potiphar atop him, the dog tore at his nightshirt, ripping it to shreds. I jumped past Dreaux and ran into the hallway, stopping near the window. Dreaux, by this time, even in his corpse-like state, had found the cane behind the door of the small room and was beating Potiphar savagely with it. The great dog took the blows undeterred and attacked his master again and again. Fearing Dreaux would maim or kill Potiphar, I attacked him from behind, grabbed his shredded nightshirt and pulled him backward, out into the hallway. He turned and faced me, glaring at me with black eyes, still grasping the cane.

I backed away from him and found myself at the window again. At that moment I heard the back door rattling. Someone was trying to force their way through the locked rear door. Theophile!

"Upstairs!" I screamed. "Theophile!"

Dreaux advanced upon me and raised the cane over his head. As I turned to run downstairs, I saw a flash of movement in the hallway as Potiphar once again pounced upon him from behind. Dreaux dropped the cane and I picked it up and struck him across the chest with it. The force of the strike carried both man and dog crashing against and through the great window. I watched dumbstruck as the two fell in an arc which seemed to last for many seconds, to the ground twenty feet below. The cane dropped from my hand and landed next to them.

Potiphar had hit the ground first. I heard him whimper a little, and quiver. Dreaux lay motionless for a moment, then rolled over onto his stomach, a liquid and indistinct form. With some difficulty, the dark form stood. I squinted impotently at the body that should have been Dreaux, but seemed one instant formless, and the next solid and distinct. He grasped the cane which had fallen beside him and began to beat Potiphar across his head and face until the great dog lay still.

"Dreaux... no!" I heard myself saying.

I was aware suddenly of running footsteps, and in an instant Theophile appeared at the northeast corner of the house. He ran toward Dreaux and was upon him before he could turn to face the onslaught. Theophile rammed my husband with his forearms, knocking Dreaux forward and forcing him to drop the cane. Theophile grabbed the cane almost before it hit the ground and, with one sickening blow, resonating like striking a log with an axe handle, crashed it against Dreaux's temple, killing him instantly.

Theophile stood over the two still forms in the moonlight for a moment. He looked silently up at me. He then walked down the gentle embankment to the gravel bar on the River Aux Vases and tossed the cane into the water. It was quickly carried away. He returned up the hill and called up to me:

"A few field stones hereabout. That's what he hit when he fell. I need to get back to town ahead of you. No one can know I was here tonight. You'd better get dressed. You'll have to go see the sheriff."

"Yes," I said.

Theophile quickly disappeared into the darkness.

I returned into my bedroom and sat at my vanity. The room seemed to form anew around me. I needed to get dressed, and then I would have to try to saddle the mule by myself. I had never done it before. The house was silent except for the ticking of the clock on the mantle downstairs, and that one sound seemed irrelevant to the stillness that hung on the freezing walls, furniture and windows of the old house. The house, which was now mine, but somehow angry and hostile. The walls seemed to shrink and the ceiling press down upon me. The fire in the iron stove had long since gone out. My hands and feet were aching with the cold: a cold I had never felt before.

He Knows

Donatien tried to return Mrs. Heuygens' gaze with the same intensity and earnestness she had directed at him for the past twenty minutes, but he found it exhausting and impossible to maintain. For him it was an uncomfortable and uncustomary effort, but for the old woman, it seemed to be her natural way of looking at people when she spoke to them.

"Do you think it odd, Mr. Thibault, for an elderly woman such as I to wish to hire a male companion your age?"

The sunlight glinted off the snow outside. The reflection coming through the large parlor window glared off the old woman's white hair and pale skin, making her nearly glow against the dark expanse of the room behind her. Donatien had never been in the presence of a person older than she, he thought.

"To be honest, Madame, yes, it does seem to me to be a bit unusual." The ornate chair he was sitting in was becoming uncomfortable. He hadn't expected the interview to last as long as it had. He never thought he made a good first impression on people and he was certain the old woman knew about his family's financial misfortunes. He was desperate for work and knew this kind of desperation was often distasteful to the rich.

"I would have thought you would want a woman."

"No, I prefer men. I had a young man helping me with things once, when I first came to Ste. Odile."

Donatien had looked into Mrs. Heuygens' background before coming for his interview. She had been the patroness of the New Phrygians, a prophetic sect that had come to Ste. Odile in 1892 from western New York. She and Miss Montes, the group's onetime leader, were the only two members still alive.

"It isn't fashionable to say so in this day of women's suffrage, but I find men more thorough and aggressive in taking care of business affairs."

Donatien smiled.

"I managed the banking affairs of my father's businesses," he said. "But I couldn't stop him making bad choices, in the end."

"I understand that his failures were not your fault. I think you will suit me very well."

Donatien nodded gratefully. He tried not to physically express his sense of relief.

"You further understand," Mrs. Heuygens went on, "that I expect you to live here? My mind needs stimulation and conversation at this time of life. My dear Vetta, as good a cook and housekeeper as she is, falls far short of providing those."

"Yes Madame, I understood. That will be just what I need now."

A large black cat crossed the carpet in front of the old woman and found a perch in the window next to her. Behind Mrs. Heuygens, a large, nondescript dog watched Donatien from the shadows.

"I do hope you are an animal lover, Donatien," she said.

"Of course," he lied. "I am sure these two will like me just fine."

"I have had the cat since his birth. I named him Azmiel after Miss Montes' late father. The dog is an odd fellow indeed. He was a gift from a Miss Parnell who used to teach at the old girls' academy here. He was in bad condition when she found him, and still was when he came to me. He is a dog of the old Potiphar line, she thought, that goes back to a mastiff owned by an old wild woman who lived in the salt marsh years ago. My French isn't good, but I call him Savoir. Savoir because he knows everything... or seems to!"

"A strange-looking fellow indeed," Donatien said. The dog was probably more than one hundred and thirty pounds, he guessed, and had an oddly round head and short snout. His ears had been nearly cut away entirely, as had his tail. He was exceedingly muscular. His back was unnaturally wide, and he was almost entirely hairless.

"Speaking of which," Vetta said, appearing in the doorway. "Should I walk Savoir now, Missus? He hasn't been outside all morning."

"I need you here to serve, Vetta. Just let him outside."

"Excuse me, Missus, "Vetta frowned, "but you know unleashed dogs are not allotted in Ste. Odile. I either walk him or tie him up outside a while, although it's freezing out there and he won't want to go."

Mrs. Heuygens looked magnanimously at Donatien and smiled.

"The word is *allowed* Vetta, my dear, not *allotted.* Just tie the old boy up outside for a bit. We won't leave him out long."

Savoir would not come when Vetta called him. He sat still, continuing to watch Donatien. Vetta grasped the huge dog's collar and dragged his reluctant mass out the back door. The animal walked haltingly, as if its feet were cut or burned, and the sound the feet made on the wooden floor was a sort of padded clicking, as one would make drumming fingers on a table top through a tablecloth. Out in the back yard, Vetta tied the dog to a wire strung between two elm trees.

Mrs. Heuygens had Vetta show Donatien the room that would be his. It was a turret room on the second floor at the front of the old sandstone house, overlooking Constantinople Street. The room was spacious and bright, despite the dark walnut paneling everywhere, and was furnished with grandiose Eastlake furniture.

"This will do," Donatien nodded.

"Thought you might like it," Vetta said. She grinned at him and held his gaze for a fraction of a second longer than he needed to maintain the persona of innocence he had imbued her with in the past hour. She was tall for a woman, nearly as tall as he was, and maybe a few years older. Her hair was jet black: unnaturally so. He assumed she must dye it. Her skin was fair except for a tiny purple triangle of a birthmark that disappeared into her hair behind her right ear. Mrs. Heuygens had suggested early in her meeting with him that Vetta was slowwitted and coarsely raised by a poor family out toward Lesterton, but dependable and goodhearted.

"Why did you think I would like it?" Donatien felt oddly coy in asking the question.

"I sized you up," Vetta shrugged. "I think you don't have anything now, not a piss-pot nor a window to throw it out of, but that you're used to finer things."

"Yes, that's so."

"I can tell the Missus likes you."

"Yes, I think she does."

"And trusts you already. She trusts me too. I try to be the person she thinks I am. In women, she likes simplicity, so I try to be that..."

Donatien looked at her intently. He could see he had completely misjudged her nature and personality.

"She seemed to think you are rather simpleminded. But you're not simpleminded at all, are you?"

"I know a hawk from a handsaw."

"You have some education, too..."

"Done my share of reading, though my mother was against it. Best for Missus to think I'm uncomplicated. She trusts me more that way. Just so you know. If you keep her trust, she will do very well by you."

"Your secret is safe with me! You're confiding a lot to me pretty quickly, it seems."

"Just laying my cards on the table. We're going to work closely together here. We need to be honest with each other, correct? We both want what's best for the old lady, correct? She has lots of money, but people have been trying to take it from her for years. We need to work together to protect her. We will suffer, too, if she loses everything, if you know what I mean. You'd better get your things and get moved in. And... watch out for those damned pets."

By early evening Donatien had packed two bags of clothes and essential items from his father's house and had settled into his room at Mrs. Heuygens'. For supper, Vetta made a type of potato, celery and turnip soup that Mrs. Heuygens loved, and some coarse bread that the old woman broke up into pieces in her soup. Vetta smiled at Donatien in an artless, innocent way as she served him. He had noticed the smile earlier that afternoon when they talked. All during the meal, Azmiel, the cat, brushed his body against Donatien's legs under the table, and the dog, Savoir, watched him from a front corner of the dining room.

"Mr. Ardenne, my lawyer, will be here tomorrow," Mrs. Heuygens said, turning toward Donatien. "I am making some changes to my will. I would like you to join us."

"Certainly," Donatien nodded. "I was thinking you need to notify your banks in Palmyra and Rochester that I am acting on your behalf. Perhaps Mr. Ardenne can draft something? And we should talk to the Bank of Ste. Odile, too."

"Yes, that should make it official," Mrs. Heuygens smiled.

"The cat is very friendly," Donatien said, pushing the animal away with his foot under the table.

"Almost too friendly sometimes," Mrs Heuygens agreed.

"Always got to get in front of you or between your feets when you're walking," Vetta said, removing Donatien's soup bowl. "Gonna trip somebody and break a neck someday."

"And the dog never takes his eyes off me," Donatien said, returning the dog's relentless gaze. "Savoir! I don't think Savoir likes me."

"He will in time," Mrs. Heuygens smiled weakly. "He was in poor shape when I got him. Cried every night. Sad how some creatures on this earth are chosen by God to suffer, as they are, while others prosper. If you will excuse me, I feel one of my headaches coming on. I think I'll go to bed."

"Do you need help on the stairs, Missus?" Vetta asked.

"No, I'll be fine. Just clear everything away in here. We'll meet with Mr. Ardenne in here tomorrow." Donatien pulled her chair away from the table and helped her stand. She slowly left the dining room. Savoir limped after her.

"What did she mean the dog was in poor shape when she got him?" Donatien helped Vetta stack the remaining plates and bowls.

"Covered with scars and stitches, I'm told, as if he'd been in a horrible accident," Vetta said. "Missus is wrong about him. He's not one of the Potiphar dogs. He was Miss Parnell's, all right, but no one knows where she got him. It was soon after she took up with Dr. Treves. The senior Dr. Treves. Sirach, was his name."

"I've heard of him. Scandal around his work, I remember. Surgeon and... behavioral engineer, he called himself. Isn't that right?"

"That's right. Accused of vivisection but he denied it." Vetta carried a stack of dishes into the kitchen. Donatien followed her. "Almost twenty-five years ago, Treves and Miss Parnell died in a fire at his rooms on Rouen Street. Was big news then. Before my time."

Donatien frowned. "Are you saying Savoir came to Mrs. Heuygens twenty-five years ago? I never heard of a dog that lived anywhere near that long."

"That's what I heard. But you know how people get their facts mixed up? That was never truer than it is here in Ste. Odile. The stories I've been told!"

Mr. Ardenne arrived at ten the next morning and stayed until noon. He was a fussy little bald man with manicured nails and pearl cufflinks. Donatien had the impression that Ardenne was competent and honest, an opinion bolstered by gossip and casual references he had heard of the man over the years.

The meeting exhausted Mrs. Heuygens, and after a light lunch of sliced tomato and cucumber sprinkled with vinegar and oil, she climbed the stairs for a nap. Vetta was clearing away the dishes when Donatien reentered the dining room.

"You know she's leaving you money?" he asked. "A pretty handsome amount, too."

"Yes, she told me so a year ago or more," Vetta said. "Glad she didn't change it. I was a little worried when she called the lawyer in again!"

"Just wanted to update her will. She added a codicil giving me power of attorney. She's leaving me money too. She scarcely knows me!"

"She trusts her feelings and first notions about people. She's sure you will be a trusted manager and companion. She's rewarding you in advance."

"I feel a little odd about it. Seems too much. Too generous. Almost inappropriate."

Donatien's family had struggled with financial setbacks nearly all his life. His sister Seraphica had even married old Louis Dreaux on condition the farmer transfer some of his land to their father who had just suffered another of his business reversals. Donatien knew that his new place in Mrs. Heuygens' circle would be viewed with suspicion by nearly everyone in the town. Things would be worse still if anything happened to the old woman, even a natural death, any time soon after he became the potential recipient of a windfall as a result.

In his room that night, Donatien decided it would be best not to tell his family about his good fortune. He knew his father would view these new circumstances as some possible tool with which he could allay his financial troubles: a loan or advance on his son's inheritance which he would borrow and then never repay. Donatien did not want to embarrass himself by pressing such an issue with his new benefactress. He sat on the edge of his enormous bed and pulled off his shoes. There was a knock at his door. He opened it. Vetta stood in the hallway holding a silver tray. On the tray was a warm scone, a pot of tea and a teacup. Vetta smiled.

"I thought you might want to celebrate a little!" she said.

He took the tray from her and placed it on the night table next to his bed.

"Thank you. I think I do, in fact."

He thought for a moment about inviting her in but let the idea pass. He didn't want that sort of complication just now. Vetta curtsied ironically and turned toward the main staircase. As she did, Donatien saw Savoir sitting in the shadows near the stair rail, watching him.

"Good night, boy," Donatien said, and closed the bedroom door.

It was a little before seven the next morning when the doorbell rang. If he had still been living at home, Duc, Donatien's father's old dog, would have barked at the commotion, but Savoir didn't make a sound.

When he came downstairs, Donatien found a note for him on the pier mirror near the front door. It was from his brother Urbain:

Donatien:

The worst has happened. Our sister, our Seraphica, has been arrested and is accused of murdering her husband! She came into town last night and told the sheriff that Dreaux had fallen out of an upstairs window out at their home. The coroner examined the scene and said the death was suspicious, that Dreaux's injuries were more consistent with bludgeoning rather than a fall. To make things worse, it appears Theophile, so devoted to Seraphica when they were engaged, and heartbroken when she married Dreaux, has suddenly left town this morning. Needless to say, a plot to murder the old man is suspected. Father is despondent because he knows his misadventures brought his daughter to this.

Urbain

Donatien stepped into the parlor and sat on the large sofa near the floor-length windows at the front of the house. Vetta walked breezily into the room. She still seemed to be in the same good mood she had been in the day before.

"Missus will be downstairs soon," she said. "Do you want breakfast?"

Donatien stood. "The note that came for me this morning was bad news. My sister is in trouble. I need to see my father and brother this morning. Will you tell Mrs. Heuygens I will be back this afternoon?"

The Thibault home was a five-minute walk from Mrs. Heuygens' mansion. Donatien saw Urbain watching him approach through the parlor window as he made his way carefully along the snowy sidewalk. Urbain opened the front door for him.

Urbain was a year older than Donatien, a few inches shorter, and just beginning to lose his hair.

"Father's been drinking since three this morning," Urbain said. "He's passed out in his room."

"How's Seraphica?" Donatien said, removing his overcoat.

"In a bad way. She's been denied bail. Flight risk, the judge said. She was having her hallucinations last night and says she doesn't have a clear idea of what actually happened to Dreaux."

"Not that old trouble again," Donatien said. Their sister had suffered from visions and hallucinations since childhood. She had spent many of her adolescent years institutionalized. The brothers moved into the parlor. Donatien warmed himself by the fireplace.

"We should visit her at the jail," he said.

"Yes. I have been this morning already. She'll be happy to see you. You know this case will be tried here in Ste. Odile. Whomever the jurors are, they all know us and our family problems."

"I've thought of that," Donatien said. "We'll need the best lawyer we can find. There's really nobody here in town I would think is up to it."

Urbain pushed a log in the fire with the poker. The fire flared up and sparks rose into the flue. "No, nobody in town is up to it. No one I would trust. Not with a criminal case like this. We'll have to find someone in St. Louis or down in Cape Girardeau. It's going to be expensive. I'll start making telephone calls today."

At first, Donatien thought he would tell Vetta of his family problems but not Mrs. Heuygens. But, of course, gossip would spread across town like plague, and she would find out soon anyway. It seemed better that she hear the story from him.

"I am so sorry to hear this, Donatien!" Mrs. Heuygens sipped her cup of green tea, ignoring the tiny cucumber sandwiches Vetta had prepared for her. Savoir sat in his customary spot a few feet behind the old woman, watching Donatien.

"What a tribulation for your family. Your father in particular!"

"He is distraught," Donatien agreed. He had no stomach for lunch either. A half cup of cold coffee sat in front of him on the dining room table. "I visited my sister this morning. She has suffered from hallucinations, imaginings and hysteria since childhood. She can't make a good account of herself for the events leading up to her husband's death."

"Ah, female hysteria!" Mrs. Heuygens nodded. "I've seen it before. I wondered if Miss Montes suffered from it back when I first knew of her visions. She convinced me that wasn't the case, but that sort of female malady is why I prefer the company and stewardship of men."

Donatien's attention wandered over Mrs. Heuygens' shoulder to Savoir sitting vigilantly behind her. In the shadows, the great dog's face seemed to be changing, oddly molding itself into a scowling sort of expression. The impression must be a trick of the light and his own personal distress, Donatien thought.

"You will need time to sort all of this out," Mrs. Heuygens continued. "Take whatever time you need during the day. And you'll need a decent trial lawyer, not the fussy notaries we have here in town. There is a Mr. Purviance in St. Louis who has served me very well in the past. Increase Drinker Purviance. Best man for this sort of thing. I'll write him today. He's in the Mercantile Building in St. Louis, a floor below that wonderful library they have. Have you seen it?"

Donatien was speechless for a moment. He was moved by the willingness of his benefactress to intervene but concerned about the expense of hiring an attorney a wealthy woman considered "the best". He thought of mentioning this, but decided against it.

"Madame, thank you so much," he said. "My family would be grateful for your interest in our problem. I am embarrassed to mention it to you but grateful to find you so understanding and sympathetic."

"Did you think I wouldn't be?"

"No... it's just you're bit of a mystery in town. Thought to be above the fray, removed from the concerns of ordinary people, like many who have your resources are. But you're not really like that at all, are you?"

A sense of gratitude for unexpected magnanimity washed over him. He rose from his chair more suddenly and quickly than normal. He heard something like a growl and a blur of violent motion and then felt the devastating force of the great hairless dog crashing against him. He fell backward against a pedestal holding a Chinese vase in the bay window just behind his chair. The vase crashed to the floor, and Donatien lay flat on his back, pinned by the smothering and sinuous weight of the snarling dog. Donatien knew he dared not move until Mrs. Heuygens or Vetta removed the animal.

By evening, Donatien's left shoulder was swollen and showed extensive bruising. He thought his collarbone might be fractured, but decided he would see how it felt in a few days' time before seeing a doctor. He settled himself carefully onto his bed. He asked himself: why would Mrs. Heuygens keep a pet like Savoir? An ugly, hulking, and unpredictable brute? Surely, he was much more than she needed for protection. She was safe enough in a small town like Ste. Odile, so why would she think a dangerous guard animal was necessary?

The longer he lay in bed trying to get comfortable, the more painful his shoulder became. And he started to feel angry. "What is she afraid of?" he mumbled. "Why would she need an animal like *that*?"

There was a faint knock on the door and Vetta stepped in.

"Are you all right? Would you like some more aspirin or a compress?"

"Yes. The pain is getting worse."

"I really think you should see the doctor. Dr. Isambard has an X-ray machine now. First one in the county. He can tell if you have any broken bones."

"That dog is watching me all the time," he snapped. "Why does she keep an animal like that?"

"I only know that Miss Parnell was the Missus' greatest friend in the world. When Miss Parnell asked her to care for Savoir, she looked at it as a sacred duty. Miss Parnell had some special attachment to him, as had the old Dr. Treves, too."

"But nobody knows where the dog came from?"

"Because of his size, Missus assumed he was one of the Potiphar dogs, but I know that's not true."

"He moves so oddly, and the look in his eyes when he's watching me... and he's always watching me."

When the mantel clock in the parlor struck one, Donatien was still awake in his bed. He shifted himself carefully and painfully to his right side, and suddenly his exhaustion was irresistible, and he drifted off to sleep. He dreamt of himself and Seraphica as children floating paper boats in the River Auxvasses and catching tadpoles in the springtime.

At 1:45, the chiming of the clock awakened him. His eyes drifted weakly open just as a huffing, foul breath spread over him. A great, indistinct mass of long teeth behind quivering lips was inches from his face. Dark eyes, like bullet holes in an ancient wall, penetrated deeply into his, surrounded by changing phases of expressions implying rage, violence and no part of credulity. The massive body behind the face seemed to undulate under its bare skin in the darkness. Donatien gasped and sat upright in bed, ignoring the pain that stabbed through his left shoulder.

"Savoir! How did you get in here? Out... out!"

The great dog sniffed the air a few times, slowly turned and walked out into the dark hallway. Donatien struggled out of his bed and locked his door.

Three days later, on Friday morning, a letter arrived for Mrs. Heuygens from St. Louis. Donatien had slept later than usual. He had been in pain most of the night and didn't fall asleep until a few hours before dawn. He intended to spend the morning visiting his father and Seraphica in jail, and trying to find the time to look at Mrs. Heuygens' stock portfolio later in the day.

"I've had a letter from Mr. Purviance this morning," Mrs. Heuygens said as she cracked the soft-boiled egg Vetta had just placed in front of her. I think you'll find it good news. He has agreed to take your sister's case! He'll need a retainer of one thousand dollars, but he said he will postpone other cases he has on his docket to give this one his full attention!"

Donatien glanced at Mrs. Heuygens with a mixture of gratitude and bewilderment. She looked at him as though she were awaiting a response other than the one that seemed obvious to him: how could his family possibly come up with such a sum? After a moment, he nodded awkwardly.

"Thank you, Madame. If I may use the telephone, perhaps I will call Mr. Purviance after I speak with my father and brother."

After breakfast, Mrs. Heuygens returned to her room to read and nap as she did most mornings. Vetta cleared the table while Donatien stared into his coffee cup. He had forgotten to drink the coffee.

"That offer and a quarter will get you into the Prester John Theatre tonight for a double feature," Vetta frowned. She placed Mrs. Heuygens' few dishes in the butler's pantry.

"Yes," Donatien said. "I suppose the Missus has forgotten that my father was a *failure* at all his ventures, not a success. We couldn't put our hands on one thousand dollars in six months' time. I doubt Mr. Purviance would take installment payments."

"You'll have to find someone less expensive."

"I don't think we want to employ a bargain defense lawyer. We need someone like Purviance. If my sister is convicted, the destruction of my family will be complete."

"But what choice do you have?"

Donatien stood. He walked to the large bay window and looked out at the snowy street. "I could never ask the Missus for a loan, but maybe she would give me a sort of advance on the money she is leaving me in her will."

"I don't think she will do that." Vetta sat on the window seat in front of him. "I asked her for an advance once when my mother needed her appendix out, and she wouldn't give it. Told me as generous as she likes to think herself, she isn't a bank. Loaning or advancing money to people makes them shiftless and unmotivated, she told me. Neither of us will get that money until the Missus has passed on."

"So it seems," Donatien said.

He turned from the window toward the front hall to get his overcoat and walk to the jail to visit his sister. Savoir sat just beyond the dining room door. He stared intently at Donatien's eyes as he passed, and never averted his gaze until Donatien stepped out the front door.

Sheriff Beufort allowed Donatien, Urbain, and their father to sit in Seraphica's cell for their visit. Gaston Thibault was sixty years old but looked twenty years older. Seraphica was thin, pale and distracted.

"I've decided to sell the house," Gaston said, settling onto a bench next to the cell wall. "Then we can hire Purviance or some such fellow. It will take someone like that to win a case like this."

"No, don't do that!" Seraphica mumbled.

"The property that came to me through Seraphica's marriage will be tied up for a long time and probably lost," Gaston went on, "under these circumstances."

"The house is worth two or three thousand," Donatien said. "You lose a thousand to the retainer and the rest to finish the trial. Then what? Urbain doesn't have room for you and you can't live with me at Mrs. Heuygens'."

Seraphica's face brightened a little.

"If I'm found not guilty, I will have my property. Dreaux's farm," she said. "Father and I can live there!"

Urbain sat next to his sister on her cot. He put his arm around her.

"The evidence against you is substantial," he said. "I don't think you should expect to live out your life on your dead husband's property. We need to find the best lawyer we can just to save your life."

All afternoon, Mrs. Heuygens sat wrapped in her heaviest shawl in her Eastlake chair in front of the parlor fireplace. Donatien sat on the sofa in front of the large windows and could feel cold air gusting against the back of his neck and head.

"I'm going to need some extra heat source in this big old house other than fireplaces," Mrs. Heuygens complained. Azmiel, the black cat, sat on the back of the Eastlake chair, staring into the fire.

"He's mezmatized by the flames," Vetta said, placing a tea tray on a table near the old woman.

"That's *mesmerized* my dear. So you see Donatien, as much as I would like to help you, it is against my principles to loan or advance money. If I made an exception in your case, hard luck stories would start coming out of the woodwork. I am sorry, young man."

Donatien grimaced a little.

"That's the end of it then," he shrugged.

"Vetta, would you get more logs from the cellar? I want this fire blazing all day. You can remove this tea. I don't want it now. And Donatien, would you fetch my white shawl from my room? It's at the foot of my bed, I think."

Donatien and Vetta nodded. Vetta removed the tea tray from the table, and the two of them moved past Savoir, who was nearly blocking the doorway, back toward the large entry gallery and the main and cellar stairs.

"I'm sorry about all that," Vetta said. She looked deeply into his eyes with a mixture of what seemed to be commiseration and intent. Savoir rose and slowly followed them. "We can both forget about that money so long as the old lady is alive. Best to not think about that anymore."

"I know," he agreed. "Best to be patient. But if I am patient too long, my sister will hang."

Vetta walked toward the kitchen to dispose of the tea tray and Donatien climbed the grand staircase.

It took Donatien a moment to find the white shawl among the pile of other garments at the foot of Mrs. Heuygens' bed. The wind began to howl outside, and gusts of snow clicked against the bedroom windows. He thought he would bring the quilt that was folded on the bed, too, to cover the old woman's lap. He already felt much affection for her. He understood her reasons for denying him an advance. In her position, he would probably do the same.

There was a dull crash downstairs and a thudding, tumbling sound and a faint woman's cry. It sounded like Vetta. He heard footsteps in the downstairs hallway as he ran out the bedroom door.

"Oh, good God!" Mrs. Heuygens cried. "Donatien come quickly! She's fallen down the stairs and she's not moving! Her neck looks broken!"

As he ran down the main staircase, Donatien saw Azmiel sitting indifferently in the parlor doorway, licking his left paw. Around the corner from the main stairs Mrs. Heuygens stood, blocking the cellar door. Savoir sat behind her, watching Donatien's approach.

"She's not moving, she's not moving!" Mrs. Heuygens screamed.

The frail old woman fell against the doorframe and Donatien caught her, fearing she would fall down the stairs, too. He helped her to sit on a carved bench against the rear wall. He looked down the stairs at Vetta's body, crumpled on the cellar floor. Her neck was bent backward at an unnatural angle; there could be no doubt it was broken. Donatien gathered his wits for a few seconds, then started down the stairs.

He heard a huffing sound behind him and absorbed a great crashing force against his back. He felt his head and jaw hit a stair riser as he fell and knew in that oddly dispassionate second that his jaw was broken.

He fell on his twisting arm and it broke, too. The kaleidoscopic turmoil of his tumbling body ended as he landed partially across Vetta's body on his back. He knew he couldn't move. He heard Mrs. Heuygens sobbing weakly on the bench above: "Oh, oh... no!"

Footsteps, soft and drumming, descended the cellar stairs. There was a heavy breathing above and around him. He saw Savoir crouching over him. The creature's eyes looked deeply into Donatien's. They almost conveyed peace, resolve, and satisfaction, even as his long teeth began to materialize behind quavering lips.

As Donatien felt himself fading, his consciousness evaporating into an obliterated place like the streets and hedges and ironwork disappearing under the drifting snow across the old town, he noticed for the first time, the great dog's feet. The toes were longer than they should be. Almost prehensile and curved under. They reminded him of his long-dead mother's hammer toes. The toes spread apart and moved back together in an unnatural way as the animal lifted a paw to touch the dying man. Its eyes, as they always did since Donatien had entered the old woman's house, watched his eyes relentlessly.

"You're not really a dog, are you?" Donatien gasped.

Placide

Testament of E. I. Fitz-Padgett M.D.
"Some personal record is necessary, if just for my own understanding of what has happened."
January 4, 1923, Ste. Odile jail

My argument with Dr. Gilles notwithstanding, I owe much of my success to him. I told Gilles that young Lumley could not tolerate another skin-graft so soon. I told him the shock would kill him, after all he had been through. My warning was ignored, and I warned the Lumley family. When the young man died, Gilles suspended my research. He wanted me out of his sight.

Still, Gilles had supported me up to that point. The team he had assembled were mostly Englishmen, and after the outbreak of the great war, they wanted no part in what they called "German medicine". Early in the conflict before the Americans were drawn in, I had no such qualms. As a surgeon I had become fascinated by Fischer's work in Prussia with purine and purine derivatives when I recognized their possible surgical application for transplantations.

After much work and experimentation, I came to understand that attempts at transplantations, few as they were, nearly always failed, probably because the body's own defensive biological chemistry rejected the introduced tissue. In the last two years of my medical training at Carthesian University, I became preoccupied with the possibility that purine derivatives could be made to stop the body's processes of protecting itself from this foreign matter. The university supported my research with a small stipend which also allowed Placide and I to get married and live in a tiny flat near my laboratories. After another year, just as my funds ran out, Dr. Gilles heard of my researches and invited me to England to continue them and aid him in his work to restore the limbs and visages of maimed soldiers at his clinic in London. Gilles funded my work for another year until our quarrel. Since then, I believe I have proven in my own life, out of desperation and necessity, that the derivative I have developed works. There remains only to publish the results, which I will do if I am allowed to save my wife's life, and am satisfied that she will survive, return to health, and have a normal life again. There is also the question of whether the state will allow me to live long enough to collect and write my findings.

Placide. My wife. She was always placid, indeed, serene as the famous *L'Inconnue de la Seine,* the tranquil, smiling girl pulled from the river in Paris forty years ago, whose death mask is visible in every Bohemian salon in Europe these days.

Placide and I had known each other since we were children in Ste. Odile. As a little girl, I first saw her as delicate and in need of protection, but I soon found that though timid and soft-spoken, she had strength and qualities of perseverance I lacked. Before I turned fifteen, I knew I both loved and admired her.

Although her father was a mechanic on the riverboats and was up the Mississippi and Ohio most of the year, Placide had never been more than ten miles from home when she married me and moved with me to St. Louis. This move was a great trial for her. The move to England was infinitely more daunting for her, being so far from home, but she did it, for my sake. And I would have given up my work a hundred times over, if not for her encouragement and belief in me. Even as I abandoned my surgery and focused on my researches, even as our fortunes declined and we were forced to move to that crumbling farmhouse so far from town, she never complained.

It was in early March that she fell ill.

I brought her into town to see my friend Treves, whose surgical skills were more actively engaged than mine. He found cancer in her spleen and removed the organ. Treves and I agreed that Placide could live a reasonably normal life without the spleen, as patients in his care have done before, but he warned that we should be aware that her cancer could reappear in other organs. In June, she became seriously ill a second time. By then, our automobile had broken down again, this time irreparably. We had no telephone, and I had no means of quickly getting her back into town, or to the hospital in Bonne Terre. Her pain was so severe, and she seemed to be declining so quickly, that I decided I would have to treat her myself rather than risk delay. I thought there might be some intermediate action I could take until I could get her to Treves' surgery.

"I'm worried, very worried at how quickly this is overtaking you," I told her that morning. "If only there were a car nearby I could borrow, or if I could contact Treves. You need immediate care."

"Eddie, you don't seem to know how skilled you are." She was covered in perspiration, her voice weak and breathless. "Do what needs to be done. *You* do it!"

I was brought nearly to tears by her calm acceptance and complete trust in me. I made of our dining room an operating theater. I made her as comfortable as I could on the table, I washed her, prepared my few instruments and etherized her.

As soon as I opened her, I could see an irritation and discoloration on her pancreas. At the right edge I found a tumor, aggressive and widespread. It was mostly hidden behind her stomach, so Treves had missed it when he operated three months before. No part of the organ could be saved, but she could not survive long without it. I considered what I could do.

There was no doubt the organ must come out. She would otherwise have weeks to live. On the other hand, to remove it would reduce her lifespan to mere days. I felt myself becoming dizzy as my breathing quickened and a sense of panic and dread came over me. I tried to calm myself. I listened to Placide's shallow breathing for a few moments. At length, I stood and wrapped one of my scalpels in a sterile cloth. I went into the kitchen, found a shallow metal pan in a cupboard, and chipped some ice from the block in our icebox into it. Back in the dining room, I opened the bottom drawer of the sideboard and removed my Webley revolver.

I carried these items to the barn behind our house and placed them on the clean table Placide used to sort eggs. Our two sows and boar were inside the barn sheltering from the cold. I coaxed Maggie, the hundred-pounder, out of the pen with a handful of corn. She followed me to the sorting table. As she ate the kernels I scattered on the ground in front of her, I took up the Webley and put a bullet in her skull. She dropped like a seed bag falling off a truck.

The other hogs squealed in distress and shock as I opened Maggie's abdomen and removed the pancreas as quickly and cleanly as I could. I placed it in the ice and returned to the house.

For the previous year, I have always kept a quantity of my purine derivative on hand and chilled for preservation, as well as a few items of my now unused surgical gear. I wired a bottle of the purine to the lamp over the dining table and set up a drip through a needle into Placide's arm. I waited another hour, giving the medicine time to work its way through her body.

Then, as quickly as I could, I removed her diseased pancreas and replaced it with the harvested one. I closed her wound, but not completely. I resolved to keep her sedated for a few days at least, to watch the progress of the new organ.

By evening, her temperature had begun to slowly rise. Her heartbeat was strong and her breathing regular. But as the sun was setting, her body temperature had risen to 101 degrees Fahrenheit. Fortunately, this did not get worse overnight. Sometime after five a.m. I dozed off.

After a short nap, I awoke suddenly. I checked Placide's temperature, and it had risen two more degrees. She was covered with perspiration and her breathing was shallow and labored. Over the next two hours, her breathing weakened further, and her temperature slightly increased. By late in the morning, I decided to reopen her wound and look at the organ.

I snipped my crude sutures and gained access to the transplant. All the tissue surrounding it seemed inflamed and irritated. The pancreas itself had begun to discolor; it was quickly turning a dark, brown shade interspersed with even darker spots throughout. Placide's body was rejecting it.

I collapsed onto a dining chair, and my emotions overcame me as I realized I could not preserve my wife's life. I sobbed uncontrollably for many minutes thinking about the loss of her. I thought of how the small pleasures she loved would end, and how empty life would be, how forlorn and lost I would be if I was unable to save her.

I did not move from my chair for a long time, perhaps an hour. The world seemed so bleak and empty of purpose, I did not know if I could convince myself to resume my active participation in it.

After a while, I was startled by a knock at my back door. The visitor knocked for several minutes before I understood that I was not imagining this intrusion as some sort of inner mechanism to rescue myself from the moment. I stood, walked into the kitchen, and opened the door.

Old Kraft the ragpicker stood trembling in the cold on the back step. Otto Kraft, who pushed his ramshackle wooden cart around town picking through trash for metal to salvage and sharpened knives for five cents per piece. He nodded painfully.

"Good morning Dr. Fitz-Padgett," he said, with the slightest trace of his old Bavarian accent still discernable. "Missus needing any knives sharpened today? Or you have some old copper or brass scrap you need removing?"

I didn't realize, at first, what the old man had said. My mind was in some way blocking his words, his presence on my step, and at that moment, his humanity. I stepped aside and he interpreted this as an invitation to enter my house.

"I think we do have knives to sharpen," I said after a moment. Our old butcher knife was in the sink. As Kraft walked past me to warm himself at the wood stove near the dining room, I took up the long knife and plunged it into the old man's skull. There was not the slightest bit of emotion or doubt in the act, and not a second of thought in the choice to do it. Kraft fell to the floor as blood spilled from the back of his head. He sighed a gurgled sigh and died.

I rolled him onto his back and opened his coat and shirt. His body was filthy. I washed his abdomen with a sponge, then washed it again with a clean cloth soaked in alcohol. I pulled on my surgical gloves and returned to the dining room. Placide was still breathing shallowly. I found a scalpel and returned to the kitchen. In no more than two minutes' time, I had removed the old man's pancreas. I rushed it into the dining room and quickly sutured it into my wife's body.

When this was completed, I sat on my dining chair and watched her there for many minutes. Only then did I consider the enormity of what I had done. A great sense of shame and fear swept over me, but at length the fact implanted itself in my brain that my choice was between letting my wife die or ending the difficult life of a forgotten old man. I decided I had done what had to be done.

Placide's breathing seemed to be getting stronger, and the purine drip was working well. I returned to the kitchen and dragged Kraft's body out the back door and out to the barn. I removed his clothes and shoes, and then dumped the body into the hog pen. I had seen hogs make short work of a human body during the War. With the ground being frozen, burying the old man would be out of the question for many weeks. I would leave the body in the pen for a few days and incinerate anything that was left.

I took Kraft's clothes out to the fire pit and burned them. Then I returned to the kitchen to clean the blood off the floor, and afterwards burned the rags I'd used. I then pulled Kraft's wooden cart into some dogwoods on the east side of the house so it could not be seen from the road.

As the day wore on, Placide's blood pressure improved, and her temperature dropped two degrees. I expected by evening that she would start to come out of the sedative, but all evening and all night, this did not happen. I looked into her wound and the pancreas appeared normal and healthy. I considered closing the wound permanently, but decided against it. I covered it temporarily with a sterile, damp cloth. Her temperature went up slightly late that night, but by morning was nearly normal.

All day, she did not regain consciousness. By sundown, her temperature had started to rise again. In addition, her abdomen began to appear inflamed. The purine drip was nearly empty, so I replaced it. I decided I should re-examine the organ I had transplanted. It still looked healthy, as if it were being accepted by Placide's body, yet it was apparent, from the look of inflammation on her abdomen, that something was not right. I looked again into her wound, and explored more specifically, the area of the kidneys. On the underside of both, I found spots which had not appeared concerning before. But they had changed.

The despair I had known previously, after the pancreas transplant, did not revisit me. Now I was angry, and determined more than ever, to save my wife's life. I would need more organs, and could not get them without going to town. I was sure Kraft's body had been lifeless and exposed for too long. I needed to get her in to Treves' surgery, and under the benefit of his greater skill. I could not risk another operation under the crude conditions at our home. I needed to somehow get Placide into Ste. Odile.

I retrieved Kraft's wooden cart from the dogwood bushes and emptied the scrap metal and whetstones from it. I pulled it to my kitchen door. I padded the bottom of the cart first with straw, then with several thick blankets. I wrapped my scarf around my neck and pulled on my overcoat, putting my Webley into the pocket. I removed the purine drip from Placide's arm and attached it to an upright post on the cart. Then, wrapping her carefully in our heaviest quilt, I carried her out to the cart and attached the drip.

The cart had two large wheels in back and one small, sturdy one in front. Pushing it through the snow to the road was extremely difficult, nearly impossible. The small hillside leading up to the road was rough, and I was terrified at the thought of upsetting the cart as I crossed it. The county road was not cleared of snow, but passable. There had been enough traffic since the snowfall a few days earlier to leave a few sparse tire tracks, which made my efforts a bit easier.

It was about two and a half miles to town. I doubted I could make it, under the road conditions, in an hour, but I had to try. I did not want to leave my wife exposed to the cold any longer than necessary. After ten minutes of pushing the cart, I was becoming drained and exhausted. I stopped and examined her. Her pulse seemed weaker, her breathing shallow. I felt her shoulder under the quilt but could not objectively tell if she had a raised temperature. Of greater concern, though, was her comatose state. She had not been conscious for days, and the thought began to worm its way through my mind that I may have already lost her forever. If I could get her into Treves' practice, I believed, I depended on the fact that his greater surgical skill could save her life and bring her back from the darkness to me.

I held out hope of encountering a passing vehicle, but the scarce tire tracks on the road suggested that few people were venturing out into the snow. I pulled the quilt covering Placide up to shield her face in the wind. My own face was stinging with the cold.

As I pushed the cart along, I felt myself becoming deeply exhausted in a way that would not be recoverable after a few minutes' rest. I could not afford many brief periods of rest anyway. I knew I had to get Placide to shelter as soon as possible. As my strength drained, it grew increasingly difficult to keep the cart moving straight ahead in the road. The blowing snow kept pushing the front wheel to the right, and I knew I could easily fall into the ditch now hidden from sight under the drifts.

After fifty minutes or so on the road I saw a figure approaching me on foot, coming from the direction of the town. As the figure drew nearer, nondescript in shawls, scarves and overcoats, I recognized Mae Marsh, an old transient woman who had been a familiar face around Ste. Odile for my entire life.

"Fitz-Padgett? Eddie Fitz-Padgett?" she called to me. "What are you a-doin' out on the road on a day like this? What are you a-pushin' there?"

"It's Placide. Trying to get her to town, to see Dr. Treves, as quickly as I can."

The old woman approached me. "Land-O-Goshen, what's happened to her? You can't have her out in weather like this!"

"Got cancer all through her. She's comatose. Won't come out of the ether I gave her. Have to get her in to see Treves. He has a better chance of saving her than I do."

Mae shook her head. "Treves is injured bad. His wife died, and he did something to himself. Injured bad. He ain't a-helpin' nobody these days. Your wife's gonna die too lessen you get her outten this cold. An' if she won't come outten the ether, she's gone. Gone from this world.

Happened to my little brother in the War."

I had not heard the news about Treves' injury or the death of his wife. The fact still remained that whether Treves was there or not, his practice had every piece of equipment, the gas and antiseptic I needed. If I had to break into it, I would. Of course, I still needed two healthy kidneys to transplant.

Mae leaned against the cart for a moment to rest. As she touched it, her expression changed.

"This is old Otto's cart, ain't it?" she said. "Eddie... how did you git aholt of Otto's cart?"

I reached into my coat pocket for my Webley. As I pulled it out, the hammer caught on the top edge of the pocket, and the gun flipped loose from my hand and buried itself in the snowbank. The old woman gasped and screamed a little, and with surprising quickness, hobbled off the opposite side of the road into the woods. By the time I found the revolver in the drift, she was gone.

Another quarter mile or so down the road, I passed three boys playing in the snow in a field just to the east.

"What are you pushin' there?" one of them shouted. I ignored them. As I passed, they started casually throwing snowballs and bits of ice in our direction. I thought shamefully about what I had done to Kraft and had attempted to do to Mae. And I was ashamed, too, to think one of those boys could serve as a donor. Someone's young child. And of course, to harvest one of them would have meant I would have to kill all three of them to stay free long enough to save my wife's life. I had begun to suspect, though, that Mae was right. Placide was gone, brain-dead under the sedative and never coming back to me.

I had started to tremble a little with cold and exertion. When the road became Rouen Street, I knew I was within the city limits. A few more blocks to the east and I would find Treves' surgery.

The streets of the town were mostly quiet and empty. The few people I encountered, housewives, tradesmen, and such, regarded me with some astonishment when they saw the contents of the cart. Fortunately, I was able to push through the streets more easily than the road, and I found Treves' offices quickly. I was drenched in sweat and my strength all but spent as I collapsed against his door.

The door of the practice was locked with a small, handwritten notice reading CLOSED INDEFINITELY nailed to it. Looking through the window, I could see Treves' assistant, Miss Zollhern, working at her medical files inside. I pounded on the door, and the sound startled her. She rose from her desk and opened the door. She was a plump woman of perhaps forty: efficient, humorless, but compassionate, as Treves had described her.

"Oh... it's Dr. Fitz-Padgett, isn't it?" she said.

"Yes, Miss Zollhern. I'm nearly done in. Please... I need to bring my wife inside."

"Goodness, you look frozen! Have you walked here?"

"Yes." I pulled the cart through the front door into the office. "My wife is dying. I'm desperate. She needs surgery at once. Comatose. Cancerous kidneys."

Miss Zollhern uncovered Placide's face and felt her check with the back of her hand. "Oh, my word, she's nearly frozen," she said. "It's a miracle she survived this. She's comatose, you say?"

"Yes." I removed my scarf. "Yes. I had to operate a few days ago at home. Emergency. She has never come out of the ether. I was desperate."

"You know that Dr. Treves is not here?" she rubbed Placide's cheeks lightly to warm them. "Poor man! His own wife died on the table last month despite his best efforts, and he was so full of remorse and rage that he hurt himself. He... he cut himself, and he's in a very bad way. May be blind or nearly so..."

"Yes, I heard something about it. I just need to use this facility, this operating theatre. I will try to save her myself."

Miss Zollhern helped me push the cart into the next room, the anteroom for the operating area. As she bent over Placide, carefully removing the quilt from her, I moved behind her and found a cushion from a chair near the door.

"Thank you so much for your help," I said. I removed my Webley from my coat pocket.

"Poor thing. I hope you got here in time."

"I am so sorry, Miss Zollhern." I fired the gun through the cushion into the back of her head. The cushion muted the sound a little, and down feathers spurted from the fabric. She fell across Placide's legs. I lifted her body with great difficulty and carried her into the operating room, placing her on the steel and porcelain table there.

I removed my overcoat and covered Placide with it. She was barely breathing, but her flesh was warming slightly. As I went back into the operating room to prepare Miss Zollhern's body for the organ extractions, I heard a commotion at the street door. I came back into the ante-room.

Sheriff Beufort and his deputy were standing in the doorway with their revolvers drawn and aimed at me. From where they stood, they could see Miss Zollhern's body on the operating table in the next room. I slowly raised my hands.

"Where is your gun, Doctor?" Beufort asked.

"I dropped it somewhere," I said. My voice was weak. "I might have put it back my coat pocket, I think."

"Mae Marsh told us what happened on the road," Beufort continued, as his deputy handcuffed me. "She got back into town pretty quick for an old lady. She thought you were coming here. I guess you have something to say about why you have Otto Kraft's cart. Mae said you would."

I looked at Placide helplessly. Her color had returned a little. "I didn't know what to do. She'll die if I can't operate. I needed to transplant... she needs... she's comatose."

"Mae said she was brain-dead. We can try to get her to the hospital at Bonne Terre. If she can make it. If you want to keep her alive like that. Anyway, you're under arrest, Doctor. You're not a free man." Beufort said.

"I'd keep her alive under any circumstances. Any circumstances. I'm the only one within twenty miles who has a chance to save her. I need an hour, maybe less."

"You're a murderer. You're not a free man. We can try to get her to Bonne Terre, but it doesn't seem like that's something you'd want for your wife. Doesn't seem worth it..."

"Eddie." There was a slight gasp of air, a weak sigh from the old wooden cart. "Eddie. Eddie." A familiar, loving, and essential whisper: "Eddie, I'm cold."

Saturn Devouring His Son

The House of the Deaf Man
1822

Where is Goya, they ask? Where has the sick old man gone? Where can he go to escape the horrors he has seen? Surely that's why he has gone into seclusion: escape. The horrors will always be with him, so isn't any thought of escape foolishness?

I am here. I found, so close to Madrid, a perfect hermitage. The glittering river Manzanares and above it, this solitary retreat. The House of the Deaf Man. Ha! The Deaf Man! Such a fitting name for my house. I am not the deaf man for whom this house is named, but I am deaf, deaf as a turnip, as deaf as if I lived encased in a block of ice. I do live in a block of ice, in a way. And so, I am isolated. It is said that a man alone devours himself. So be it. It is what I choose, to be here, hidden away from priests, kings, soldiers, and monsters. Only the monsters are still able to find me.

Midnight, or nearly. I should have mixed more umber today. I will mix more tomorrow. This picture will take much umber, for it is all darkness. Plenty of ultramarine, but without umber, there will be inadequate blackness, and no amount of blackness will be too much. The lamplight and candlelight are dim, and the colors as I paint them tonight are only true to this feeble light, this dimness. In the sunlight tomorrow, they will have a different character. Such is truth!

Sometimes I think the paint is its own master. It does what it will. The grim aspect of these pictures surprises even me, as if they call themselves into existence. Caprice and invention at work. These are the first expressions of the hand, the sensibility. Caprice and invention. Whatever comes immediately is the truest intention of the soul. That is what I am after now, and with these private pictures, I give this free reign. No more mendacious duchesses or stupid kings will I paint. These are mine alone, and a means by which I know myself.

What is mine alone is not for the world. No one wanted *Caprichios* except a few decadent nobles... ha, ha! Witches, monsters, the sleep of reason. The nobles can ruminate idly about these forbidden things at dinner parties, but to the bourgeois, they are too close at hand. They see the devil in their misfortunes, and to displease him could bring catastrophe. The *Caprichio*s were too near a reminder of this. And the prints on the War disasters will stay hidden. They teach a lesson (if a country craftsman has a lesson to teach), that no one cares to learn. A hog rooting for potatoes would likely be as moved by these pictures as the carpenters or farmers hereabout. So, they will stay hidden, as will these paintings. Now caprice and invention are all that concern me. These last years belong to no patron. They belong only to me.

"Why aren't your pictures smoother, more finished-looking? They are so rough and crudely-drawn." Maria Luisa said. "You have the example of Tiepolo or Mengs or Bayeu, why don't you follow them?"

The Queen as art critic. I believe I portrayed my opinion of her for all to see in the royal portrait. Oh, those royal portraits! Where can be found the caprice and invention in that profession? Still, the portraits bought this house and allow me to provide for Leocadia and little Rosarito, and my indolent son, should he need it. I am grateful.

So, what invention does this dark picture portend? What is this hemorrhage of my soul? The others I have come to understand. The crowd pictures? The individual transforms when he is swallowed into the crowd and becomes capable of horrors he could not countenance were he on his own. Men beating each other mired in a bog? Civil war writ small. Ignoramuses who will attack a foe rather than save themselves.

But what of this one?

These eyes are wild, but I will make them wilder. A little white lead... there. Bigger, more horrific. Is it fear or insanity I have represented? They are often one and the same. Do these eyes follow me? They seemed to watch the brush approaching just now. It must be exhaustion. I shouldn't paint so late at night, though these pictures are alien to the daylight. I have hoped they won't frighten little Rosarito, but she must learn to live with them, because they must... certainly must, come into being. My soul is at stake!

The sleep of reason. You filthy old Pagan, fearful, superstitious. Gobbling up your own helpless child so he may not grow to usurp you. Are you insane from the unspeakable act you commit, or wild with fear for failing to do it? One horrible alternative versus another. I swear I heard an exhalation from your putrid mouth and smelled briefly a fetid, dead stink of the remnants of other children rotting in your teeth. But who are you?

I never much loved Josefa. It was provident to marry her. As she was Bayeu's sister, it was a good match for me. It opened doors: the tapestry works and royal patronage. For thirty-nine years, she managed my household, bore my children and buried all of them but Xavier, and accepted her life as it was. If I dallied with milkmaids or duchesses, she abided it. If I lived with her or apart from her, she abided it. I wanted to treat her better, but I couldn't. I could never manage to do it. How can someone so complacent be loved? She was the boot-scrape at my back door. Did she ever hate me for it? I can't say. Could she have ever hated me enough to consume me as this antediluvian monster does his son?

No, no, she couldn't hate or fear that much. She had half my flaws, or less, so no...

The body of the decapitated child moved slightly closer to the dripping mouth, didn't it? No, impossible. I should stop for tonight and look at this again in the morning. Helpless child!

When Napoleon claimed to be marching on Portugal and brought his army into Spain, his soldiers were everywhere. Charles was a weak king and Ferdinand his son, evil, so I thought the French were a boon. Reason and enlightenment in Spain, at last! But the people were suspicious and revolted. On the road to Saragossa that summer, the soldiers had preceded us. As we drove past a shepherd's house a few miles from the city, we saw a soldier tear an infant from the arms of its mother. He gave the child to another soldier nearby. The child screamed in abject fear, its arms flailed in confusion and pathetic inability to act in any defensive or self-protective way. So completely was it at the mercy of the violent and inescapable tableaux which was, at that moment, confusing and terrifying it. The soldier dropped the child unceremoniously to the ground and bayonetted it. Its mother, screaming in her emotional agony, was shot by the other soldier, and only then did I see, on a hillock above the shepherd's cottage, the naked bodies of two decapitated and mutilated men nailed to the trunk of a gall oak tree. We drove on—it was Zapater and I—knowing better than to stop and intervene or even seem to have noticed what happened. We passed the cottage quietly, hoping to remain unmolested.

Just past the cottage we saw the genesis of this horrific scene. On the ground, bound to a rail, was the nearly naked corpse of a French soldier. The hands had been cut off and the head bashed in, and a shattered shepherd's crook protruded from the bloody rectum of the carcass.

How may the demons in the military ranks or the demons flailing grain on the hillside be perfected? The question itself is nonsense. Circumstance *makes* cowards and monsters of us all.

I will send for Dr. Arrieta in the morning. I must need a tonic for my nerves because I swear this old monster, as I paint him on the wall, is leering at me. It is *me* you are devouring, isn't it? I am the helpless child devoured by the ordinariness and prevalence of evil. Do what you will! Once you are painted and defined on this wall to see as I wish, in the physical world, you can no longer devour me from within. You will be exorcised! Depicting you is how I disarm you.

Impossible! How can a deaf man hear? I remember what hearing is like, and I swear I hear a grunt, a slurp... wet-sounding as an oaf chewing with his mouth open. Enough for tonight. I must go to bed. I will put out the lamp, and the candle is almost spent. I must find my way carefully to my room.

That dark form against the wall. That must be my cloak and hat. Yes, my cloak and hat on the peg. Could almost be the goat-headed Baphomet, the Great Goat presiding over his profane ceremony. You

I have exorcized, demon. You are on the wall adjacent to Saturn. Depiction has, as I planned, trivialized you so that you cannot be a transforming, ill-defined monster inside me. I have *fixed* your nature and image on that wall.

Yet, I could almost testify that I hear the chanting of the initiated around the Great Goat. They yowl their release from the oppression and injustice of life, of the Church and the Inquisition. Here, in this dark circle of initiates, I have freedom and release, they say. I am allowed the madness of celebration, and at those moments, I am as free as a lunatic strolling naked in an asylum. No judgement, no punishment.

Agh! Rosarito! Again, you have left your wooden cow on the floor for me to trip over. When Leocadia brings you into my room in the morning to wake me, I must scold you, though I hate the thought of it. I will simply remind you to collect your things at the end of the day. We need order to replace chaos in this house.

OH! GOOD GOD ROSARITO! Your wagon! Just around the corner! Another trap for me! I may have broken my kneecap and fractured my shin. Agh! I won't be able to stand for a while. The candle has rolled away... not too close to the drape to start a fire. Good God, that child! What I abide in her! The temperance her sweetness buys. I don't think anything is broken. I'll lie here until I catch my breath then try to stand.

My mind isn't clear. This has shaken me.

It's just a wisp of a smell. It's the smell of Saturn's vile breath I smelled before. In this darkness, I can't locate it, but it had the thrust of exhalation. And sound... the wet sound that should be impossible for me to hear. If I push myself a few inches I can reach the candle. There. Still lit.

Now... what is there to see?

The wild eyes! The body spreading over me! That gray mouth dripping its putrescence! I fixed you to the wall... to devour your son for eternity and be purged from me. I can't get my breath... I must calm myself or my senses will abandon me. You, monster, are pinioned there on the wall now and helpless! You MUST be there. I put you there to be done with you...

I'll see. If I can get on my feet again. Back across the dark room to the wall where I left the monster. My knee, my knee! YES! You are still here, still devouring the innocent that was once Francisco Goya. And your wild eyes, the eyes of a now aged fiend, are back in their place, watching my fear and distress. Fear and distress. They are in your eyes too, and the eyes are familiar. They are aged, and they must be mine... also. It is I who eats the child's carcass, who gorges with that gray mouth wet with contagion.

I will do no more to this picture. It is no exorcism. It is no triumph of invention, but a timorous concession to it. It is not trivialized by its placement on the wall, no. Nor will it ever be so, so long as mothers scream helplessly, and infants, confused and terrified, die in the grass.

Mal Ardents

No, Dad, I'm not going to kill you. I know I threatened to when you threw me out, and there was a time I would have done it, but no more. Whether you deserve it or not, I've decided it's not up to me. That idea, that preoccupation with revenge was destroying me. Forgiving you is just self-preservation. You have to live with the kind of man you were, father and husband, if you have any part of a conscience left.

I know you're in this old cavern of a building somewhere. Scary place. Haunted, Mom used to say, and I can believe it. Odd sounds, the blizzard, the wind howling like it is. I'm going to keep talking to myself, just for the company. Maybe you'll hear me coming.

Dr. Treves knew you were despondent, depressed, and afraid of me. He thought you might go into hiding. I've searched the old house on Mal Ardents Street and your other properties around town. This old orphanage is the last thing you own. Lots of places for you to hide here. This is the last, perfect place for you to hide.

I hear movement downstairs. I know it's you, son. I tried to hide the fact from you that I bought this old building. It was a secret transaction. Didn't want the family to know. But someone is downstairs three floors below me. Who would come out at night in a snowstorm and break into an abandoned building, except for a man with a mission to fulfill? I know it's you, Henry.

This room here, this was the Infirmary, I think. Torn wallpaper, anatomical chart on the wall. Little brown girls being indoctrinated by the nuns, brought here for their scrapes and cuts. Some died of diphtheria, I remember Mom saying, and measles. Academy of St. Perpetua. Then the orphans came, and they changed the name to Phrygia House, but the nuns stayed. Until the Church lost interest in this place and its mission. Nothing here in this room.

This room next door looks kind of official, like an office. Maybe the principal was in this room. The Mother Superior. Are you in here someplace Dad? You'll freeze in this rambling old place. Hasn't been heat or electricity in here for years. No place for an old man as weak and old and sick as you. Weak and old.

Abusive fathers never seem to foresee that timid sons can become angry men. You didn't foresee that, I know. "A man who hates himself will hate anyone who loves him," Mom used to say. But, if I could only tell you, you have nothing to worry about. I *don't* forgive you, on second thought. You don't deserve it. You are just irrelevant and ridiculous now. Old and vulnerable. The time when you were important or fearsome is long past. Self-preservation, like I said, and to show you I'm not the person you are.

I hope you'll give me the chance to explain myself when you find me. If you find me in this labyrinth of a place. Who doesn't make mistakes in this life? Aren't I being punished now? Who has ever committed an offence bad enough to deserve what is happening to me?

Dr. Treves told me everything when I got in town yesterday. With the blizzard, I didn't think I'd make it, but after his telegram, I knew I had to come. He bought his new fluoroscope machine just to study your case. First one in Ste. Odile County. He studied you for months under the machine. He couldn't believe what he saw.

We always thought it was odd there were so many twins in the family. Four sets of twins in the same generation. You were one too, though your twin didn't develop. Not at first. Treves told me that spot on your back, that hair-covered mass was your twin. Somehow it didn't die, and your body didn't absorb it. It was just dormant until eighteen months ago, when it began to grow again. Incredible. Dormant for seventy years, then active and growing. Stealing nutrients and energy and life from you. To his amazement, Treves says it is the twin that is absorbing *you*.

Who has ever suffered so much, Henry? My body is being ripped apart from within, is being replaced by the monster growing inside me. God's punishment for the misery I have caused? It seems so. I will probably die in this tiny, freezing room, hiding from my children. What a coward I am! I should face my accusers and accept whatever comes from the two of you. Instead, I am in hiding with my gun under my pillow, when I should not even defend myself. I would give whatever I have left to have one last peaceful and loving moment with you, son. I would preserve that in my mind for the rest of my days, and it would be all I need. I need that. Is it too much to ask?

This must have been a classroom. I think the snowfall has gotten worse just since I've been here. Just a few more rooms to check on this floor.

Treves asked me a question he said you wouldn't answer for him. He wanted to know about Ida. Poor little Ida. My little sister. What a horrific, short life she had. The doctors in St. Louis recognized the condition immediately: *harlequin ichthyosis*. The thickening, cracking and discoloration of the skin, the blindness as the eyes film over. Her eyelids and mouth turned inside out, the struggling just to breathe. You rejected her. You denied her and left her at this very orphanage to die, so affronted by her condition that you called her a demon, a devil, and you refused even to pay for her care. The nuns could not refuse her. She died after five days. Then you abandoned us.

And yesterday, Treves told me, that the twin growing inside you and replacing your body with its own has this condition, too. The fish mouth, the cracked plates of skin, the bulging, sightless eyes, the suffering: these are what you can expect. You may be there now. I will soon know.

I hear you on the stairs, Henry. The stairs to the second floor. I can hardly see anything now. Just blurs and shapes most of the time. I don't think I will be able to see your face very well if you find me. My eyelids and mouth have turned inside out from the swelling of my skin, as Treves told me they would. My skin is thickened and cracked into plates with wet fissures in between. Yes, your sister had this condition and I hid her away here. I know that walking these halls, she is on your mind now. I reviled myself too much in those days to admit I could produce such a child as little Ida. I couldn't stand the thought of it, so here I am, suffering what she suffered. But as for you, Henry, and also Virginia, my two healthy children, who needed to love me in spite of it... you two and your mother: What can I say to you?

They should tear this old building down soon. Not much more use could be had out of it. It would cost a fortune to make it useable again. I guess Virginia and I will inherit it, unless you've cut us out of your will, Dad. And you probably did that. Even though she's in State care now, I think she will be well someday, after you're dead, and if there's any inheritance to be had, she'll be taken care of. *If.*

You never cared for your family's needs, only your own. You had no use for me in your businesses, so you cast me aside. You get what you can out of a person, even your own children, then you're done with them.

If you're in here someplace you must have a lantern and a kerosene heater, otherwise you'd freeze. I want to find you and get you out of here. Back to our old house. This is no way to die. No, not even for you... Dad. I looked all around outside the building before I broke in. I didn't see any light in any of the windows.

Mom loved this old shambles of a building. Since she grew up just across the street, it sparked her imagination. She wondered about the lives of the girls who were schooled here and, later, about the orphans. She told me once she thought the place was haunted, and there were stories back then that it was. She loved sitting among the old sunken graves where the nuns are buried under the avenue of cypresses. She wanted to be buried there, too. But she wasn't destined to be buried in any hallowed or consecrated ground, was she? Suicides are forbidden. Virginia and I always knew it was your fault. Indirectly. You were long gone by then, but Mom somehow convinced herself that your destructive nature and the collapse of our family were ultimately her responsibility.

I could hear Virginia crying in her room on the night of the funeral, crying so loudly that I think many of the neighbors on Mal Ardents

Street could hear her, too. I helped her understand that you, Dad, are made in such a way that you can feel nothing but disgust for anyone who loves you, just as Mom had said. In some way, Mom herself had forgotten that.

The rest of these rooms look like dormitory rooms. I guess all the classrooms were on the first floor. With all these broken windows and the wind howling through here, I doubt you'd be on this floor.

You're getting closer now. You're on those creaking old oak stairs leading to the third floor. I'm at the north end of the hall if you make it down this far, but my lantern is turned down low and my door is closed. I don't know if I can speak to you when you come. I can see a little better now, a few details. I would love to see your face again, Henry. I would love to make something like a smile at you with this fish mouth of mine: something you recognize as a smile. If you want to kill me, you'll do it, but I will be smiling at you when you do, if you know it or not. If I can't see your face, I'll think of that perfect baby boy you were. Despite how I destroyed my family, I was proud of you all. But even I know that doesn't mean much now. Not to you, and certainly not to Virginia inside her lunatic asylum. A young and vigorous man has the strength to defend his mistakes and shortcomings, to be entrenched in them no matter how wrong they are. An old man who has outlived his time has no such twisted luxury. He is at the mercy of those he has wronged. If I could have one more perfect moment with you, I would preserve it, and that would be all I would need for all the time I have left.

The third floor. You're either up here or nowhere in the building. This is how selfish you are. You hide in this freezing old building to preserve the miserable life you've had. If I were you, I would want it over, want the memories obliterated for good. But not you. You see something to preserve in all this destruction. Something to be preserved at all costs, and I'm not sure why I want to help you.

More dormitories, ghosts in every freezing room, I think. The daughters of slaves, the daughters of displaced Indians, then orphans. Cast-offs from the orphan trains or unloved little monsters like Ida. They all left something behind here, I can feel it.

Nothing in this room. How could children live in these tiny spaces, two or three to a room? Across the hall there; it looks like there might be a light in there.

I think I've found you, old man. Yes, there's a little light flickering. You're in there. I'm not here to hurt you. Yes, I hate you, but I have put it in the past. I will do what I can to comfort you and reassure you and make your last days... easier. You are my father, after all...

You've found me. I can see well enough to see the horror in your eyes at the sight of me. I want to speak to you, but I can't. My fish mouth will no longer make words.

I am the same monster your little sister was. This is my punishment for abandoning her. I can see it in your eyes. But there's something else there, too, thank God. Compassion. From that comes forgiveness. The look in your eye shows me, shows me the kindness in your heart. This is the moment I have prayed for. This is the moment I want to preserve...

This is my gun Henry. If there were any expression possible in my face anymore, you'd see it's not aimed at you from fear. It's love and thankfulness. This moment... to be frozen in love and thankfulness.

Hakudo Maru

When the earth shook, Haru Noda awoke from a dream of his dead son, Kaito. Haru opened his eyes in the dark. He lay on his back, and as he awakened, he knew that the shapes he saw in the gloom were the timbers of his roof, not the ribs of his *wasen,* the boat from which he drew his living. Haru often dreamt of Kaito and the boat since his son had fallen into the ocean two years before and drowned.

Haru stood. He lit his oil lamp. His wife Emi still slept on the mat, snoring peacefully. Their grandson Naoto, a boy of six, slept nearby. He had not moved since he had gone to sleep many hours before. Haru placed his lamp in front of the alcove that held the *Kamidana,* their household shrine. He touched his lips and prayed for the spirits of all things, especially those of Kaito and his wife Amai, who had died giving birth to their grandson. Haru knew his aging eyes were slowly failing him, especially in the dark, so when a web-like mist or miasma seemed to form just above the shrine, he was not sure it was really there. He had seen the mist before in the dark and often prayed it was not the anguished soul of his son. He strained his eyes to see in the darkness, and the mist was gone. Haru thought he heard an angry groan, but it could have been Emi mumbling in her sleep.

"May the spirit of my son find peace and bear no grudge," Haru whispered, "and may his spirit never become *aragami,* seeking revenge for lack of gratitude among the living, for his sacrifice!"

As Haru finished his daily prayer and wondered why he had awoken, the earth shook again, and he remembered. He thought of Admiral Perry of America, who had visited thirty years before and had made such demands on the Emperor and the high lords and that *Namazu,* the great catfish, had risen from the depths of the ocean to cause a *tsunami* to punish the country for conceding to the aggressors. The earth had shaken like this then, Haru remembered. And at that moment, he realized he was hearing a dull roar far out over the ocean, dim now, but growing louder.

Haru knelt at his wife's shoulder and shook her gently.

"Emi, wake up!" he said. "You must wake up. Take Naoto and go up the mountainside. There is a *tsunami* coming!" The old woman roused herself and sat up.

"I have felt tremors," Haru continued, "and heard a roar out at sea." Movement and voices could be heard outside the small house. Other villagers had read the signs too and were waking their neighbors.

The front door opened suddenly and Daichi Ito, a neighbor, stepped in.

"Ah, you're awake," he said, "Everyone felt the quake. We are going up the mountainside before the wave comes!"

"Thanks to you, Daichi," Emi said, rising to her feet. "We will pack now and join you soon." As Daichi closed the door, Emi moved to her grandson still asleep on his mat and shook him gently. "Naoto, wake up!" she said. "Water's coming, we have to go up the mountain!"

The boy groaned and rubbed his eyes. He sat up, confused. "It's still night," he said. The boy yawned and reached for a small wooden steam engine lying nearby which Haru had made for him, based on a drawing they had seen of such a machine in America.

Emi removed a small pack hanging on the rear wall and began filling it with *anpan* buns and dried black bream. She also placed a small jug of water and pouch of salt in the pack, as she had done for fifty years for her husband's midday meal.

Haru moved toward the door. "Get Naoto as high up the mountain as you can," he said. "Fifty *shaku* or more, at least. Go as high as you can go. Impossible to say how high the water will be." He could see the terror in his wife's eyes as she understood what he was telling her.

"You are coming with us!" she said.

"No. You and I cannot move *Hakudo Maru* to high ground in time. We cannot move it up the mountain. We must save the boat, or we're done."

"You're an old man!" Emi screamed. "You cannot..."

"If I don't get the boat to deep water in time, it will be destroyed."

Emi composed herself. Haru could see that she knew he was right. The boat was everything. After the deaths of Kaito and Amai, they had no family. If the boat was lost, they would be elderly beggars in a poor and isolated prefecture with a child to raise.

Haru continued quietly. "If I am not far beyond the breakers and over the deep before the surf is drawn away from the shore... it will be too late. I must go now."

Emi removed the cotton pack she had just filled with food from its peg on the wall. She handed it to him.

"I won't need that," he smiled. "You take it. There may be no food for you here... afterwards." Emi quickly filled a second pack with the same items.

"Take it." She insisted.

Haru kept the two hinoki-wood oars, carved for his father nearly seventy years before, safely hung above the door jamb. He respectfully lifted them from their perch and whispered a prayer to their *kami*: "May these oars serve me well another day, and may they not break or be lost in the storm to come."

Haru's house was nearer the water than most houses in the village. The full moon hung beautifully over the shimmering sea, and from its position, Haru thought it must be four or five hours until dawn. *Hakudo Maru* sat on timber wedges nearby. Haru put the oars inside the boat and began to drag it toward the ominously subdued surf. He could still hear the dull roar out over the ocean. It was louder now than before, and Haru thought about the great wave rolling under the moonlight far out to sea, gaining fearful strength as it approached the shore.

Once in the water, Haru set the oars in the oarlocks, sat in his place on the middle thwart and began to scull the boat toward open water.

"The boat is everything," Haru thought as he pulled the oars. Though it had the gleam and polish of age and use, *Hakudo Maru* was as sound as it had ever been. The planks of the hull, butted together, and the seams sawn through for a perfect fit, had never leaked in over seventy years of use. Kaito would have inherited the boat if he'd lived, and Haru was certain it would have served his son into his old age, as it had served him. Kaito had loved the boat, and still felt the exhilaration of manning it out on the ocean: a feeling that had faded away in Haru over the years.

As his arms weakened and his legs thinned and cramped at too much exertion, Haru's exhilaration had turned to apprehension and mild dread. The dangers of the sea seemed vague to him when he was Kaito's age; now they were foremost in his mind. His son's eagerness and enthusiasm sustained him in their days on the water, Haru found, and sometimes he remembered what it was to possess those feelings, and he was grateful. He had once believed he would work in the boat a few more years until Naoto was of age and could help, then he would pass the *Hakudo Maru* on to his son, and he would take his rest.

It pained Haru's left shoulder to row. When Kaito was alive, he shared the rowing and the two of them could fish with nets and catch red and black bream, pilchard, and others. But these days, alone on the wide sea, his body slowly failing him, Haru only fished with hook and line and hoped he would not snag a yellowtail or some large fish he could not land alone, and have to cut his line away.

Haru watched the shore slowly disappear in the moonlight. A few faint lamplights could be seen making their way carefully up the mountainside. Emi and Naoto would have had time to get some elevation by now. He was comforted that their lives would be saved, but dreaded to think what would become of the village under the wave. If Haru did not survive the night, he prayed that his neighbors would show charity to his widow and grandson.

Naoto had just turned six years old the week before. He had never known his mother, the beautiful Amai, a child herself when the boy was born. He was only four when his father had drowned. He wept for days and would not eat. Emi had always been both mother and grandmother to him, but the loss of his young, loving, and vigorous father damaged him and wounded his spirit. He grieved for months until, slowly, the comfort of habit and routine, and the protection of his grandparents, seemed to heal him.

Haru had always thought the boy would eventually join Kaito on the boat and continue the tradition of his family. Kaito had noticed, however, and Emi agreed, that the child had a love for mechanical things and mathematics. Emi had repeated to her husband many times that if the boy has such an aptitude, it is there for a reason. Their duty to him was to place him in a university in Tokyo, not in a boat on the ocean.

The sea shimmered in the moonlight ahead of the boat, out to the horizon, but was black as pitch and unfathomable on either side. Haru did not like being alone on the water at night. Alone on the night sea, he felt more vulnerable to the terrors of the depths. He hoped to die before he ever saw *Umibozu*, the black, bald sea spirit, or *Isonade*, the great capsizer of boats whose tail is only ever seen above the waves. Some nights the dark ocean seemed alive with spirits and fearsome sea-beasts, monsters he dreaded less actively in the days when Kaito sat with him in the boat.

For another hour, Haru rowed until his shoulder ached and he was certain he was over very deep water. His body trembled from exhaustion, but he knew if he had not rowed out far enough, to a place where the growing wave had not yet built to a great height, he would not be able to row the boat over it, and he would be lost.

The angry voice of the ocean was much louder now. Haru could see the irregular ridge of the wave building at the horizon, glistening in moonlight at its center and tapering off to darkness to the north and south. Now there was nothing to do but head the boat into the coming wave and wait. Haru had no way of knowing, but he felt in his heart, that he was sitting over the spot where Kaito had gone into the water two years before and drowned.

Haru wept. It was evening when it happened. The sun was down. A storm was coming, and the water was getting rough and they had decided to head back to shore. Kaito was pulling in the empty net when a large wave arose suddenly and crashed into the side of the boat, nearly capsizing them. Haru could see a rogue wave building strength behind the first one, and he knew he had to turn the boat prow into the wave or be lost. Haru manned both oars and was bringing the boat about when Kaito stood to get a better grip on the net.

Haru breathed a prayer, "The boat is everything, so may it be saved," as he pulled hard with his right arm and pushed with his left. He saw Kaito go over the gunwale and into the water, but he could not stop maneuvering the boat until it was facing the wave. The wave hit the boat and nearly turned it end over end, but it righted quickly as the wave passed. Haru jumped from his thwart and peered over the gunwale into the dark water. He could see nothing. He stripped down to his *fundoshi* and threw himself into the sea. He saw nothing but darkness beneath the precious boat he had saved. Kaito must have become ensnared in the net and been drawn down in the storm current. He was gone.

Haru watched the swell of the ocean approaching him in the moonlight.

"Forgive me Kaito," he whispered. "You are one of the *Funayuri* spirits lost at sea because I chose wrongly at that moment." He wiped the tears from his eyes. In that instant, a movement caught his attention. At first, he thought it must be a reflection of moonlight on the water, but then he saw it was something else: a faint glow of light under the waves. The light moved under the boat from right to left, then toward the prow, behind him. He had often seen shoals of jellyfish and plankton glowing underwater at night, but this was something different. The light was small, and moved too quickly, almost instantaneously and erratically, to be a shoal of animals.

The light vanished. Haru thought of looking over the gunwale for it but decided he didn't want to see it again. He began to grow fearful. It wasn't the approaching water that frightened him, that was a natural thing he knew and was prepared to face: it was something else. He looked in the cotton pouch Emi had packed for him. His mouth was very dry and as always, she had packed a small clay jug of water for him, along with dried fish, salt and *anpan* buns. As he sipped the cool water and replaced the cork in the jug, he thought he heard a breath being exhaled. He froze as he realized he felt a hand touching his back.

Haru could not move. He knew the boat was drifting and he must bring the prow around to face the oncoming water, but he could not move his arms to do it. He resisted the urge to look behind him. There should be nothing there, but if he was wrong about that, he didn't want to see. The pressure on his back moved upward. It no longer felt like a solid human hand, now it was more supple and formless.

He heard more breathing, and a humming that sounded like the grief-stricken threshold to a wail. Haru saw that the swelling water was almost upon him. He pushed the oars and managed to point the prow of the boat out to sea again.

The boat mounted a swell ten or eleven *shaku* high. There would be several more of those before the big wave passed under him. As the second wave approached, Haru felt the pressure against his back become a tendril that rose to wrap itself around his neck. He could see nothing at all extending over his shoulder and around his neck, but the pressure increased. He wanted to pull it free, but he needed both hands to man the oars. The second wave hit and threw the prow of the boat high enough that it pointed directly at the moon. He needed to row as hard and fast as he could into the coming great wave, or he would have no chance of topping it before it threw the boat over backwards.

Haru gasped for breath. He quickly grabbed at the tendril choking him, but there was nothing for his hands to grasp. He stretched out his neck and tried to fill his lungs with air. Pain stabbed through his back and shoulder as he strained at the oars. He had only a minute or two to head off the growing wave approaching him. He planted his feet against the ribs of the boat and pulled again and again against the creaking oarlock and the straining hinoki-wood oars.

With the choking tendril and the exertion of rowing, Haru felt himself getting lightheaded. He knew he could not pass out before he topped the great wave. The mountain of dark water grew out of the sea behind him, like the monster *Namazu* emerging from the depths. Haru pulled and pulled at the oars until he was certain he could not pull hard and fast enough to top the wave. Then, immediately, he felt the fulcrum of the *Hakudo Maru* shift and fall downward at the prow, righting itself. He had climbed the wave. From where he sat to the horizon, the sea was calm, but behind the boat, toward the shoreline, the great wave roared on and grew in height as it overwhelmed the shallow water.

"May Emi and Naoto be safe," he murmured. "May the village and my neighbors be spared." As he sat upright to stretch his back, he realized that the tendril was no longer around his neck. He rubbed his throat and breathed deeply. "*Onryo*," he said. "The vengeful ghost of my son has..."

Haru's skin prickled, and a stab of fear shot through the core of his body. An armless, unseen force had lifted him off the thwart. No definable appendage grasped him. It was as though his ribcage, his lungs, his neck and head were at war with him, and then, bent on terrifying him, were willing him upward. He was six *shaku* above the boat. Now ten. He was too numbed by fear to think, except that he believed this force meant to drop him in the sea.

The force suddenly released him, and he fell, dropping onto the gunwale and tumbling into the water. He struggled to the surface. His body trembled with exhaustion, and he thought he had broken his shinbone against the gunwale. He flailed against the air and oar, to clamber over the edge and back into the boat.

"Please *Onryo*, please Kaito, let me be..." He fell back into the boat, gasping for breath. He needed to get back to shore as quickly as he could. This was a place of vengeance and anger, and he had to leave it.

As he grasped the edge of the thwart to pull himself up from the floor of the boat, his face arose over the gunwale. There, having arisen from the water, facing him over the edge of the boat no more than the width of a hand from his frozen eyes, was a face as black as the bottom of the ocean must be at that terrifying moment. The head was bald and glistening in the moonlight. The mouth undulated pink and wet. The eyes red-rimmed, fathomless as space and filled with infernal rage.

Haru cried out in anguish and buried his face in his hands. He wept. He knew this spirit meant to keep him here, and that he would never see his wife and grandson again. The sea had calmed greatly, and after many minutes, Haru found the courage to look up. The face was gone. He sat himself on the thwart and considered whether he should even attempt to return to shore or surrender to the will of the spirit. He rubbed his left shin. It was certainly broken. He thought of the villagers who would survive the *tsunami*. The priest would gather them at the shrine on the mountainside and perform *Harae*, the purification which would allow worship and the rebuilding of the village.

Then Haru's mind returned to the night Kaito had died. Grief and shock had filled his heart. He remembered his anguish and his grieving, but he also remembered there had been no purification, no cleansing of the impurity of the tragic death. Kaito had found no peace because Haru himself had failed to provide it.

Haru removed his water jug from the cotton bag and the pouch containing the salt. He poured the remaining water over his hands and shook them dry. He then poured the salt into the palm of his right hand and scattered it over the rear thwart of the boat, where his son had gone over the side.

"Kaito, my son," he said, "through my great and sinful error I have failed you. I failed you in my grief. I was so overcome I did not purify your death, your loss. The anger, unrest and displacement you have known since, is through my great fault. Accept this purification now, and forgive me. I pray to join you soon in that dark world, which we will make bright with our communion and happiness." He touched his lips and wept.

A weight seemed to leave his body, and an oppressive miasma lift from the boat, and the old fisherman's brain. For a moment, all was quiet across the water.

But soon, in the distance toward shore, Haru heard a great crashing of waves. Behind him the sea was still and silent. A pink ribbon of light was just beginning to show at the horizon. He rowed toward shore. If his left shoulder gave out and his broken shin pained him too much, he could wait and just drift in. It would take hours, and by then the timbers and shattered boats and household goods of the destroyed village would be drifting past him before the surf brought it all back to the beach. But he didn't want to wait. However painful it was, he needed to be home. He wanted to see the lanterns and torches coming back down the mountainside, to embrace his wife and grandson again, and offer thanks for their safety. And he wanted to find bricks or timbers to drag his boat onto to protect it from the beetles and worms on the ground and the high tides that would, if he were ever less than vigilant, drag it out to sea.

Zana

Abkhazia, 1890

When Zana could feel in her body that winter was coming, and Genaba would allow her to walk alone to the ice-crusted banks of the Mokva nearby to wash herself, then, more than other times, she thought of the first child. She was a child herself then. Her people, the *Abnauayu*, as Genaba called them, cast her out when they found she couldn't speak and was slow to learn their ways. She was a danger to them if she was difficult to teach or could not warn them of the approach of the men, the Others. They agreed they must abandon her, but not before Ukurt, the leader, mated with her, so that even if she was left behind, she could fulfill her duty as a female to birth more *Abnauayu*.

She would have six more children over the years, as a slave and pet of many masters, including Genaba. The first two died after she washed them in the icy river when she delivered them on the riverbank, and bit through their cords, as her mother had shown her. The next four were taken from her by the Others and raised as their own children.

When Ukurt cast her out, her mother cried and pleaded with him that she had only seen thirteen winters and could not live alone. Ukurt was not moved. He said the girl was backward and a danger to the clan. She was given time to learn the plants and animals she could eat, how to dig a shelter and to avoid the Others, and to vanish into the world to hide herself from them. She learned these things, but much more slowly than other children before her, and Ukurt still said she must go. Then, all that remained was for her to choose her *mahtkm'ai*, her companion to guide her and comfort her in the next life. Zana thought that of course her mother would accompany her and destroy her fears at the moment of her crossing over to that time after her death. But she could not say her mother's name aloud so listeners could hear, so none could repeat the name and make it true.

When Ukurt was certain Zana was pregnant, she was sent away from the *Abnauayu*. She was glad for the infant inside her because she would not be completely alone in the world for the next few years. The dark spirits troubled those pushed from the group more than those who stayed within it. This worried her. She knew she must deliver a healthy baby and do her best to protect and shelter him.

In her body, she felt the winter coming and knew she must move further down the mountain. In the lower hills there were acorns and brown clover and iris bulbs to eat, as well as goats, voles and shrews, when she could catch them. But there were also many of the Others, so she would have to hide herself well and vanish into the world in their presence, as her mother had taught her.

She followed a river that washed down from the high snows. She found a place where the river slowed to a stream and gathered itself into pools full of fish. The mud of the banks was black and gray like her skin, and red flowers dying of the cold on hillsides were the color of the hair on her legs and arms. She knew this meant she should stay here and make this the place of the birth. She dug a hole in the sloping riverbank and decided this would be where she would stay until the child fell into the world.

As her belly grew larger and she felt her power and energy draining into the child, she knew each day she must put herself in the state of *tnak'ashtbet*. This was the place beyond pain which her mother had shown her, a place she must find in her mind to push back against the cold of winter, and where she must go on the day of the birth.

She easily caught fish most days in the pools. She found that voles were easier to catch than shrews or hamsters. One evening, as she was resting in her shelter, a hyena dragged the carcass of a goat to the riverbank in front of her. She startled the hyena and it ran away. She was glad that it was alone.

The goat was one of those kept by the Others. It was small, but the flesh was tender. Zana knew she should not hunt those goats, even though they were easy to catch, because the risk of being seen by the Others was great. But as the child grew heavier inside her and she didn't have the quickness to catch the smaller animals or the energy to catch the larger ones, she knew she must take the risk to keep her strength up for the birth soon to come.

Early the next morning, she swam the icy river and climbed the eastern bank toward the low fields and foothills. She quickly came to an enclosure of logs and mud where many goats were grazing. The day was still: her scent did not carry east in the breeze and warn the goats. She hid herself behind a medlar bush near the enclosure. A female goat and her kid wandered toward her, and in an instant Zana had grabbed the female and broken her neck. The kid bleated, and stood frozen for a moment, then ran toward the opposite end of the pasture and the rest of the herd. As Zana turned away from the pasture, she saw an Other at the far end, herding the goats. Zana watched the goatherd as he noticed the kid running toward him. She saw him look further up the tree line, until his eyes fixed on her. He stood motionless as she disappeared into the shadows.

Back at her shelter in the evening, Zana tore the skin from the goat carcass and ate the raw flesh until she was full. She hung the rest of the meat high in a tree for the next day and hoped a lynx would not find it. Afterward she was exhausted.

She went to sleep as soon as the sun went down and dreamt of the child inside her. She saw him come out of her in the river and climb onto the mud of the bank on his own. His skin was gray as an afterbirth and the hair on his body was fine and red. Because she couldn't speak, he spoke to her with his mind only and asked her if, when he was grown, she would return him to the clan so he could be the father of *Abnauayu*. She called him The Gray Boy, and she knew if she ever returned him to her people, she would have to abandon him there and live the rest of her life alone. She was outcast, and would never be allowed to return to the clan.

She awoke from the dream as water pushed out of her and she knew it was time for The Gray Boy to fall into the world. She walked to the water's edge as the sun was rising. A great rosefinch sang in a pine tree across the river and water could be heard falling over boulders further upstream. Otherwise, there were no sounds. Zana stood ankle-deep in the river. Her stomach contracted powerfully, and she felt movement inside her. Her stomach contracted again, and then, easily and effortlessly, The Gray Boy fell out of her. She caught him and slid him into the cold water.

He looked just as he did in her dream. Proof, as her mother had said, that dreams are true. Tears streamed down her face and she laughed. She laughed again, silently, when he made a little cry and took a breath. He would be able to speak and live with her people if he wanted, even if she could not. This proved she had not passed her curse, her flaws on to her son. Her gladness overwhelmed her.

She sat in the shallow water and washed The Gray Boy. She washed the blood from her thighs and from between them, though the blood continued to seep and stain the water around her. She examined the little pale body. Legs, arms, head, back, and stomach. Everything was perfect. The tiny arms flailed stiffly and uncertainly, fearful in the spoken world. She pressed him against her chest, and he was comforted. She felt drained and weak. She wanted to rest in her shelter. Her breasts hurt and she felt a powerful need to nurse The Gray Boy.

She stood slowly. She was unsteady and trembled a little. The great rosefinch had stopped singing and the sound of the falling water seemed more distant than before. There was another sound now coming through the trees from the east. She realized she had been hearing the sound for a few moments before she recognized it, and it sent a stab of fear through her: dogs.

It was Sergey Ardzinda who captured her: a name she was soon to learn, and a face that would be in her mind for the next forty winters. The dogs were his, and they led his gamekeepers to her. It was Ardzinda's goat Zana had killed, and his goatherd who had seen her the previous day. As the dogs rushed across the river toward her, she could not think what to do to save The Gray Boy. She tried to climb the tree in which she had hung the goat carcass, but her arms were not strong, and her head wasn't clear. She reached weakly for a branch and felt the child slip from her grasp. A large mastiff had him before he reached the ground. Another dog attacked the first and the two fought over the small body. The last she saw of her boy was a tiny gray foot, motionless in the frenzy surrounding it, vanishing back into the world of darkness.

Zana's scream could not escape her body. She dropped from the tree and fell upon the dogs. She snapped a neck and crushed a skull as the pack tore at her, driven wilder by the blood on her thighs. She felt a blow to the back of her head, then another. As her consciousness faded, she saw the goatherd with a cudgel striking her. She grasped a handful of his long hair and ripped out a large circle of his scalp. Two more of the Others beat and screamed at the dogs trying to stop them from tearing her to pieces.

When she awoke, she was in a freezing muddy pit. The one she would know as Ardzinda was looking down at her. The goatherd, with a bloody cloth tied around his head, and the other two who had helped capture her, Ardzinda's gamekeepers, were with him. All but the goatherd were smiling down at her, talking and laughing. Zana had never seen Others this closely. They were small and pale and ugly. Their faces were narrow and pinched, and their teeth discolored. She guessed she must have been more than a head and neck taller than any of them.

Though she still felt the pain of giving birth, she was a little stronger now. The blood had dried on her thighs and she wanted to wash it. She touched her still painful opening and found there was fresh blood newly spread over the dry patches. But there was something else there, too. She had been mated with while she was unconscious. She looked back up at the Others, these men, and wondered which had done it, or if all of them had.

For the first week or more, Zana raged at the Others whenever they would show themselves over the rim of her pit. These men feared her, she could tell. The gamekeeper called Yuri threw food down to her twice a day: hares, ducks and geese, or fish. On the first evening, he threw down a cloth he seemed to want her to cover herself with. She ripped the cloth to shreds. Yuri looked at her differently than the other men. He was older than the rest. He had a long gray beard and a shaved head which he covered in a fur hat most of the time. There was curiosity and familiarity in his glance. And kindness. It seemed as though he alone among the Others had knowledge of the *Abnauayu*.

Many times, Zana heard Yuri talking with Ardzinda in an agitated manner. Sometimes she could see them over the edge of the pit, and though she didn't know their words, she knew their talking was about her. One morning, a few days after the full moon, Yuri tied a rope around the trunk of a pomegranate tree and lowered himself into her pit. She watched in amazement as he came down. She did not expect any of the men to dare to come close to her. At the bottom, Yuri looked at her cautiously. She towered over him. He had a second rope thrown over his shoulder. They looked at each other for a moment, and after he seemed satisfied she was not going to harm him, he approached her and held out his hand. She brushed the back his hand with hers to show that he had nothing to fear from her. He removed the rope from his shoulder and she immediately understood what he meant to tell her. If she would allow herself to be bound, she would be hauled up out of the pit.

She looked into his face for a long while. When she was certain she saw no bad purpose there, she stepped toward him and extended her wrists for him to bind. He smiled at her and quickly tied her wrists, extended the rope to her ankles, then up under her arms. He touched her shoulder and said some words in a soothing manner. Then he called something up to Ardzinda above. Soon the upper end of the rope had been tied to an ox and Zana was slowly hauled up to the edge of the pit.

At the top, four men, including the goatherd she had injured, grabbed her and pinned her to the ground. She struggled and grunted at them for a moment, then lay still. She did not want to be thrown back into the pit.

She lay on the ground and Ardzinda stared down at her. She bared her teeth at him, and he struck her in the jaw with the end of a cudgel. She looked closely into his eyes and saw emptiness there. This was the Other who had caused the death of The Gray Boy. This one was her enemy.

The four men lifted her from the ground and carried her to a strong enclosure of green logs and wattle which looked newly built. Yuri had climbed out of the pit by then. He followed them into the enclosure, and when Ardzinda and the others had laid her on the ground and hurried out, locking a heavy gate behind them, Yuri spoke soothingly to her and cut her bonds. She stood slowly. There was sadness in Yuri's face, and she could sense that he wanted no part of her captivity.

Yuri alone brought her food twice a day. Once more, he brought her a cloth to cover her body with, but she refused to do so.

Soon many Others began coming to Ardzinda's estate just to see her. They sometimes laughed and jeered at her and their children threw rocks and sticks to taunt her. She bared her teeth and growled and barked at them because she could do little else. She saw no way yet to free herself, and she did not want to go back into the pit.

One evening in the spring, Ardzinda brought many men to his estate. It troubled Zana; she could not tell why, that none of the men brought their children or wives this night. The men gathered outside Zana's enclosure and she became afraid. If they meant to harm her, she could kill many of them easily, but then she herself would be killed. Ardzinda's pack of hunting dogs were all loose around the enclosure, barking savagely at her. This was unusual, and it seemed it had been done as some measure of protection for the men gathered around her.

Ardzinda removed a wineskin from his shoulder as Zana had seen him do many times. He had let her taste the wine once and she liked it. He took a small, folded paper from his pocket and from it emptied a powder into the neck of the wineskin. Then, to her surprise, he tossed the skin over the wall of the enclosure. She grabbed the wineskin eagerly and carried it to the sleeping pit she had dug for herself. She uncorked the skin and drank the contents quickly. It was delicious.

Ardzinda soon threw a second skin into the enclosure. As she drank it, the men laughed and joked among themselves. She finished the second skin in a few minutes and realized quickly that she could not stand or keep her balance. A great pain shot through her head and she felt herself toppling over onto the ground.

When she awoke, she was sick and in pain. The sky was gray with the sunrise. She was not in her sleeping pit, but in the middle of the enclosure, and there was blood on her hips and legs. As she sat up, she realized most of the pain she felt was in her inner thighs, and she understood that all those men the night before had mated with her. Her morning food came very late that day, and a goatherd boy brought it, not Yuri. She never saw Yuri again.

In a few weeks, Zana knew she was pregnant again. By summer, Ardzinda was allowing her to leave her enclosure unbound, so long as one of his armed men was nearby and his dogs were tied up.

When the second winter of her captivity came, her child was born on the riverbank, and moments after she washed him in the icy river, he died.

By the next autumn, it seemed that Ardzinda had become bored with Zana, and he gave her to another landowner who removed her further down into the low country. Bagapsh, her new master, was older and kinder than Ardzinda. He treated her well and did not imprison her in an enclosure. He offered her freedom many times, but after a few months living in his fields, she decided that staying among the Others was better than her old life of living alone in the mountains. She knew now she would always live among these men.

Bagapsh allowed Zana to run with him when he hunted deer. One evening, the old man fell from his horse and down a steep hillside as they rode home. Bagapsh died the next morning. A few days later, she was taken away to the lands of another man.

Over the many seasons since she was banished from the *Abnayu*, she lived with many masters and had been moved many times. By the time she became the property of Geneba, she had forgotten much of her early life. She could no longer tell from watching the rivers and the sun where the home of her mother and her people could be found. She knew if she ever changed her mind about living among The Others and decided to run away and return to the mountains, she was not sure if she could find them.

Geneba treated her well and never confined her. She allowed him to mate with her freely and it was he who ordered that her newborn babies be taken from her at birth to save their lives. Genaba's wife and the other women on the estate hated Zana and never allowed her in the big house, but Zana enjoyed roaming the fields and woods with Genaba, hunting deer with him or watching over his cows, sheep and goats.

Zana lost count of how many seasons she lived with Genaba. But as she grew older and was never allowed to see the children she had borne, except at a distance with the peasant women raising them, she thought more of The Gray Boy.

Her body was changing. She noticed she was not as strong as she had been many seasons ago. Her back, arms and legs hurt, and she found it more difficult to put herself in the *tnak'ashtbet*, the place beyond pain. It had grown clear to her, though, that The Gray Boy had become her guide and comfort in the next life, her *mahtkm'ai*. And she had decided she was ready, at last, to be with him.

She had never learned to understand many of the words of the Others. But on an evening late in the fall, when Zana could feel in her body that winter was coming again, she heard Genaba and his wife say the name "Ardzinda" several times. Zana wondered how it was Genaba would know of Ardzinda. At first, she worried that Genaba meant to return her to her old master, but she felt this was not likely. She knew Genaba's estate was her right place and that she was meant to live the rest of her time in the spoken world there.

Ardzinda must be a very old man now. Perhaps he merely wanted to see her again to see if she had prospered under other masters. Or perhaps he felt shame for his treatment of her when she was first captured, and for the brutal death of The Gray Boy. His shame, if he felt it, was meaningless to Zana. His cruelty and brutality remained; they were put into the world by him, put into the lives and memories of many. If he felt regret, to those who suffered, it meant nothing.

Zana started to keep watch on the hillside behind Genaba's gate, hiding herself among the spruces. The hill overlooked the narrow and gated wooden bridge that crossed the Mokva River on Genaba's estate. It had always been her favorite spot in the region, and the river, the trees and the rocky chasms always made her think of the day The Gray Boy was born.

On a cool evening, as she was preparing to walk back to her sleeping pit near the house, she heard dogs barking beyond the crossroads, toward the village of Tkhina. She watched the road for many minutes as the sun went down. After a while, an indistinct figure on horseback appeared on the road: a very old man, it seemed. As the figure grew closer, Zana began to recognize the posture, the fur cap and beard, the greatcoat of the rider. It was Ardzinda. As she watched him a sense of peace came over her. Everything, every moment in her life was in its place as it should be. This moment meant something important and further moments beyond this one would be empty and without meaning.

Some distance behind Ardzinda, Zana saw two more men on horseback following him. The great pack of Ardzinda's hunting dogs followed the two men, fighting and playing among themselves and occasionally nipping at the horses. Zana made her way quickly down the hillside, hidden by the spruces, as Ardzinda crossed the bridge. She did her best to disappear into the world as she came down, and the old man did not see her.

Ardzinda cleared the bridge just as his men and dogs were entering it on the other end. Zana ran from her cover on the hillside and closed the bridge gate behind him, tying it fast with a leather strap. Before Ardzinda could turn, Zana pulled him from his horse onto the ground. The dogs had seen, before their masters, what was happening. They were barking wildly and quickly ran the length of the bridge. They crushed against the gate a few feet from Zana, and she knew in a moment they would be upon her.

Ardzinda, on the ground, looked for a moment into Zana's eyes. It seemed for a second that he meant to smile, but as she stared down at him, she knew he could not mistake the rage and pain in her face. She extended her hand to him. Confused he took it. Before he could move his legs to get onto his feet, she placed her foot against his ribs. Her grip tightened and with a gristly snap, she pulled his arm from its socket and dropped it on the road. He groaned and gasped and fell back to the ground.

The dogs were wild with the smell of blood and one of them had nearly chewed through the leather strap. Zana sat in the road facing them. In a moment, if her spirit was right, she would find her *tnak'ashtbet* and hardly feel the pain to come. And soon after that she would again be united with her beloved Gray Boy, and try to understand, with his help, why she had taken so long to come to him.

The Dark Walk Forward

Lucie told her son he should call the bandaged man Daddy. She told him that this man, this stranger, was his father. The boy had little memory of him, and with the man's whole head wrapped in bandages, there was no face for him to recognize. The boy didn't seem to think it odd that he had no father at home since his mother took such good care of him. He never thought a father was needed. Lucie said this man had gone off to war and been terribly hurt. Burned. She had not spoken much to the child about the man because she never expected to see him alive again. She thought it best. The man survived the War, though his face had been burned away in a battle, burned so badly, the doctors had taken skin from his legs and sewn it onto his face. He had gone through a long recovery in another country.

Now he was home. Daddy.

Though Lucie called the boy Trieste, he knew his real name was Charles, and that he was named after his father. He knew he was four years old, but not like other children. He could not speak like them or play with them. Their noise and energy made him scream, and he could not tell them what was the matter when he screamed, so Lucie kept him away from other children. She moved him far into the country, away from the town of Ste. Odile. She told him she would teach him everything he needed to know herself. He tried to learn numbers and letters as his mother taught him, but he had a hard time remembering them and using them in the way she wanted him to. Especially numbers. He seemed to only be able to see them as things that were oddly alive and able to duplicate or reduce themselves endlessly, not as just marks on paper. He had always loved the old story of the salamander his mother told him, of how it was born from fire and crawled out of burning logs. When his mother wrote "3 + 2" on a paper, Trieste saw five individual salamanders wriggling out of a flame in his head, and he knew the answer to the problem was 5. Lucie slowly understood her son's way of seeing things, and she was patient and full of love for him. Even at four years old, Trieste knew this.

Their small house in the Saline Marsh was their own world apart. They had pullets and geese and a garden, and a big, fighting terrier to keep the foxes away. Trieste named the big dog Rudy Benko, a name that popped into his head the moment he laid his eyes on it, that afternoon when their friend Marie gave him to them.

Their only neighbors lived a long walk north along Saline Creek: Genevieve Gothard the wildcrafter, and her husband Mesmin.

Genevieve had given herbs to Trieste's mother to cure her sadness and others which were meant to calm the boy himself and make him better able to be near other people and learn more easily. None of these remedies seemed to work. But after they had lived in the small house a while, Trieste seemed calmer and he was learning a little better and he noticed his mother became a bit more cheerful. Trieste's duties were to gather the eggs from the chickens every morning and to feed Rudy Benko. He enjoyed doing these things and felt that when he did them, he was adding to his mother's happiness.

Trieste made one friend in the few times he'd attended the Church of the Holy Mandilion in Ste. Odile. Her name was Ady Stauffenberg, and she was one month older than Trieste. Ady's mother, Marie, owned a car, and every few weeks she and Ady would come out to visit them. Ady's calm and patient nature never upset Trieste or made him wish she were gone, and Marie and Lucie were great friends and always had many things to talk about.

Two months before his father was due home, Marie and Ady visited them. The mothers had coffee and toast with preserves in the kitchen while Trieste and Ady sat on the front room floor, cut pictures from magazines, and pasted them onto paper to illustrate stories they invented. It was one of their favorite things to do. They had made four story books illustrated with pictures this way. They were only allowed to make their picture books where their mothers could watch them. Once they had gone into Triste's room and set one of their books on fire. Trieste tried to explain to the mothers that he no longer liked that story book, and since he couldn't stand the idea that it would still be in his home after he no longer wanted it, he needed to burn it. Lucie told him it was the only time she had ever thought of spanking her son.

"He has been in London for many months," Lucie said, refilling Marie's coffee cup. "He's had five surgeries to rebuild his face. He has been under the treatment of a Dr. Gilles. Harold Gilles, who has been treating soldiers with horrible injuries from the war; facial disfigurements, burns, shrapnel injuries, and the like. Charles' face was nearly burned away. Dr. Gilles is experimenting with a procedure where he replaces burned skin with skin taken from other parts of the victim's body. It's called reconstructive surgery, but they never look... the same. In fact, in spite of the surgery, the victims still look quite grotesque, I'm told."

"Those poor men! Who would think a thing like that would work?" Marie said, sipping her coffee. "It almost sounds like the Frankenstein story in real life! Oh, Lucie... I hope that wasn't the wrong thing to say! I say such stupid things sometimes. Charles has written to you?"

"No. He is unable. He has lost sight in one eye and is nearly blind in the other. There is an orderly caring for him, Mr. Hogue, who has written me of Charles' progress. He says Charles is a shattered man, shattered... of course. Unpredictable and full of rage. Mr. Hogue hopes being home and with his family again will be restorative to Charles and

give him peace and make him the man he was before the war. But...
how can that be? Marie, how can Charles ever be a father to Trieste
again? How can he be a father to a child like that?"

The day Trieste's father returned to his family was a very hot August
day. They could hear, above the sound of the cicadas, the car coming
from some distance away, and so Trieste and his mother walked out
into the yard to watch for their visitor. The car was a green sedan with
U.S. GOVERNMENT on the license plate. The car pulled off the road
in front of their cottage and parked on the dry grass of their front yard.
Trieste grabbed his mother's hand and held it tight.

"Is this Daddy?" he whispered to his mother.

"Yes, it's him," she said. "He has suffered very much. We must do
what we can to understand him and make him feel welcome and... at
home."

"But why does he have to come and live with *us*?"

There were two men in khaki military uniforms in the front seat of
the sedan. The driver got out of the car and opened the rear door. The
dark form of another man was visible in the back seat. The other
soldier approached Trieste and his mother. He was carrying a red
folder and a small leather bag. He touched his hat.

"Mrs. Barre? Lucie Barre? I'm Lieutenant March."

"How do you do, Lieutenant. I didn't expect..."

"I'm a liaison of the War Department with the office of the
Supervising Surgeon General of the Public Health Service. As Dr.
Gilles of the British Army performed experimental reconstructive
surgeries on some American service men, the War Department and
the Supervising Surgeon General have agreed to track the physical
healing and psychological progress of these subjects and to keep Dr.
Gilles and his associates informed so that their treatment of future
wounded can be improved. Private Barre... your husband, was one of
the more severe cases and is of great interest to Dr. Gilles and Dr.
Trevellian, the alienist. They felt they were making no new progress
with his mental state, his depression, and that keeping him confined in
a hospital wouldn't be a real test of his ability to re-assimilate back into
his old life. They thought he might do well to be back home with his
family. This is all experimental."

"Experimental!" Lucie said. "But what are we... how are *we* to cure
him? My son is special, unusual. He can't cope with this."

"He is your husband, ma'am. It will do him a world of good to be
with you and your son again," March interrupted. He knelt down and
looked Trieste in the eye. "You're Charles, Jr., are you? You must be
glad to have your daddy home?"

Trieste looked quickly at March and frowned. "I don't know who he
is," he said, and buried his face in his mother's apron. March stood.

"He needs your care and kindness, Mrs. Barre," he said. "He won't
recover without them. Here is his file." He handed Lucie the red file
and leather bag. "Remove his bandages tomorrow and do not reapply

them. In the bag, you'll find morphine and instructions for its use. Also extract of aloe if he needs it. Keep him out of the sun and in a calm state. Don't cook if he is in the kitchen with you. He is terrified of fire, as you would expect. There is a journal in this folder. If you would keep a record of his progress, the Supervising Surgeon General will be in your debt. We need to gather information about these men. It's all new country to us. I'll be back to check on him in a month and bring you fresh supplies. You don't have a telephone?"

"We're not rich, Lieutenant."

The dark figure in the back of the sedan stepped out into the sunlight with the driver's help. Charles had become alarmingly thin and stooped, but seemed taller than when Lucie had last seen him. His head was wrapped in bandages. The driver took his arm and helped him walk slowly toward the house. Trieste broke away from his mother and ran inside.

"He's nearly blind," March whispered. "He has some vision left in his right eye, especially of things directly in front of him." Lucie walked slowly toward her husband.

"Charles," she said, touching his arm, "I never thought we'd see you again."

"Neither did I, Lucie," Charles said. His voice was wet and vague, and his words were barely understandable. Lucie held his arm for a moment. She was uncertain about or unwilling to express any further affection.

The driver handed Lucie a small suitcase.

"We are going to leave you now, Private Barre," March said. "I'll see you in a month. Remember, healing will be slow, and your family wants the best for you. Understand this is difficult for them, too." March and the driver returned to the car and in a moment were out of sight along the dusty road.

Charles made a wheezing sound and swallowed hard. Lucie held his elbow and guided him into the house. At the front porch step, he tripped, and she steadied him. "You know I'm as good as blind?" he snapped at her.

"I'm sorry Charles. I didn't think."

"I'm sorry. That wasn't much of a greeting, was it? Why did you move out here anyway? So far out here away from town?"

"It was best for Trieste. Charles, Jr."

"The boy has to learn to adjust, like I do."

In the front room, Lucie led Charles to his old chair, and he collapsed into it. He exhaled loudly as he sat. Lucie sat opposite him on the sofa. Charles' mouth was not bandaged. His lips were swollen and pink and his teeth looked elongated and discolored.

"Are you hungry?" Lucie said. "Can I get you something to eat?" She stood.

"Just some water. Where's my son? I can't say how much I have missed the both of you."

"He's here. He may need a little time to get used to having you..."

"Where is he?"

Lucie could see Trieste's shadow from where she stood, behind her bedroom door. "Trieste, honey," she said, "Come here. Daddy wants to see you. He missed you."

"His name is Charles. Don't you want to call him by my name?"

"It's his nickname. It's what he's used to. Let's not argue about this now. Let's get him used to having you... to being a family again." Lucie walked quickly across the front room toward her bedroom door. She held her hand out toward Trieste and after a moment he took it. "Come on, son," she said.

Lucie led him into the front room. Trieste pressed firmly against his mother, refusing to look at the strange, bandaged man.

After a moment, Charles spoke:

"You don't remember me, but I'm your father." The words were garbled and indistinct. "Can you look at me?"

Trieste whispered to his mother: "I can't understand what he's saying."

She knelt down beside him. "He said he's your father."

"I *know* he is!"

"You'll be able to understand him better as time goes on," Lucie said. "You have to get used to each other again. It will take time, as Lieutenant March told us."

"I know you don't know what to make of me, especially looking like this," Charles said. "I won't force it. We have time. All the time we need. Right now, all I want to do is rest. Lucie, I want to lie down for a while."

Lucie watched him walk into her bedroom, kick his shoes off and collapse onto her bed. He had chosen the right side, her side to sleep. She went into the kitchen and heated up some succotash for Trieste.

The next morning Lucie cut the bandages off.

Charles had had a restless night and Lucie didn't sleep at all. Their double bed seemed suddenly small to Lucie, and she didn't see how she could ever get accustomed to sleeping with him again. When he touched her shoulder, she flinched and moved a few inches away from him. A few times she felt herself drifting off to sleep, but at those moments he would gasp for breath, or say something about their wedding day or Trieste's birth at Bonne Terre Hospital, and how they loved their new son, loved him even more as they realized the infant didn't respond to them and connect to them as a normal baby should.

In the morning, Charles said he was anxious to get the bandages off, and he insisted that Lucie do it before breakfast. Charles sat at the kitchen table while Lucie rummaged through the kitchen drawers, looking for her scissors.

"Trieste," she said, "where are my scissors? You and Ady were using them..."

Trieste walked silently into the kitchen holding the scissors in his left hand. He was sucking his thumb.

"Oh son," Lucie said, "don't tell me you're sucking your thumb again. You stopped that months ago!"

"Get your thumb out of your mouth!" Charles said. "Are you a baby?"

Trieste ran into the front room and hid behind the sofa.

Lucie carefully placed the scissors blade under the bottom edge of the bandage and began to cut. As she cut an odor of suppuration escaped from underneath. She turned her head away choking and thought she might vomit.

"On with it! Finish it!" Charles demanded.

Lucie slowly continued cutting, holding her breath for long stretches at a time. The interior surface of the bandages was wet and stained pink and she shuddered when her fingers brushed against it. In a few minutes she had cut the saturated cloth completely away.

"Oh, Charles!" she exclaimed, before she knew she had said it.

It was not a face, but a mask of misplaced thigh skin, which looked now like a crust of dry mud spread across missing features with holes for eyes crudely and unevenly punched through. It looked nothing like the face of a natural man, but like a hideous impersonator in a disguise haphazardly put together. The eye-holes were mismatched: the right one small and round and the left one distended and oblong, incompletely covering the damaged flesh underneath. The left eye was obviously sightless: a gray film covered it. The right eye fluttered and blinked painfully. The lips were swollen and red and stretched out from the elongated teeth, which were always visible. The nostrils extended above their normal limit, well above the tip of the nose. There was a patch of hair left at the top of the head. Lucie gasped, and she heard her son in the front room crying. Rudy Benko was barking excitedly at something in the yard.

"Are you in pain?" Lucie asked after a moment. "Do you need the aloe?"

"I am always in pain. Look at me. How could I be anything else? Get a soft cloth and dry off the seeping areas. And shut that dog up. What the hell is he barking at?"

Lucie did as he asked. She dabbed carefully at the pink eye orbits, lips and ears. "Trieste, see if you can quiet the dog down," she said. Trieste went outside.

Charles whimpered almost inaudibly. He picked up a hand mirror he had brought from his wife's dresser and looked. "Oh," he said. The word trailed off into a sob.

He stood and walked into the front room, drawing shuddering breaths as he tried to mask his emotions. Trieste came back inside and moved behind the couch. The dog had stopped barking. Charles sat in his chair and slouched against the back.

Lucie saw that the wet skin of his neck was touching the fabric. She thought to ask him to let her put a towel behind him, but she kept silent.

Rudy Benko started to bark again. Trieste ran outside and came back in immediately.

"It's a possum in the tree," he said. "Rudy Benko always barks at possums. I can't make him stop."

"Son," Charles said. His voice was weak. "Charles, come here. Charlie... Trieste. Come here a minute."

Lucie walked into the room. She stood at the back of the couch and held her hand out. Slowly, Trieste took it. He stood.

"Son," Charles said. "You need to look at me. Look and get used to it. The doctors can't do no more for me. This is as good as I am ever going to look. We'll all be together from now on, so you need to get used to me. I know we can do it."

"But momma and me moved here," Trieste said, clinging to his mother's side. "You weren't here when we..."

"Where my family is, is my home. I am here, and I want you to get used to it. I am the only father you're ever going to have. All right?"

Trieste nodded his head.

"I've been home since yesterday and I haven't had a hug from my son yet. Now, I don't expect you to, not right away, but you could shake my hand." Charles extended his right hand.

"Give him more time, Charles," Lucie said. "This is so much for him to adjust to."

Charles exhaled painfully and dropped his arm, and seemed suddenly angry. "It's an adjustment for me, too! This is my family and my house. I am here to stay so everyone better adjust! Look at me, son. *Look!*"

Trieste looked timidly at his father.

"Get used to me and my face, boy. Get used to it, because I am here to stay."

"I *know!*" Trieste mumbled. "You said it before. You keep saying it."

The next morning when Trieste got out of bed, he found his parents were up already, his father sitting in the front room having coffee. Lucie arose with her husband and made the coffee, serving it to him on the sofa. He sipped the hot liquid loudly, dribbling much of it on his chest from a mouth that never seemed to close completely. She returned to the kitchen to make breakfast. Trieste did not like the sound his father was making, and he went back into his room and put his fingers in his ears.

After breakfast and after Lucie had cleared things away, she prepared for Trieste's lessons for the day. In a kitchen drawer she kept a book of the alphabet, a book of arithmetic, geography, reading, and penmanship. She stacked these on the table next to an Old Tecumseh tablet and a wide carpenter's pencil, newly-sharpened with a paring knife. Charles watched her as he refilled his coffee cup, then returned to the front room.

"Why are you teaching him this stuff now? He's only four." he said.

"He's very bright," Lucie said, "but he has his problems and I want him to have every advantage. He'll need every advantage. No time like the present."

"If you treat him like a freak, he'll always be a freak," Charles said as he shifted painfully on the sofa.

"He's not a freak!" Lucie said, looking angrily at her husband. "Don't call him that! Don't say that so he can hear it!"

"He needs to be in school with other kids. When the time comes, I want him in public school. If he doesn't learn how to be normal, he'll never be normal. It's just stubbornness in him, as I see it. What will the future be like for him if you coddle him like this?"

The phrase stuck in Trieste's head: *What will the future be like?*

"Charles, you don't..." Lucie stopped herself. She needed to be calm for Trieste's lessons. If she wasn't, he couldn't concentrate, and he would learn nothing that day.

"Don't think you can put me off, Lucie," Charles went on. "Don't think you can drop the subject or change the subject and then do what you want because I forgot about it. It's not just the two of you and me in the background keeping out of your business... I love him, too, in case you've forgotten. We both decide what's best for him, not just you..." Charles' voice faded away. This burst of emotion had exhausted him.

A week after Charles' return, Trieste found he could stand to be in the same room with him. If his father spoke a few words, Trieste could tolerate it, but if Charles spoke more than a few sentences or tried to reprimand him or his mother, he ran from the room, disappearing under a bed or up a tree in the yard. This would enrage his father at first, but he didn't seem to have the energy to sustain his anger.

In the second week after Charles' return, they had visitors. Bill Wiek, wounded at Argonne, had lost his right eye, part of his jaw, and his right arm below the elbow. He had spent most of a year in a bed next to Charles' in the hospital in London. Both men found they had developed a taste for brandy while in France, and Wiek had promised Charles that if they both recovered, he would present his friend with a case to celebrate the fact. As good as his word, Wiek had just been mustered out at Fort Dix and was being driven by his younger brother, Les, back to his home in Galveston.

Lucie offered the Wiek brothers dinner, but they declined, saying they would eat back in Ste. Odile where they had a room in which to spend the night before they continued their trip in the morning. Trieste stayed in his room, and after an hour of attempting to be polite and cordial as the men finished a bottle of brandy and started another, Lucie left them and sat with her son on his bed, reading to him until they both fell asleep.

In the morning, Lucie found the front door standing open and Charles asleep on the sofa, drooling from his twisted, red mouth and snoring loudly. He smelled of alcohol. She decided to leave him there, undisturbed, for as long as he needed to sleep.

Just after ten o'clock, Charles woke, walked out onto the front porch, and vomited violently onto the Rose of Sharon bush. Then he went back into his room, got into his bed, and fell asleep again.

At noon, Trieste took his alphabet book, a pencil and tablet out to the front porch. He lay on his stomach on the well-swept boards to practice writing his letters. A small squealing sound on the north side of the house was followed by barking as a possum ran past the porch and up the maple tree in the front yard. Rudy Benko was right behind the possum, barking wildly, nearly catching the animal before it skittered out of his reach. The dog stretched up the tree trunk as far as he could reach and continued barking excitedly.

"Rudy Benko, shut up!" Trieste yelled. "You're being too noisy!" The dog continued to bark nonstop for many minutes.

Suddenly the front screen door flew open, and looking back over his shoulder, Trieste saw his father standing behind him, holding a heavy revolver that he had seen in his mother's chest of drawers once.

Charles had not noticed his son there, lying on the porch. Trieste saw in his head what would happen next, but he could make no sound to stop it.

His father raised the gun and shot. Rudy Benko yelped and collapsed to the ground. Charles shot again, and red spray blew from the dog's head onto the tree trunk.

As Charles lowered the gun and turned back toward the house, he saw that Trieste was on the porch and had witnessed what he had done.

"Charles!" Lucie screamed as she rushed out the front screen door. "Are you out of your mind? Are you insane? How dare you!"

"Can see well enough to shoot a damn dog... if you thought I couldn't," he mumbled. "Damned dog that wouldn't shut up." He walked back into the house, feeling his son's eyes on him all the way.

Trieste made no sound. He put his thumb in his mouth.

Lucie looked at her son. He looked back at her, his expression as blank as when he had watched the first snowfall last winter. His mind had vanished into some other place, as she had noticed in him more and more as he got older.

"Son, I am so sorry..."

Lucie took a spade from the shed behind the house and buried Rudy Benko under the tree where he died. Trieste tried to help her, but she sent him to the back yard until she finished the job.

Late in the afternoon, Lucie put a pot of water on the stovetop and began to cut up potatoes into it. Trieste sat at the small kitchen table drawing the troll under the bridge from the story of the Billy Goats Gruff his mother had read to him the night before. As Lucie set the table, she noticed Trieste's troll was nearly bald with a tuft of hair at the top of his head, and he had a single eye. As Lucie watched him, Trieste drew a circle around the eye.

"Momma," he said, never looking up from his drawing, "why does he have to live with us?"

"You should stop asking me that question, son. He will be here from now on because he belongs here. We all just have to get used to each other. I'm sorry about the dog and sorry you saw that happen. All I can say is, your father is not himself yet. He would have never done something like that before... You'd better put that away," she said, nodding toward his drawing. "We'll be eating soon."

Taking a match from a box on the shelf above the stove, Lucie struck it and lighted it. The blue flames engulfed the bottom of the cooking pot. A terrified moan came from the kitchen doorway. As Lucie and Trieste turned, they saw Charles falling backward against the china cabinet in the dining room.

Lucie gasped.

"Oh Charles, I'm so sorry!" she said.

Charles groaned in pain and struggled to get to his feet. "Lieutenant March told you about that! He told you not to light a fire near me!" he screamed.

"I didn't *see* you there, Charles! If I had known..."

Charles stood silently for a few moments. His breathing was erratic, and he appeared shaken.

"I'm all right. I'm all right," he said. "Not your fault. I came to say I'm sorry about the dog. I wanted to say I'm sorry to both of you, especially you, son. A terrible thing to do..."

Trieste said nothing and continued to draw. Trieste was learning that he could stop hearing the arguments his parents had or anything they said. He could make himself stop listening and think about other things and places no matter how close or loud his parents were. He sat at the table, his drawing in front of him, and he watched the blue flame roiling under the pot. He imagined he saw a salamander, newly-made and perfect, wriggling free of the flames.

In the evening Charles, said he was thirsty and needed a drink. He took a bottle of brandy from the pantry, opened it with some difficulty, and returned to his chair in the front room.

As Lucie cleaned up the kitchen after supper, headlight beams flashed across the wall. The front door was open, and she recognized Marie Stauffenberg's gray Ford. Ady pushed open the passenger door and jumped out of the car.

"Who is that?" Charles demanded.

"It's Marie Stauffenberg and Ady, her little girl. They are friends of ours. I can't imagine what they are doing here now." Lucie dried her hands and hurried out the front door. "I'll see what they want, Charles. You can just stay here, I'm sure they won't stay..."

Trieste ran out the front door ahead of his mother and out into the yard. He hugged Ady, who seemed surprised by his excitement. Lucie followed close behind him.

"Marie, what a surprise," she said.

"I'm so sorry to drop in on you like this," Marie said, " We haven't seen you in a while, and we had to go by Ady's grandma's to get her prescription filled, and I wanted to return your juicer. I found mine under the sink! And I wanted to see how things are going with Charles back..."

"Oh, Marie," Lucie said in almost a whisper, "This isn't a good time. He has been drinking. He has taken up drinking..."

With a terrified whimper, Ady suddenly ran to her mother and hid behind her.

"Child, you like to have knocked me over..." Marie began.

"Why are they here, Lucie?" Charles had appeared on the porch. His speech was noticeably slurred now. "Don't you want them to come in?"

"Momma!" Ady was in tears.

"Be still, honey," Marie whispered. "I'm sorry Charles. I never just drop by. I'm Marie Stauffenberg. Rude of me. We're going. We're going now."

"Go on then. If you're sure you don't want to sit and talk... have a face to face..." Charles mumbled.

Marie looked at Lucie for a long moment but said nothing more. Marie helped her terrified daughter back into the car. In a moment, they were gone.

Charles went back into the house and returned to his chair. He took another long drink of the brandy, spilling much of it on his shirt.

Lucie and Trieste remained in the dark yard for many minutes. Lucie knelt down next to her son.

"Ady was frightened," she said. "She wasn't expecting to see your father like that. We didn't have the time to warn her, did we? People who don't understand what your daddy has been through won't understand..."

"I know, Momma," Trieste nodded. "People will always be scared of him because he looks like that. Grown-ups and kids. Always. And we will always have to live with him." He took his mother's hand. "Come in with me." He led his mother up to the porch and into the front room.

To Lucie's surprise, Trieste led her to Charles. The two of them stood in front of Charles for a few moments.

"Well?" Charles said, at last.

Trieste looked directly into his father's dead eyes, which he had never done before that moment.

"I want to know why you want to live in a place where nobody loves you."

"Trieste!" Lucie gasped, as she pushed the boy behind her.

Charles stood in a rage. He reached drunkenly for his son, but Lucie pushed him away, and he fell back onto his chair.

"Go to your room, Trieste!" Lucie cried. "And lock the door!"

Trieste did as his mother told him.

Trieste heard a crash as though a chair had been thrown over. "You turned him against me!" his father screamed. "You haven't done anything to make this work!"

"I won't argue where he can hear us," Lucie said. "Come outside."

The back screen door opened, and Trieste could hear their voices out in the dark yard, fading slowly as they moved toward the woods. He looked out his window but could see nothing beyond the small oval of light from the open kitchen door on the black grass. Their voices were further away now, but he could still make them out as they moved toward the salt marsh.

"You hate me. You wish I had died over there..."

"That's nonsense Charles! You can only see your own pain. You haven't tried to understand what *we* are going through. What about *us*?"

Trieste heard his mother make a sound like she had made once when she tripped on a root and fell. A little moan of muffled pain. Then he heard nothing at all for a very long time.

The darkness was silent, and suddenly Trieste felt there must be silence across the whole world. Everything was quiet and muffled, and he knew was alone. Knew he was the only living thing in the dark world, a ruined world, and that things as alone as he was, could never find happiness.

After many minutes, Trieste heard the back screen door open. He heard footsteps outside his bedroom.

"Go to bed, boy," his father said.

"Where's Momma?" Trieste said. "She reads to me."

"Not tonight. She's upset. She's walking to... cool off. Go to *bed*!"

Trieste sat on the floor under his window. He knew his life was now broken and could never be repaired. He knew he was alone, or worse: he knew he could do nothing but share his life in this small, isolated house with this hideous man. Trieste knew this was impossible.

Trieste did not move from the floor for more than an hour. He didn't expect to hear his mother come home again, and she didn't. He could hear his father snoring in the front room, and he knew he would be snoring still in the morning and that his mother would not be there with him. He opened his door and went into the kitchen. He pushed a kitchen chair next to the stove and found the box of matches on the shelf above it.

As soon as he entered the front room, he could smell alcohol. It was a smell that was familiar to him now, and which he never wanted to smell again. His father had spilled much of it on himself as he got drunker, before he fell asleep.

Trieste approached the grotesque man snoring in his chair. For a moment he watched him struggle to draw air through his swollen lips. Fire could never make something as perfect as a new salamander, he knew: it could only make a monster like this man.

Trieste struck a match and when he dropped it on his father's chest, he was surprised at how the flame leapt up as though it were anxious to be born.

The man, Charles, who called himself father, awoke suddenly and screamed. He swatted frantically at the flames, screaming and crying in pain and terror. His panic spread the flames across his alcohol-soaked body, and he fell to the floor, setting the sofa alight, screaming as he was consumed.

Trieste ran into his room and crawled under his bed. He knew the flames would never reach him. He knew it because there was no such image in his mind showing that he would be hurt.

In a little while the fire had died down and there were cars in front of the house. A man out on the highway had seen the smoke above the trees and had come to help. He had sent another driver to get the fire department and sheriff in town. The man was a farmer who had been to a tavern. He came in through the back door and found Trieste in his room, still hiding under his bed.

In a short time, the Sheriff was there, and a fire truck, but since the fire was nearly out, they just watched the scene to make sure a fire didn't grow or spread. Soon after that, a large woman in a black car arrived. She told Trieste she was from the State and that she was there to look after him and take him to a safe place. The large woman was very kind and had a soft voice, which made Trieste feel less alone. The woman gathered some of Trieste's clothes and a few wooden toys. She asked him if he was ready to go. The only answer he could make was, yes, he was. After all, he knew he could not live in a half-burned house alone. The thought would have frightened his mother, and he would feel very bad to frighten her. He moved toward the front door.

The large woman's hand was on his head, gently guiding him toward the waiting sedan. He stepped across the threshold out into the night. With her kind encouragement, he started the dark walk forward toward the car and to all the ruined years to come.

Acknowledgements

I never published a piece of fiction until I was thirty-three. I never really wrote a serious piece of fiction until then. As a teen, I had scribbled in a notebook: half-baked ideas and unresolved narratives. Like a lot of teenage boys who turn out like me, I read horror and science fiction. I loved H. G. Wells, Verne, Poe, Lovecraft, and scores of others. By fifteen, I had read the classic Modern Library collections from the 1940s, *Great Tales of Terror and the Supernatural*, and *Famous Science Fiction Stories: Adventures in Time and Space*.

Two of my idols from that time were Ray Bradbury and Isaac Asimov. I wrote to both of them through their publishers. I asked the usual young fan stuff: where do your ideas originate, why do you repeat certain images and metaphors, what advice... et cetera? I was surprised to get responses very quickly from both of them. Imperfectly typed postcards arrived within two weeks of my sending my letters, both signed in ink. Asimov's was in ball point pen, and Bradbury's was some sort of fountain pen, which was an interesting retro choice for a futurist, I thought.

Both responses were gracious and understanding of my obvious naiveté. Asimov's was no-nonsense and to the point and amounted to: "There are really no new ideas under the sun. What matters is how you make an idea your own." Bradbury's, on the other hand, was more pastoral and leisurely. He remarked on his style and how it developed and how I had pointed out that many of the machines he describes have animal-like characteristics, something he said he hadn't considered before. Even at fifteen, I doubted that statement, but thought it was nice of him to say.

Armed with these epistolary validations from two personal heroes, I scribbled in my notebooks pretty frantically for several years. But by the time I was a senior in high school, I had discovered poetry, and somehow that art form's ancient pedigree and succinct terseness elevated it to a level of sanctity and importance that fiction had not yet achieved, in my thinking. Over the next few years, I made plodding imitations of Yeats and Auden and many others, won a few minor honors, and had a few minor publications until playwrighting came along and I embarked on a whole new set of imitations.

In college, I had discovered the work of William Faulkner, Flannery O'Connor and James Joyce, and those left their mark, though I still was not thinking much in terms of 'fiction' for myself. Finally, at age thirty-three, the notion finally hit me and stuck. I got a great idea at work one day and couldn't get it out of my head until I wrote it down. My daughter Megan had just been born at home (yes, that was intentional) and I wondered about creating a narrative around the idea that a character, a backwoods woman, cannot predict or control *what* she gives birth to. The result was my first fully realized story, "One Happy Family".

There was really only one place I wanted to send the tale. T. E. D. Klein was editor of *Rod Serling's The Twilight Zone Magazine* in those days. Klein loved the story, paid me what seemed like a princely sum for it, and it appeared in the October 1983 issue. A few months after that, I got a letter from renowned anthologist Martin H. Greenberg asking to include the story in an upcoming collection he was putting together to be called *A Treasury of American Horror Stories*. He offered seventy-five dollars up front and a miniscule royalty, and I jumped on it. A few months after that, I could mention, in my future cover letters, that my work had appeared along with tales by Stephen King, H. P. Lovecraft, Richard Matheson, and Robert Bloch.

I didn't exactly build on that success though. Publications were sporadic. There were way fewer options then, and many were tiny and ephemeral. I appeared in small publications that came and went, like *Eldritch Tales, The Horror Show, Charon II, Spectral*, and many others.

I realized early on that the fiction I responded most to was often "regional". There was Flannery O'Connor's South, Faulkner's Yoknapatawpha County, and, in horror, Lovecraft's mythic New England. As a young kid, I had always been interested in the history of, and my family connection to, the old French colonial village of Ste. Genevieve, situated on the Mississippi River a few miles from where I was born. I wondered if I could create an infernal, fictitious version of the old town. I noticed the old French female name of Odile on many gravestones in the ancient cemetery, so I decided to call my village Ste. Odile. I wanted to introduce my cursed town in a spectacular way. I wanted something that paid homage to my lifelong love of gothic horror fiction. In 2010, my historical horror novel *The Black Garden* was published.

It was well-reviewed and well-received, but not widely promoted. Response was positive enough that I started contemplating a sequel, and to that end, my wife Cindy and I travelled to Alsace and discovered, quite by chance, that there is a real Ste. Odile, a mountaintop retreat dating to the eighth century. For several years before and after this discovery, I have been writing what I call my Ste. Odile stories, many of which appear in this volume.

A couple of years after my debut novel, my illustrated children's book about Bigfoot, *Annette: A Big, Hairy Mom* was published by New Babel Books in the U.S. and by VF Libris in Croatia and Stella in Slovenia. Writing this novel and its sequel was something I didn't foresee in my creative sensibility. I have never had so much fun writing anything, and have no doubt I will visit this region again.

At about this time also, I had the notion to write what was, for me, a new kind of horror story: a type that deals in equal parts with supernatural and *possibly* supernatural "horrors", as well as the day-to-day horrors of isolation, loneliness and self-revulsion. Thus my story *The Little Dead Thing* was born. The tale immediately found a home at G&H Publishing, who also enthusiastically took the next one, *Porphyria*, in this new series, and credited me with helping their small company survive its first year, due to their popularity. Publisher C. P. Dunphy even called me "A great, undiscovered voice in horror fiction."

The stories I have been writing since are all in this same vein. Their enthusiastic acceptance out in the publishing world has been most encouraging and certified that yes, I have something to leave behind in this life. My wife Cindy has been a most patient fan and enabler, as have my many friends and readers over the years.

Eternal thanks to Andrea and Dark Owl Publishing for believing in and even loving these stories. Gratifying to know that all these years of work were serving the function of bringing me to your attention. This has been a dream association!

Gratitude hardly covers the debt I owe my longtime editors Anne Makeever and David Lancaster, consummate professionals who always make a hopefully good thing so very much better. And then there are my kids, Megan and Evan, always supportive and proud of what I try to do. Their pride and support have almost been all the encouragement I needed through all these years. More to come, guys. I promise.

John S. McFarland
Ste. Odile, 2020

Editor's Note

The image used on the cover of this book is of Second Lieutenant Henry Ralph Lumley, a pilot during World War I. You may have noted his name in the story "Placide", included herein.

Young Lt. Lumley's plane crashed on the day he passed his pilot's test. He survived, but with serious burns over his entire body. Lt. Lumley suffered from the loss of his left eye and could hardly see out of his right one. His fingers were burned to where he lost his thumbs, and his legs were burned enough to restrict his movement.

Lt. Lumley became a patient of Dr. Harold Gillies, who was working on facial reconstructive surgery using skin grafts, pioneering these techniques in the early part of the twentieth century. His work was incredibly important in helping men who had been severely injured during the War. The photograph depicts Lt. Lumley after some of his skin grafts were healing. Gillies's work was still experimental, however, and to be one of his patients meant a lot of pain and endurance to see it through. Sadly, Lt. Lumley succumbed to complications from his wounds and the surgeries two years after his accident, suffering heart failure.

Lt. Lumley is not the only real person to grace these pages. The radium girls, the lead miners, various WW1 soldiers, surgeons, religious devotees, so many of the author's characters are based on men and women who are a part of human history. Some sacrificed themselves for the greater good, some did not know the consequences of their actions until it was too late.

But overall, Mr. McFarland handled his characters with grace and care, bringing honor to the memories of the real-life persons they embody. While his collection is harrowing, we are reminded of the fragility of life, yet also how fortunate we are to live in this modern world. And we thank those men and women for their intelligence, skills, and immolations so we may live better lives as their descendants.

Andrea Thomas, Editor
Arizona, 2020

About the Author

John S. McFarland's short stories have appeared in numerous journals, in both the mainstream and horror genres. His tales have been collected with stories by Stephen King, H. P. Lovecraft, Robert Bloch, and Richard Matheson. His work has been praised by such writers as T. E. D. Klein and Philip Fracassi, and he has been called "A great, undiscovered voice in horror fiction." McFarland's horror novel, *The Black Garden*, was published in 2010 to universal praise, and his young reader series about Bigfoot, *Annette: A Big, Hairy Mom*, is in print in three languages. His story collection, *The Dark Walk Forward*, is his first.

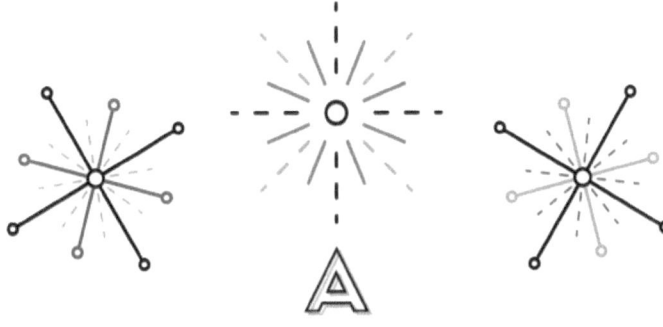

A CELEBRATION OF STORYTELLING

The Anthological Festival of Tales

58 stories by 39 authors designed to honor the art of writing by
including a fair, festival, or celebration in each telling.
From fantasy to sci-fi, from thrillers to mysteries,
we know readers will truly enjoy this feast of fables.

Now Available from   Dark Owl Publishing, LLC

www.darkowlpublishing.com

We all know how the stories go:
An unlikely hero will gather a member of every race and every nation
to discover the Fallen Lord's dark secret and cause his defeat.
But Adal is the most unlikely of heroes,
and the stories must be satisfied with the company he leads.
Will the Fallen Lord turn the tales
of the Storied Lands against them?

THE KEEPER OF TALES

STORIES ARE ALIVE.
THEY WILL BE TOLD.

an epic fantasy adventure by

JONATHON MAST

Coming from Dark Owl Publishing, LLC

March 1, 2021

www.darkowlpublishing.com
Where quality fiction comes to nest.

COMING MARCH 1, 2021!

From Dark Owl Publishing, LLC

THE LAST STAR WARDEN

Tales of ADVENTURE and MYSTERY
from Frontier Space, Volume I

BY

JASON J. MCCUISTION

AUTHOR OF
PROJECT NOTEBOOK

www.darkowlpublishing.com

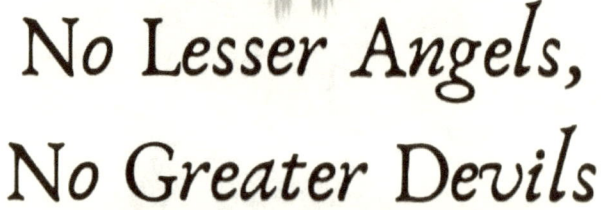

No Lesser Angels,
No Greater Devils

*Beautiful and haunting stories from
the unique and relatable prose of*

Laura J. Campbell

Coming May 1, 2021 in paperback and on Kindle

Dark Owl Publishing, LLC
www.darkowlpublishing.com